Lenity

By

D. Baird Manchester

Blessings!
D. Baird

xulon
PRESS

For the glory of my Lord and Savior, Jesus Christ

"I tell you the truth, some who are standing here will not taste death before they see the Son of Man coming in his kingdom."

-Matthew 16:28

Chapter One

There is no place I haven't been; no thing I haven't seen; no situation that's new to me. Or so I'd arrogantly assumed before that cool, overcast day in Chicago.

My job is to watch, to witness, to wait. Acting only with express permission. Yet, even so, even knowing the risks of straying from my path, in the moment I reacted as any young, adrenalized man would have: I saved the girl's life.

It was an average Tuesday afternoon rush hour in the city. I stood on a crowded corner of Russell Street, waiting for the light to change, not sure I wanted to face my lonely penthouse just yet. Thinking, in fact, that it might be time to pack it up and move on. Fall in Chicago serves as a harbinger of the long, cold winter ahead, and late October in the States always means an increase in activity for me.

Thailand might be nice… or Palestine, I thought. I'd been away from the West Bank and the sea for far too long. I could feel a gravitational-like pull on my heart. *Perhaps it's time to go home.*

My thoughts were broken by a disturbance in the crowd, a wave of pedestrians roiling toward me, shouts and panicked cries. A man near the center brandished a gun, as did the pursuing police.

My pulse rate jumped, but fear was no stranger to me. Neither were moments like this. I stepped off the curb, shielded by cars parked along the street but still closer to the traffic rushing by than was comfortable. I tried to gauge whether the light would change before the chaos reached me.

No, I decided.

Most of the people around me had noticed what was headed our way and shrank back into the folds of the nearest building. Others rushed to cross with traffic now, hoping to outrun the gun.

That's when I noticed her: a young woman intently texting on her cell phone, rocking slightly on her too-high heels. I felt a flash of recognition, but realized that I did not know this girl. What I'd 'recognized' was a moment occurring that would become an important memory. It had happened to me before.

The girl stood between me and danger, oblivious to what was coming.

What is *coming*? I wondered, looking up the street again. The gunman was closing fast, his eyes wild and white, his tongue lolling like a rabid dog's. *Does a demon have him? Will it recognize me if it does?* I averted my eyes just in case and hoped he was making his choices for a different reason.

He took no notice of me; he had Text-Girl in his sights.

She was so young, so isolated in the crowd, so completely unaware that he'd be on her in three strides... in two.... He lunged, shoving her hard, using her small body to propel himself in the opposite direction, around the corner.

She flew forward off the curb, shrieking, and stumbled beyond the protection of the parked cars.

I moved without thinking, barely registering the blaring horn and squealing tires. I launched myself at her from the opposite side, countering the forces that would have otherwise sent her under the wheels of a red SUV that flashed by so close, I could feel the heat off its engine.

The momentum of my tackle slammed us against the hood of a parked car, setting off its alarm. I regretted that I could not have been gentle about it. I heard her breath escape, followed by short gasps as she struggled to get it back.

I scrambled off of her as two of the police officers arrived to help. The others, presumably, still chased the gunman. I felt relieved: not to be alive exactly, but that the dangerous man hadn't once looked at me.

Text-Girl took two more quick breaths before breaking into heart-wrenching sobs. I reached out to her, but instead, one of the officers took my outstretched arm and led me to the sidewalk.

I relayed my perspective of the events. Even though he'd seen the whole thing, he was very demanding about the details and meticulous in writing them down. He even asked me to repeat some of my words, causing me to wonder if he couldn't understand my accent.

When his questions ran out, I asked, "Would it be okay if I went over and talked to her, now?" I glanced to where Text-Girl was sitting, on the back bumper of the ambulance. They'd wrapped her in a blanket. She held a rumpled tissue in her fist. The other officer stood close to her in a protective, fatherly, kind of way.

"I guess," the policeman answered. "Just let me make sure they're done talking first." He sauntered over, spoke briefly with the other officer who nodded at him. When he turned back to me, it was to wave me over, but he didn't wait for me. Instead, he and his partner walked toward the front of the ambulance.

I approached slowly, eyes lowered. Text-Girl's crushed phone lay in my path. It, evidently, had not escaped the SUV. I carefully stepped over the broken bits. When I looked up again she was staring at me. She offered a weak smile and patted the place beside her as if it were a park bench.

I closed the distance between us, but didn't sit.

She was beautiful, with the fresh, flawless skin of someone just out of her teens. With one hand, she gracefully swept her long, ash-brown hair behind her ears.

Our eyes met.

I blinked, stunned by the unusual color of her eyes, the exact shade of the sea I'd sailed when the world was new to me. *So many times. So long ago…*I felt drawn into their depths, almost lost there. I managed to ask, "Are you all right?"

Her eyes widened briefly, a certain reaction to my accent that I'd come to expect. In answer to my question, she nodded, biting her lower lip and averting her gaze.

The gesture caused a clenching in my gut, a familiar response. I'd always been especially sensitive to vulnerability in others. I'm sure that's why I'd been given the job I had been given. However, combining that with the reminder her eyes had brought of my longed-for homeland, and the result was disconcerting. I had to take a moment to compose myself.

I looked at my shoes, incredibly uncomfortable wingtips, which I hated wearing. I wondered why I'd chosen them today; I hadn't been in court. "I'm sorry if I hurt you," I began.

"You saved my life," she answered, her voice of an unexpectedly deep timbre. She waited for me to look up again before continuing, "Sorry if I didn't seem grateful. I was really freaked out! I hadn't understood what was happening, why you grabbed me, until Officer James explained it." She half-chuckled. "Guess I was in my own little world there."

"You seem a lot calmer now," I said, noting a complete turn-around from a few minutes ago.

She scratched her pencil-thin eyebrow with a French-manicured nail. "I feel strange. I think I'm in shock?" It sounded like a question, as if I might be able to confirm that assessment. "It's all so weird, you know?"

She glanced toward the gathered, gawking crowd. "You wouldn't happen to have a cigarette, would ya?"

"I don't smoke," I said, sounding apologetic although I hadn't intended to.

She nodded. "I'm… was… *am* trying to quit…. Wouldn't want to end up looking like my mom." Her eyes widened once more. "My God! Did I just say that?"

My fingers clenched, a reflex to the use of His name in that way. I exhaled slowly. "Look, I… I just wanted to make sure you are all right. I should…." I motioned toward the sidewalk.

"Well, hey, don't go until you at least introduce yourself, okay?"

It took a moment for me to recognize I was blushing. That hadn't happened in a very long time. "Sorry," I said, "I guess I'm a bit shell-shocked as well."

I held out my hand. "I am Jaden." *At the moment*, I added to myself. *Have to keep things truthful, at least internally.*

She took my fingers into her soft hand. "That'll be easy to remember."

"Ah… I… I'm sorry?" I stammered as she released me. "Most people find my name odd."

She squinted at me. "Your eyes," she said. "I would have called them emerald green, but jade works, too. Jaden."

I tried to smile. It had been ages since a woman had made me so uncomfortable.

"I'm Carly, by the way," she added.

"Well." I swallowed loudly. "I hope to see you again, Carly, under less… horrifying circumstances."

"It's a date," she said brightly. "I'm free tomorrow night."

My mind reeled at the unexpected offer. She was young, beautiful, vulnerable and interested in me. A combination I generally ran from. I couldn't think of anything more creative to say than, "Oh."

"You're not married or anything, are you?" she asked, adding, "'Cause I checked for a ring."

I gazed at my left hand. "No," I whispered sadly, "never married."

"Well," she continued, "people are gonna ask me about my savior, so…."

I interrupted forcefully, "I am *not* your Savior!"

She looked at me carefully for a moment and then mumbled, "Whatever, dude."

I felt ridiculous. She hadn't meant anything by it. "Carly, I'm so sorry…. I'm not myself just now."

She looked down, twisting her hands together. "Yeah. Me neither."

I was surprised by a sudden compulsion to touch her, to cup her chin or place my hands on her shoulders. I didn't.

"I'll uh… I'll see you around?" I'm not sure why I phrased it as a question. Maybe I needed affirmation that her interest had been real.

"Sure," she replied, not looking at me, not affirming me in any way.

I sighed quietly and walked away, knowing that I would try, but I would never, ever be able to forget her eyes.

Chapter Two

Sometime after midnight, I was lying in bed unable to sleep. Instead, I indulged in an intricate fantasy I'd created, one in which I'd said, 'yes' to a date with Carly.

My King suddenly spoke. As ever, I did not see Him, but there's no mistaking His voice: calm and exuberant, low and high, beautiful and terrifying, underlain with endless love. It filled my darkened bedroom with invisible light in the deepest part of the night.

"Timon," He used my ancient name, "I am displeased with you." It wasn't the first time He'd spoken this phrase to me; it wouldn't be the last.

Not sure if He was speaking in generalities, or if He was commenting on the daydream He'd just interrupted, I rolled out of bed and fell to my knees, my forehead resting on the floor. He didn't sound displeased; He never did, but He couldn't lie.

I answered Him, "Your kingdom come, Lord. Your servant awaits."

"Today, I called Carly Bell Benson to my throne." As He spoke her name, I saw her as He sees her: a thousand nuances of creative and edgy, sharp and witty, vulnerable and beautiful, chary and lenient. But she was more than a list of traits. He'd created her to embody the sea of my homeland, deep and vast, at times boiling and thunderous, at times smooth and silent. Brilliant in the sunlight. Murky in the shadows. Able to buoy up any load or tear apart anything caught in her wake. A bounty of good things swam in her currents. A force for destruction lurked below her surface. If you looked just right, you could see it all in the blue of her eyes.

My breath caught as a wave of affection mixed with desire swept through me. Irrepressibly, my heart hammered in my chest. Never had I experienced attraction at such a level.

My Lord continued as if He hadn't noticed my reaction, "She did not come…. And you neglected to ask for permission before interfering."

I had. "Forgive me, my King," I whispered. "I acted on human impulse."

"You are forgiven, my son."

"Why did you… reveal her to me in this way?" My voice remained as weak as my knees, my breath shallow. Fortunately, there was no reason to get up from the floor and plenty of reasons to remain there.

"You need to know her, Timon. I will call her again."

"She isn't…." I knew I shouldn't mention this, but if I was going to, I had to rephrase it as a question. "Is she sealed to your kingdom, my Lord?" Over the years, I'd become able to recognize His Spirit at a glance. I did not recall seeing it in all the depths of her eyes.

I felt His love flowing into me, now. Calming the rather fierce rush I'd felt for Carly. His love carried understanding and sympathy, but He didn't answer. He was right not to; that answer was between the two of them.

He must want me to introduce her to Him, though, I thought. *What other reason could He have for wanting me to know her this intimately?* Just thinking about her brought another tidal wave of emotions crashing over me, desire chief among them.

I groaned. Human love... lust... whatever it was this time, was not meant for me. I thought I'd reconciled that fact years ago. But I could no longer imagine the world without Carly Benson in it. I needed her in the way I needed the Mediterranean Sea, and so I pleaded, "May I speak with her once more, my Lord? Before you call her again?"

My request pleased Him; I could feel it in a tingling down my spine. He rarely gave me orders, but He appreciated it when I understood His wishes.

"She is fortunate, that you would ask for such a thing." He paused as if to think, but I knew that was purely for my benefit, to give me a chance to think.

In that moment, I remembered that He already knew this conversation and its outcome. For that matter, He'd known that I would save Carly off the street corner, long before He'd called her name. Plus, He'd shown me her soul, a match to my own. It meant something pivotal was about to occur. I couldn't guess what that 'something' was, but I knew that Carly and I were to be an integral part of it.

"You may speak to her again," He pronounced. "But I need her here. Very soon."

I exhaled my relief. Time was tricky with Him, though. What did 'very soon' mean to an eternal being?

I didn't ask Him where or when I'd see her; I trusted Him to work that out.

"Thank you, my Lord," I answered earnestly. "All praise, glory and honor to the King!"

He didn't leave me. He never did. But He was silent after that.

I crawled back into bed, but I still couldn't sleep. I stared into the black night, imagining Carly's face, floating in the void above my head. I recalled the way He'd said her name. In that moment, her entire being, her soul itself, had come into existence in my mind. I felt as if I now knew everything about her. Not her circumstances or experiences, but her character. Combined with the pre-existing physical attraction, my need to be with her was suddenly absolute and unconditional.

I should have gone to my office the next morning, but I knew I wouldn't be able to focus on the stacks of contracts awaiting my appraisal. Instead, I phoned my assistant, Brittany.

"Hey, Britt," I responded to her much more professional salutation. "Is there anything on my docket today that Madison can't handle without me?"

"Playing hooky again, Jaden?" she chided.

"I may be needed elsewhere," I explained.

She hummed as she reviewed my calendar. "You're in luck. Adam canceled your afternoon appointment."

Adam was one of my law partners. We were supposed to meet about an upcoming court appearance. "Did he reschedule?"

"Not yet."

"So I'm free?"

"Looks like. Will you be in at all?"

"I doubt it."

There was the slightest pause before she said, "See you tomorrow, then."

I'd caught the hint of disappointment in her voice, but chose not to acknowledge it. "'Bye, Britt."

After hanging up, I offered my Lord a quick prayer of thanks for the free day, a request that He lead Brittany to a man who could care for her in ways that I couldn't, and a plea for Him to lead me to Carly.

In preparation, I sorted through my experiences, choosing and practicing the words I would say to her, the best of my arguments, anything that would not give me away in the process.

This was not my normal *modus operandi*. I usually spent time with people, living as an example of the Christ's servitude and endless love, sharing it with them as I got to know and understand them and their circumstances, so that I could present them with a logical place to invite the Savior into their lives. I didn't feel like I'd have time for that with Carly, though. I'm sure that's why He'd let me hear Him speak her name. It gave me a place to start, since otherwise, I knew next to nothing about her.

At nine o'clock, I finally showered. Afterward, as I wiped down the foggy mirror, preparing to shave, I stared at my reflection for a moment and wondered why I couldn't suppress the attraction I felt toward Carly. I'd done it before with other women.

What can I offer her? I wondered for at least the millionth time in my life.

It didn't take much to trigger memories of the last time I'd let myself fall in love: Ingrid. Stockholm. I still checked in on her once in a while, although I'd never allowed her to see me. Not since the day I'd said goodbye, on my way to India. No doubt, she thought I was dead… if she thought of me at all. She was a great-grandmother now. Her husband, Anders, had given her the life I could not. She was nearing the end of her days on Earth in peace.

I focused, again, on my reflection. Time had not aged me. My skin was as smooth and clear as it had been on my 28th birthday. It was a lighter shade at the moment, an effect of cooler climates, but essentially, the same.

My hair was still solid black, not a single gray hair, not ever. I wore it just long enough to curl around my ears and collar, but I refused to incorporate the styling products my current hairdresser insisted on selling to me.

My eyes were a clear, bright, glittering green. *Not really like jades at all*, I thought, smiling as I recalled Carly's observation, her unusual voice, her own amazing eyes. Excited that I might see her again soon, I spread shaving cream along my jaw.

I dressed casually, in nondescript khakis and a coal-colored mock-turtle. The cotton fabric clung to my torso. Something I'd noticed that women noticed. The wingtips were left in my closet in favor of well-worn loafers. It was a good day for walking.

I wondered what Carly would be wearing when I saw her again. I couldn't remember what she'd had on yesterday; I'd been too mesmerized by her face. However, I could remember her small body, pinned briefly beneath mine against the hood of a black Audi.

With great care, I pushed that memory aside, replacing it with one of the last time I'd dated, and what I'd been wearing that day. I shuddered, relieved that styles had so drastically changed over the years. *Except for stiff, dress shoes*, I thought, preferring the bare-foot-in-the-sand days of my youth. Today, my feet and my clothes would be comfortable, if not my soul. The last thing I grabbed before leaving home was an olive-green trench coat.

I wandered fairly aimlessly over several blocks of the downtown area, not knowing where or when I would see her. Not even knowing if today would be the day. I ignored all street signs and landmarks. I simply flowed along with the stream of others, hundreds of people, all on their way to someplace else, and most of them in a hurry to get there.

It was a warm day for October, but windy. I left my coat open and kept out of the shadows as much as possible, enjoying the sunshine. There were still remnants around town from last Sunday's marathon. I scooped up a stray paper cup and a couple of empty gel packs and carried them until I found a trash bin, and then I had to find a public restroom to wash my sticky fingers.

A few blocks off the marathon route, I stopped to read theater posters and an advertisement for a design exhibit at the Museum of Science and Industry featuring the work of Emilio Ambasz. I'd met him not long ago, in Paris, and smiled at the memory. He did his best to unite the natural world with industrial products in order to meet the ergonomic needs of humans. I greatly admired his efforts.

Another flyer caught my eye, this one for a Saints and Demons exhibit at the Art Institute. Someone had decided that would be perfect for the upcoming Halloween holiday. I shook my head. No doubt something like that would draw my enemies in.

Menus taped to the windows of various restaurants caught my eye. It was lunchtime, and I was getting hungry. Not in the mood for the Japanese restaurant in front of me, I crossed the street, walked a block, turned the corner... and there was Carly, coming straight toward me.

Her hair was tied back in a high ponytail, whipped by the wind. She wore a pink pinstriped shirt, fitted at her narrow waist, over cream-colored, billowing slacks with heeled leather boots but no coat. Her mouth came open slightly when she saw me. I grinned in response.

She was walking with a friend, a taller woman a few years older than Carly, and not nearly as attractive. The friend had artificially-blond hair, too short for the French braids she'd forced it into. Little spikes popped out all over her head. The two ends stuck straight out in back. She kept her hands pinned to her sides to keep her skirt from flying up in the breeze.

Carly exclaimed, "My hero!" as I closed the distance between us.

"You look well today," I told her.

"Yeah, like, thanks to you." Carly placed her palm briefly against my shoulder as she turned to her friend. "Jen, this is that guy who threw me against a car yesterday."

Her choice of words startled me, and her casual contact felt more like I'd been struck by lightening. Combined with the fact that she was even more beautiful than she'd been in my dreams, I found it hard to tear my eyes away from her. But eventually, I did.

"I'm pleased to meet you, Jen," I said belatedly, offering my hand.

She'd noticed the pause, but shook my hand politely with a brisk, "Hey." Then she leaned into Carly and whispered, "You were right about the accent. Oh, my *God*!"

I cringed for a number of reasons as Carly elbowed her friend. She looked at me apologetically and asked, "Are you going to McDonald's, too?"

We'd met right in front of it; I hadn't even noticed.

"Yes," I answered, thinking, *I am now*. I wasn't a food snob, but the whole idea of fast food had never made sense to me. Of course, I, literally, had all the time in the world.

Jen, in an overly animated gesture, smacked her palm against her forehead and said, "Carly, I just remembered; I *brought* my lunch today.... See you back at the office."

"Je-en," Carly slurred, but Jen was already backing away. She winked at Carly and then twirled away from us.

"I'm so sorry," I said when Carly looked back at me. "I didn't mean to interrupt."

She shrugged. "Jen's cool.... I may even like her better than I thought."

The door to McDonald's opened. The man coming out paused to hold it for me. I thanked him and then said to Carly, "Ladies first."

"You obviously don't know who you're dealing with," she replied and slipped inside.

Carly wouldn't let me pay for her lunch, and I didn't press the issue. I watched with a smile as she dropped her change into the clear, plastic box collecting for Ronald McDonald House. I put in a few dollars myself.

We'd both ordered salads. She got hers with a Diet Coke. I made a different choice, which she began teasing me about as we carried our trays toward an empty, almost-clean table.

"That chocolate milk, dude?"

"Vitamin D *and* calcium," I answered.

She laughed. "Perfect for a growing boy."

Is that how she sees me? I shook my head in response to my own thoughts and chose not to reply.

"So, I'm glad I ran into you," I said casually, waiting for her to sit before I did. "How are you doing today?"

She bobbed her head. "Yeah. Better, thanks…. You?"

"Couldn't sleep," I told her truthfully as I slid into place across from her.

She smiled a sympathetic smile, perfect and dazzling. *Probably professional whitening,* I thought. She'd admitted to smoking, after all.

"Seriously, it was a scary situation, what happened yesterday," I began. "If you need to talk…."

"Do you work around here?" she asked before I'd finished speaking.

Okay, I thought. I could take a hint, even a more-subtle one if given the opportunity. I replied, "On the Loop, actually, but I had some business uptown this morning," *true enough*, "and decided to walk. It's such a beautiful day."

She nodded. "So long as you don't mind the wind."

"What about you?" I prompted.

She quipped, "I don't mind the wind at all."

I opened my mouth. No words came out.

She giggled. "Dude, you're too easy! The look on your face!"

I shook my head. People never teased me like this, but it absolutely thrilled me that Carly would. "Sorry…. You…. You're like no one I've ever met." More than the clichéd 'breath of fresh air,' she was more like the wind in a sail I'd vowed never to unfurl again. I took a deep breath. "And that's saying a lot, actually."

I continued, enunciating each syllable, "Do you work near-by?"

"Yep." She turned her attention to her meal, choosing the chicken and vegetables, leaving the lettuce untouched.

"And... what kind of work do you do?" I asked.

She rolled her eyes. "The boring kind."

"I see.... I get the feeling you don't like talking about yourself," I noticed.

She didn't even look up.

The place had grown crowded and noisy; perhaps she hadn't heard me. I bowed my head and silently asked God to bless my meal and to guide my words. When I opened my eyes, Carly was looking at me curiously, but only for a moment. She promptly turned her attention to a carrot slice speared on her black, plastic fork.

I let her eat, picking through my own salad.

Our eyes met several times over the next few minutes, both of us quickly glancing away. The next time it happened, she blushed and I chortled.

Her eyes darted back to mine. "What?" she asked.

"I just...." I searched my mind for something she might relate to. "I feel like I'm back in middle school."

She giggled. "Me, too! My... relationships... usually don't develop this way."

"No?"

"Can you believe it? Men don't normally sweep me off my feet on street corners."

"I don't believe it," I joked along with her.

She chuckled and then looked away with a heavy sigh. "I usually meet guys at… this or that bar…. My relationships last just long enough for one of us to slink away from the other's place in shame a few hours later. I'm usually too embarrassed to return their calls…. That is, *if* they call."

She might have been looking for judgment from me, but she wasn't going to get it. "If it makes you feel any better," I told her, "you're the first girl I've *ever* swept off her feet." *Too bold*? I wondered, holding my breath.

Her eyes snapped up, glittering like sunlight on the open water. The corner of her mouth quirked into a slight smile. "I wish I didn't have to say this, but my desk is calling," she said, suddenly rising.

"Oh. Sure. I'll walk you back." I leaned over to gather the bits of paper napkin a neighboring toddler had shredded and dropped to the floor beside my chair, adding them to my trash.

When I looked up, Carly was gazing at me with raised eyebrows. "Isn't there someplace you need to be?" she asked.

"Not really."

She eyed me skeptically for a moment longer and then shrugged. "Okay. I've gotta do one thing, first."

I followed her, dumping our trays and getting back in line. When she ordered a burger to go, I assumed it was meant for Jen.

Therefore, it caught me completely by surprise when, as we walked down the street a few minutes later, she paused beside a homeless man who sat bundled in a dirty blanket with his back against the cold stone of a bank building.

"Spare a dollar?" he asked, not quite meeting our eyes.

Carly knelt smoothly at his side. "I got this for you," she said sweetly, handing him the white paper sack. "Eat it while it's hot, okay?"

He nodded, curling his cracked fingers around the bag.

I should not have been so surprised. After all, I knew what kind of woman she was. *Are you certain she's not already yours?* I asked Him in my mind.

Are you? He replied.

He was right to remind me that I couldn't see into her heart the way He could.... But I still hadn't seen His Spirit in her eyes, and that was generally an absolute for me.

I gave the homeless man five dollars. "For dinner," I told him as Carly walked away.

"Do you know that man?" I asked curiously, as soon as I'd caught up to her.

She shook her head. "I just buy an extra burger and give it to the first homeless person I see. There's always someone new.... And it helps me, too," she added after a thoughtful pause. "I may never find someone to take care of me, but I can do a little to take care of someone else."

"Wow," I replied, truly stunned by her sudden candor. "Want to talk about that?"

"Not really."

She hadn't so much as glanced at me through our exchange, and I knew better than to push her. Instead, I nodded my understanding as we walked on in silence.

Carly stopped at the next corner and looked up at me. "We're here," she said, motioning vaguely.

I held her bright eyes with mine, trying to see beyond their unusual color. "Can I see you again?" I asked, surprised that it sounded a lot like begging.

Her eyebrows rose. "I dunno…. Maybe."

"You said you were free tonight," I reminded her.

"When did I say that?"

"Yesterday."

"Hm…. Well, I wasn't lying, but…." She squinted at me. "You didn't seem all that interested."

I didn't? "I wasn't myself yesterday…. Can you meet me at Farfelle d'Amoré at eight?"

She bit her lower lip again, but this time, over a grin. "Yeah. Yes, I can."

I held up my index finger. "My treat this time."

She made the 'okay' sign and headed across the street. I didn't try to follow her.

Chapter Three

I had nothing scheduled for the rest of the afternoon and couldn't bring myself to go to the office. I might get stuck there, even though they weren't expecting me. And, besides, the weather was too perfect to waste reading tedious contracts. So, I called in a reservation to the restaurant and then chose to check out the Ambasz exhibit. I'd always wanted to see inside that museum. I loved 'old' architecture. It had a way of transporting me back through time.

I stepped up to the curb, hailing a cab. The driver was pleasantly surprised when I requested my ride to the Museum of Science and Industry in his native Arabic. He responded heartily and began talking about Jordan, his homeland. He told me that he missed the country and his extended family very much. He and his wife had moved to Chicago with their two young sons after she was accepted into the Rosalind Franklin University of Medicine and Science.

He said he was proud of his wife and happy to have escaped the too-close-for-comfort war and the many refugees flooding across the border. However, even though he'd been a banker in Jordan and spoke English fluently, he had not been able to find similar work in Chicago. He'd resorted to driving.

He told me how unfortunate he found the American bias against mainstream Islam, blaming that for his lack of a better job. Even in a large community with an established Islamic culture, he felt isolated. He worried for his children.

I could empathize. When he finally gave me a chance to speak, I told him I was originally from the West Bank. He immediately assumed that I was Palestinian. I didn't correct him, although I did tell him that I was Christian and not Muslim, which didn't faze him at all. I hadn't expected it to.

He voiced his opinion on the fate of the West Bank, wishing, as I did, for peace among the people living there. When he fell into a contemplative silence, I leaned my head against the cool pane of window glass and silently prayed for him and his family as well as for my own homeland.

The city gardens slid by as the taxi traveled south on Lakeshore Drive. Out the other window, Lake Michigan was a hazy grayish-blue stripe along the horizon. It held no interest for me. The color was all wrong.

A short seven miles later, I'd reached my destination. I paid my driver, wishing him well. As he pulled away, I jogged up the short flight of steps and entered the old Beaux Arts building, built for the World's Columbian Exposition held here in 1893. I'd missed that one, but only by about twenty years.

Inside, most of the building's turn-of-the-last-century details had been removed, disguised or diminished. It felt very modern, with high ceilings, lots of plate glass and chrome, an open, free-flowing floor plan, even L.E.D. panels announcing the screening times for various IMAX films.

I took it in and then sighed my disappointment. With every passing century, much was gained, but I also knew a lot was lost. I'd come here hoping to remember a slower, less complicated time.

After paying my entrance fee, I headed up the stairs. The Ambasz exhibit was neither large nor exciting. It featured office cubicles, lighting and ergonomic chairs. There was a case displaying flexible pens and toothbrushes and another case filled with engine parts.

A handful of design students milled around, taking notes from bland information boards, which dully discussed Ambasz's unusual twist on otherwise ordinary items. The exhibit barely touched on the man's return-to-nature thinking.

I found myself a bit bored. I remembered him as a man of quick wit and contagious enthusiasm. I'd read an article once that described him as a design poet, as fitting a description as any I could come up with. None of those things seemed evident in this exhibit. It was disappointing.

Carly has a quick wit, I remembered, wondering what her take on flexible pens might be.

I checked my museum map and decided the more historic exhibits might evoke those feelings I'd come here to find. I started with the museum's oldest permanent exhibit; I'd heard wonderful reviews of the Coal Mine tour and wanted to see it for myself. Even though I had to wait in line for half an hour only to be packed into a dark elevator with about fifteen field-tripping middle-schoolers and our sweaty tour guide, it didn't disappoint.

We stepped off the elevator into a claustrophobic underground cave. As our guide began discussing the mechanics of coal formation and extraction, I marveled at the layers of limestone that shaped the walls and ceiling around us. How subtly the colors changed! Nothing in the natural world failed to enthrall me, not even black and gray rock.

I wondered if Carly had ever been here. I could easily picture her among the twelve-year-olds, twisting her hair and popping her gum like the girl standing beside me.

But she would be more interested than that, wouldn't she? I wondered. *Especially in light of the recent mining disasters.* I could imagine her taking on this cause, lobbying for stricter enforcement of safety regulations.

I didn't daydream long. I was fascinated to learn about the technology of coal mining, and how it has improved over the years. Our guide took every available opportunity to demonstrate how safe mining has become, from methane detection to cave-in protection. He assured us that, despite recent events, most mining operations were quite sound.

Still, I found it hard to believe that people would volunteer for this dangerous, loud, dirty, claustrophobic work. I found myself praying for the men and women laboring in such places all around the globe.

After my tour ended, I returned to the brightly lit, wide-open exhibition space and spent a few minutes wandering aimlessly. I'd noticed the Yesterday's Main Street exhibit on my way into the mine. It comprised a few storefronts, re-created from the early 1900's, through which one could peek at history without disturbing it. I chose to visit that area next. I'd hoped to relive a bit of my own Chicago history, but the first window I came to, a clothing shop, seemed overwhelmed by the large open space of the museum. It wasn't possible to fully drift into the past. Still, the re-creation was accurate. I passed some time staring into the display windows, spying many familiar objects, particularly in the drugstore. I shivered when my eyes fell on a straight-blade razor. That thing brought back some painful memories.

Within the exhibit was a functioning ice-cream parlor, Finnigan's. I stopped by for French-Vanilla ice cream and closed my eyes while I ate it. Working hard to tune out the modern language all around me, I imagined Carly here, dressed in a lacy Edwardian gown, her hair piled in the style of a Gibson girl. The daydream didn't work, though. Carly's personality differed greatly from that of a classic Gibson girl.

I remembered our date and checked my kinetic watch, wishing briefly for calligraphed numbers on the face and a knob to wind. Although I hadn't seen much of the museum, I had only a couple of hours left to enjoy the weather before I'd have to head home to get ready.

Outside, I followed the walking path south along Cornell Avenue and entered Jackson Park, heading for Wooded Island. Feeling warm, I removed my trench coat and draped it across my arm. I tipped my head to the sunshine and inhaled the breeze off the lake. It was fragranced by the decay of the fallen leaves, which lined the path and reminded me of what I do like about autumn in the Midwestern United States.

An ornate Japanese gate, marking the entrance to Osaka Garden, drew me in. I startled and scared away a couple of college kids who'd come here, apparently, to make out. They left me with the whole garden to myself. I hadn't even known it existed.

I naturally slipped into prayer as I wandered, surrounded by His creation. The gravel path meandered around perfectly planted flowerbeds, bridged a large lily pond and climbed up to a pavilion where a musical waterfall provided rhythm for my prayers.

I thanked God for the beauty and vastness of His world, and for all He'd allowed me to see of it. I thanked Him for the human creativity and ingenuity required to build this particular piece of paradise and for the insects, birds, squirrels and chipmunks that called it home.

I was still praying when I left the garden and resumed my stroll around Wooded Island. I prayed for myself, for my taxi-driver and for all of the University of Chicago students milling around me, quite probably ditching class as I was ditching work.

I excused myself, *Prayer is my real job after all.*

My Lord said nothing to contradict me.

I began praying for Carly, which dissolved almost instantly into daydreaming about Carly. I could picture her eyes, her lips, the wind filtering through her straight, silky hair. I could almost hear her smoky voice teasing me about chocolate milk and my other foibles. I could almost feel her soft, warm hand in mine....

The physical attraction was strong, but this wasn't the first time I'd had to deal with my humanity interfering with my work. Certain options simply were not open to me.

Like long-term relationships... or physical ones. I'd reconciled myself to that truth long ago. *And anyway, she's little more than a child*, I reminded myself, *while I'm a very old man.*

My young man's body protested, and I changed my thought pattern again. My Lord had placed us on the street together yesterday so that I could share His great love, not my own.

I opened the 'Carly file' in my mind, determined to separate the physical from the spiritual. We were both charitable people, and that is where I would find our greatest connection.

Imagining the conversations I wanted to have brought her voice back into my head. With her voice, came her eyes, and I was undone once more. It was too great a temptation to imagine her here with me, strolling hand in hand.

Before I knew it, I had walked the longest loop on Wooded Island and found myself heading back toward Cornell Avenue. Lost in my daydream, I hadn't paid attention to where my feet had taken me.

If I'd been more alert, I would have noticed that, suddenly, the sky seemed a little darker, that the wind seemed a little colder, that the birds had stopped singing, that I was alone on this path near the road.

If I had been more alert, I would have noticed the straw-colored 1989 Chrysler sedan, oddly pulled off onto the shoulder of the northbound lane of Cornell.

If I'd been more alert, I would have felt the dark eyes peering out of that car, willing me to gaze into the window.

Trinity! my Lord whispered urgently into my addled brain.

I knew that He wasn't talking about Himself. I also knew that Trinity was not an enemy to face unprepared.

The signs I'd missed before came together rapidly. I shut down all thoughts of Carly and forgot all human desires. This job required the focus of a neurosurgeon.

"Grant me the use of Your Spirit's power, Lord," I prayed, "that I might send this beast to judgment before Your throne!"

I felt surges of adrenaline and testosterone, but knew those to be reactions of my own body. I wanted to feel the cold, tingling electricity that would indicate His Spirit's power was working within me, but it did not come. Instead, He answered as He has each of the countless other times I've encountered Trinity.

"Not today, my son."

I ground my teeth, grunting in frustration. Why would He allow this evil to continue plaguing His Earth? Both of us knew that, if I kept my concentration, I could destroy Trinity with a single command backed by the Lord's power.

I wanted to fight so badly, I nearly forgot that, on my own against Trinity, I was pretty much helpless. I even took a few more confident strides toward the vehicle as the car's passenger door opened and the shadowy figure within moved.

What are you thinking? I screamed at myself as my reflex for self-preservation finally kicked in. Knowing that Trinity couldn't recognize me unless it saw my soul, and that it couldn't see my soul unless we made eye contact, I turned my face away and bolted to the west, crossing Cornell behind the Chrysler, both blessed and cursed by the lack of traffic on that normally busy street.

I heard the car's door slam, and the engine rev. The tires squealed as the driver pulled a U-turn.

I fought my rising panic. This thing that called itself 'Trinity' as an affront to God was in fact, three demons that had blended and bound themselves into one very powerful monster. It usually borrowed a human host to get around and to influence others. It discarded its hosts violently once they were no longer needed.

Even though it could not possess my body, nor anyone's in whom the Holy Spirit of God resided, Trinity could attack me physically. Even if I had been granted full use of the Spirit's power, it could still send me to my King's throne. It was one of the few things on Earth that could.

Without proper concentration.... I stopped that thought, not wanting to admit that I'd been so distracted by my daydreams that I hadn't even noticed the signs of the demon's presence. I didn't want to think that my obsession with Carly might be the reason my Lord had withheld His spirit from me.

You know it isn't, He assured me.

I tossed my coat away so that I could move more freely. "What is *it* doing in Chicago?" I cried as I ran. My last encounter with Trinity had been in Paris, many months ago.

My Lord sent me a memory of a poster I'd seen earlier, the one advertising the Saints and Demons exhibit.

Figures, I thought sarcastically. Trinity had come to see itself on canvas, to revel in the admiration of humans enthralled by its twisted beauty. It lacked for nothing in the vanity department.

Since the car had to — or at least, chose to— stay on the roads, I used creation for cover. Once the driver had committed to westbound Midway Plaisance, I angled north, racing across the remaining stretch of park.

I dove behind a row of bushes, landing flat on my stomach. I both heard and felt the air whoosh from my lungs. As I struggled to regain my breath, I parted a few branches in front of me so that I could watch Stony Island Avenue.

The car turned north and slowly rolled by my hiding place. I waited until it had passed the 59th Street intersection and then pushed myself up and sprinted across the road behind it, racing for the University of Chicago campus.

The driver saw me. The car accelerated. I didn't know if it would turn around again or try to cut me off on a different street. I didn't wait to find out.

My pulse pounded. I gulped for air. My muscles felt tight and strained. Not because I lacked conditioning, but out of sheer panic. I stayed off the pavement as much as possible, cutting around buildings, pushing myself to go faster, begging my Lord to reconsider granting me access to His Spirit.

He didn't.

My eyes flashed around quickly each time I had to come into the open or before I crossed a street. I saw one patch of yellow, but didn't pause to determine if it was the Chrysler. I didn't even register the exact color.

I prayed for my life and for a safe route and for a safe harbor.

This, He provided.

I skirted the perimeter of the Laboratory Schools, slipped between two buildings I had no inclination to look for the names of, and there, dead ahead across Woodlawn Avenue, rose the Gothic, ivy-covered architecture of Rockefeller Chapel.

I charged across the street, not watching for traffic of any color, fixated on the wide-open double doors and oblivious to everything else.

The chapel's narthex folded me in, encasing me like a cocoon as I crossed the threshold.

Safe!

I doubled over with my hands on my knees, drenched in sweat and panting. My eyes stung. My whole body ached.

I was lucky to be alive, and I knew it. Within two weeks of Halloween and with a Saints and Demons exhibit in town, I'd allowed myself to get distracted by a woman.

Idiot! I called myself and then pleaded to my Lord, *Forgive me; forgive me; forgive me.*

"Can I help you?" a gentle voice asked.

I straightened, blinking at the man who'd spoken, wondering if he was the pastor of this place. No symbol marked him as such. He wore casual clothing. Silver-streaked his conservatively styled hair. His dark brown eyes were filled with concern, although he did not otherwise indicate that he'd noticed the sweat-stains, the dirt or the leaves caught in my hair.

He held a brownish-green tweed jacket folded over one arm, as if he'd just been heading out. It reminded me of my trench coat, which I wasn't about to go back for.

"I… need… a place… to pray," I panted at him.

He reached out to me, but did not touch me. With the other hand, he gestured toward the sanctuary. "May it bring you peace," he said, adding, "Would you like me to pray with you, son?"

I was usually the one making that offer. My soul relaxed. "Not today, Sir," I replied, "but I very much appreciate your offer."

He nodded, motioning again to the sanctuary, and then went on his way.

I entered the light-filled nave, humbled, and took a seat in the first pew I came to.

There were many people roaming through the sanctuary, though no one noticed me. Most of them stood gawking at the architectural details. Normally, I would have been as well. But instead, I closed my eyes, placing my elbows on my knees, my head in my hands. Quietly, I waited for Him.

Love flowed all around me. Love so great, I wondered if I'd ever been loved before.

Timon, He whispered.

My tears fell, caught by my own hands. I wasn't even sure why I was crying. Because I'd nearly been caught by Trinity? Because I'd allowed myself to become distracted by Carly? Because I'd failed my Lord? Because He loved me anyway? Because I was physically and emotionally drained? *Yes, all of these*, I concluded.

"Forgive me," I whispered aloud.

There is nothing to *forgive*, He assured me.

Maybe not yet, I replied, silently now, *but, obviously, I'm the wrong person to help Carly. Send her someone who….*

He interrupted me. *Is this your choice, Timon? Have you decided not to meet with Carly tonight? You wish to let her go?*

Put that way, I had to stop and think about it. Carly would be at Farfelle d'Amoré this evening. Could I really stand her up? Could I live without ever really knowing the sea that was Carly Benson?

I was still thinking about it when my Lord added, *You've never made a choice that I could not manage, Timon.*

But won't Trinity hunt me now? I couldn't endanger Carly, even if that meant hurting her.

It may, but Trinity has never made a choice I could not manage either, He reminded me.

I knew that was true. I took a deep breath and said, *All right. I'll meet with Carly this evening as planned.*

Very well. He's reply sounded pleased, but He didn't say, specifically, that He was.

"Thank you," I whispered.

Chapter Four

When my cab pulled up in front of Farfelle d'Amoré that evening, Carly was already waiting, leaning against the stucco-coated building. Her purse, the strap held tight with both hands, swung between her knees. Her head bobbed in rhythm to the Italian music being piped out through a speaker above her head. I couldn't suppress an image of waves rolling rhythmically against a rocky shore as I watched her move.

I'd arrived a few minutes late, but less than five. A surprising statistic, given my race home to shower and change before catching a taxi back north. My heart was still pounding hard.

She hadn't noticed my cab yet, so I used the excuse of paying my driver with a credit card to study Carly for a little while longer. She'd left her hair down, which I liked, but she had on far more makeup than she needed. Her eyes were shadowed in smoky grays, the lashes thickened and black. Her lips were painted an unnatural crimson. The blush on her cheeks was false this time.

My eyes strayed to her soft, rose-pink sweater dress. It fit perfectly over her petite frame, emphasizing every curve and plane. As I'd noticed earlier in the day, she was more beautiful in person than she could ever be in my memories, despite the unnecessary makeup.

Careful, I warned myself. Then, to lighten my own mood, I asked Him, *Why did you have to make her so perfect? Why did you choose to make her like the sea?*

I could sense Him beaming in response, but there was no answer.

I slid from the taxi, fixing my smile, vowing to control my thoughts. I walked purposefully toward her.

"I'm happy to see you again, Carly," I said, keeping my eyes on her face now.

She looked, at first, as if she might have a snappy retort, but then her expression changed to something more serious, and she said, "You, too.... Everything okay?"

I forced myself not to shudder. "Does it show?" I asked.

She raised one eyebrow, nodding.

"Let's just say I've had a bad afternoon and leave it at that."

She smiled supportively and hooked her arm around mine, as if we were old friends. I guess we were. Sharing experiences of terror binds humans quickly, and whether she knew it or not, she'd been with me through two in a twenty-four hour period. We walked into the restaurant, saying nothing more.

When I'd made the reservation, I'd requested a private table. The hostess didn't disappoint me. She led us to a high-backed, mahogany booth in the back.

The place fit the stereotype of 'Italian Restaurant' perfectly. The bench seats were covered in red leather, the table in a red and white checkered cloth. There was even a basket of thin, twisted breadsticks waiting for us. The room was dim, lit mostly by candlelight.

It felt right, sitting across a table from Carly again. The hours we'd spent apart, even the horror of Trinity, faded as if I'd dreamt it all. My pulse-rate slowed; my confidence returned.

"How was your afternoon?" I asked casually.

"Boring." She quickly changed the subject. "I'm having trouble placing your accent. It's not quite Middle-Eastern, not quite European." As she spoke, she rested her forearms on the table and leaned toward me.

"I've lived all over the world," I told her, holding my shoulders stiffly against the seatback. *How can I keep a clear head with those eyes just inches away?*

"Italy?" she asked.

Ah, sweet Mediterranean… "Sí."

She grinned. "Then you can tell me if 'Farfelle d'Amoré' really means, ' pasta of love.'"

I chuckled. "If you translate it literally."

"Like, what other way is there?"

I felt myself fall toward her, until I'd mirrored her pose. I couldn't help myself; her sparkling eyes, like sunlight dancing over warm waves, had drawn me in. *Don't think; just dive.* "In Italy," I explained, "food and love are part of the same package, closely intertwined. The name is meant to evoke an air of romance."

She smiled at that. "Where else have you lived?"

I shrugged. "Everywhere."

"But where?" she pressed.

"I doubt you could name a place that's *not* on my list."

Her eyes flashed at the challenge. "Tanzania?" she guessed.

I replied in Swahili, "Ndiyo ndiyo," nodding my head, and okay, showing off a bit. "But that was awhile ago."

"No way!" she exclaimed.

I shrugged again. "Most of my time in Africa has been spent in Sudan, Rwanda and Ethiopia." *At least recently*, I added to myself.

Wide-eyed, she whispered, "Doing what?"

"Philanthropy." Sensing her interest, I continued, "In Rwanda, for example, I worked with a group of medical relief workers, headed by a couple from southern Wales. He was an internist, and she was a gynecologist. I spent three months with them, traveling to various refugee camps."

"That must have been tough-but-amazing," she inserted, truly awed.

"It was a challenge," I agreed, "but there were many miraculous moments, too. I remember, we were working near a town called Munigi when a twelve-year-old boy arrived, having dragged his injured mother and baby sister on a homemade litter for over fifteen miles! He was so ill, he could barely stand, but he wouldn't let us look at him until after we'd convinced him that his family would be okay.

"His mother had been beaten, both of her legs broken. The baby was malnourished, but not sick. Turned out, the boy was worse off than either of them. He had malaria, an advanced case. It was touch-and-go for days, but thank God, we were able to cure him. We left him as strong physically as he'd been mentally on the day he'd arrived at our camp."

I was glad to share this story with its happy ending, and the event was recent enough, I didn't have to edit much out, except that I was the pediatrician who'd diagnosed and treated the boy and his baby sister.

Remembering the Prichards, the couple I'd worked with there, always brought a tinge of longing. I'd been envious of their marriage, watching them share the joys and trials of their work, drawing strength from each other through each difficult case. I couldn't count how many times on that trip I had wished for someone to put her arms around me.... And then I'd gone to Iran, where things had gotten worse.

I could have easily fallen into despondency with those thoughts, but Carly, having hung on every word of the first story, pressed me for more. I always have more. As my stories unfolded, I added more of my faith, until I felt I was fully illustrating God's love rather than anything I'd done without Him.

She didn't question it. Her enthusiasm never waned. She plied me with question after question.

At last, I felt that I'd monopolized the conversation for far too long and said, "So, that's what I was doing in Africa."

"Wow, dude, that's the life I dream of!"

Wow, indeed. Suddenly, I saw a vision of us on the edge of the jungle, bringing medicine and hope to the world's most needy people. Longing for a partner threatened to overwhelm me again.

I broke the spell she had on me by sitting up straight.

"Why'd you come back?" she asked, making assumptions that I didn't correct.

"I got a little burned out, actually," I admitted, frowning. "For every happy ending there are dozens that are… not so happy."

She nodded her understanding, but then said brightly, "Don't go getting all glum on me! New topic…. How many languages do you know?"

I didn't have to force my smile. "A few." *All of the human ones.* I'd received that gift at Pentecost.

She squinted at me. "You must be older than you look."

The comment caught me by surprise, just as I was, in fact, considering how very long I had been alive. I laughed, hard, like I'd never heard a better joke. All the tension of the day drained out of me.

"What?" she asked suspiciously. "Why is that so funny?"

I composed myself. "Mostly, I just needed an excuse to laugh. It's my turn to ask a question, I think."

"Oh, is that how this is gonna go?" She tipped her head and looked at me from under her darkened lashes. My heart rate jumped in response. It had been so long since anyone had flirted with me like that, I'd forgotten how to react appropriately.

"It's only fair," I quipped, trying not to give myself away. "What were you doing on Russell Street yesterday?"

"Like, you can ask me anything at all, and that's what you want to know?"

"You'd rather not say?"

"No, I'll say." She paused. "Actually, I don't really know. I normally take the 'L' home after work, but Jen had asked me to meet her for drinks. When she didn't show up, I went outside to look for her. I was out there, texting, trying to find her, when *bam*," she clapped her hands for effect, "some oaf shoves me out into traffic!"

I nodded, wondering if she'd noticed the gun. "Oaf?" I echoed.

"As in *off*ender."

Yeah. She'd seen the gun.

"My turn," she continued.

"Whoa, I've been talking all night! And you've already asked a million questions," I pointed out. "I want to know more about you."

She shrugged. "I answer the phones at Scheoff Publishing. I've lived in Chicago my whole life, never been beyond the suburbs. I'm still cohabiting with my mom. Dad's ancient history. That's the whole story."

I doubted it. "How old are you?" I asked. She seemed so young. Too young for me to be so interested in, in fact, but I couldn't help myself.

She raised her thin eyebrows. "Truthfully? ... Twenty." She wasn't lying. I could usually tell. She continued, "How old are you?"

It was such a natural thing to reply, "Twenty-eight." I'd said it thousands of times in hundreds of languages. *Neither the truth, nor a lie.*

"Not so old after all," she said, seeming pleased.

Our waitress returned for the third time to take our order, and I felt ridiculous apologizing to her again for not being ready. Although we'd had plenty of time, neither of us had so much as cracked open a menu. I promised myself that, no matter how bad the service was for the rest of the evening, I'd double my ordinary tip.

Carly, meanwhile, was scanning the wine list. I plucked it from her hand and returned it to its holder. "We'll have water," I told the waitress then asked her to come back for our food order, promising we'd be ready. To her credit, she did not roll her eyes at me.

Carly leaned forward and whispered, "She wouldn't have carded me."

"That's hardly the point," I answered.

She looked surprised. "You don't drink?"

"Not when my dinner partner is under-age."

She shook her head, but said nothing more until the waitress returned, at which time she ordered Tortellini Alfredo and then pouted over her manicure.

I ordered the first entrée on the menu, in fluid Italian, without thinking. I was worried that I'd just ruined both my first date in almost a century and, worse, any chance of speaking with Carly about matters of spirit. *And it had been going so well*!

"Why are you looking at me like that?" she asked once we were alone again.

"I think you're mad at me."

She twirled a strand of her hair. I couldn't help remembering the young girl in the mine exhibit.

"I'm trying to figure you out.... Jaden." She said my name slowly. I was relieved to hear it. With her frequent use of 'dude,' instead, I'd wondered if she'd forgotten.

"It's different, isn't it?" she asked.

I blinked. "What is?"

"Your name. It's different."

"Hebrew, actually."

"You're Jewish?" She considered it for a moment. "You're a little taller than most, but I guess you look sort of Jewish."

"I was once," I answered, sensing a possible opening.

She scoffed. "You can't stop being Jewish!"

I took a chance, knowing the word I was about to use carried a lot of baggage with it, for some people, anyway. "I'm a Christian now."

How odd, I thought, realizing that it had been easier for me to say that word to an Arabic man than to an American woman. To my relief, it didn't put Carly off.

"Well, then," she replied, "you're a... what's it called? Messianic Jew."

I felt my eyes widen. "Yes, that *is* what it's called, but I'm surprised you know the term." I rushed to add, "Not a lot of non-Jewish people do."

She shrugged. "I read a lot… working for a publisher and all."

"Ah." I nodded. "That makes sense. However, I am not a Messianic Jew. I'm a Christian." I inhaled to go on, but before I could, she spoke again.

"I'm not anything; I don't have time for God."

"We know," I replied. *Idiot!* I called myself, even as the words were leaving my lips.

She sat up straighter, blinking. "We?"

All of my carefully planned phrases evaporated. I looked down. "Sorry… I'm… close to God. A little closer than most people."

"Like… you're a priest?" she asked, sort of hopefully, as if that would excuse me of my word choice.

"Not a priest or a pastor, but like that. I pray a lot." I could save this. I forced myself to meet her eye. "Carly, I have to ask you…. Do you think… what happened yesterday might have been God's attempt to get your attention?"

She stared at me for a while. "You know, Jaden, if you were really all that close to… you know, *God*, …then you'd know that, in my life, I've faced far more horrifying things than traffic."

Show me, I asked Him, but He didn't.

"You really aren't feeling your mortality after that experience?" I pressed.

She looked away. "I don't have time for metaphysical crap, either."

I briefly pressed my knuckles to my lips, and then said, "Look, Carly, I've spent a lot of time in prayer over this, and I feel very strongly that yesterday wasn't an accident... And perhaps, I wasn't supposed to interfere. God has these things planned.... Jesus called your name.... Death is still coming for you."

She laughed, but nervously. "Like, the guy with the black cloak and sickle?"

"I'm serious."

"Yeah, seriously scaring me." Her eyes sought the door, a long way off.

"I'm sorry. I don't mean to," I assured her. "It's just that... maybe you should find the time to explore matters of the spirit."

Her wide-eyes shot back to mine. "Because you think I'm about to *die*? Jesus Christ!"

I stiffened and begged, "*Don't* profane His name!" I couldn't tell her, at least not now, that doing so in my hearing caused me physical pain, like a heart attack. I did add, "Please," as softly as my gritted teeth would allow.

She rolled her eyes, so I closed mine for a moment. When I'd relaxed enough to force them open, she was staring at me, intently, with a look that conveyed her assurance that she now knew exactly why I was single, and that she needed to escape as quickly as possible.

"May I try to explain?" I asked hopefully.

She replied with, "You know, Mental Health Chicago is just a short cab ride away."

"Please?" I begged.

Her shoulders lifted slightly, but her expression didn't change.

I went forward anyway, "You heard me talking earlier about my time in Africa and the work I was doing."

She nodded slowly.

"Well... I'm kind of like a missionary. I spend a lot of time in prayer, and He, ah... Jesus, that is... guides me to the people He thinks I can help. He granted me some time to try... to talk to you about Him, and..." *Why am I babbling? What am I even saying?* I sighed and concluded, "I'm not doing too well with that, am I?"

Cautiously, she asked, "Do you talk with Jesus often, Jaden?"

I shrugged, casually, I hoped. "Sure.... Lots of people do, you know."

She nodded but pressed, "Does he talk back?"

I answered tentatively, "Yes."

"Out loud?" It didn't come out as an accusation, but as if she might be open to the idea.

I cringed anyway as I considered lying. I dropped my gaze to my hands, twisting them together in my lap.

"Jaden?"

I looked back at her and whispered, "What happens if I say... sometimes?"

She nodded, sadly, "With all your flinching and cringing, I kind of expected you to.... Does Jesus tell you what to do?"

I shook my head. "He just gives me information and lets me decide what to do about it."

"So," she continued carefully, "if he said something like, 'Carly needs to die,' you would then *decide* what to do about that?"

I felt almost as shocked by her implications as I had been by the sudden appearance of Trinity in the park today. I managed to croak out, "No!"

I cleared my throat and continued forcefully, "It's nothing like that! How can you possibly think that I would hurt you? Or anybody!"

She shrugged. "I don't know you at all, dude. So, thanks for yesterday, but...."

The waitress appeared with our meals. Carly smiled politely as the dish of tortellini in cream sauce was set before her. She finished her sentence, maybe not as she'd intended, after the woman left. "Let's just eat and say goodbye, okay?"

Very soon, He reminded me.

"Carly, I have to...."

"Stop! You have to stop," she ordered and popped a whole tortellini into her mouth.

I sighed, dropping my gaze to my hands once again. *What's happening to me?* I had, in my long lifetime, spoken the good news of Christ Jesus to presidents, kings and emperors, powerful men. Some had even wept at my words. Why couldn't I talk to one young woman in Chicago?

The difference, I realized, was that those men had been ready to hear it. Carly wasn't. I was rushing things. *Bad idea.*

I lifted my head to start over and noticed a strange look on Carly's face... and that she was rocking slightly… and turning purple. Grunting, she motioned frantically to her throat.

"Carly!" I cried, jumping from my seat. In one motion, I pulled her up, bent her over my fist and performed the Heimlich, not for the first time, but certainly, for the most desperate time in my life.

Chapter Five

At the restaurant manager's insistence, an ambulance had taken Carly from the restaurant to Saint Joseph Hospital. This was strictly a precautionary measure. She was going to be all right. She had politely, but pointedly, asked me not to follow her.

So, I'd gone home alone, but not really alone. My Lord spoke in His beautiful and terrifying voice as soon as the penthouse's door closed behind me.

"Yet again, Timon, you did not ask for my permission before you intervened."

He didn't sound angry, but that didn't mean He wasn't. I had now rescued Carly twice without His consent or even His input, and I was supposed to know better. Action without prayer: a very bad policy, indeed.

I dropped into submissive position right there on my entry rug. "Your kingdom come, Majesty. Your will be done…. Forgive my impetuousness, but I knew that her life was in your hands. My efforts could have been in vain."

He replied, "It is as you say."

I couldn't stop myself from asking, "What would you have done in my place?"

His laugher was real this time. It sounded like pealing bells, filling the room. "You remember me well," He admitted. "Although, you might also do well to remember that I never acted, not once, without my Father's blessing, even if you didn't hear me seek it." He let that sink in and then asked, "What will you do next?"

What indeed? I doubt she'll be willing to see me again. "I think she needs some space," I answered without really answering.

"Yes," He agreed. "You will have to wait on her choices, even after you've made yours…. But remember, I need her very soon."

Why should Carly have to die? I wondered. *To convert Jen? To reunite her parents? To torment me with desire and loss for the rest of my life?*

My Lord, of course, heard my thoughts. "Ah, Timon, my son, I never grow weary of you…. But of course you know, it is none of those things."

"I know," I answered.

"Do you also know that the time I have set for you and Carly to be together is a gift to you both?"

I was humbled. "Thank you," I whispered. I dared not ask how long the gift would last.

"I love you, Timon."

I knew it. I felt it. I loved Him, too.

I went to my office on Thursday morning and tried not to think about Carly, tried not to remember her leaning languidly across the table from me, my eyes lost in hers as I shared my experiences of Africa... before I'd messed it all up. I tried not to think that the damage I'd done might be irreversible.

But every time I successfully pushed Carly from my mind, Trinity snuck in. A potential vehicle for my own death loomed cold and foreboding on the southern horizon.

I gazed out my window in that direction, wondering, *How long will it stay in Chicago? Will I have a chance to fight it? Or will God continue to allow it to roam free? Will I be forced to run again?*

Thoughts of Trinity made me shiver. So, I imagined Carly's eyes once more and the warmth of the sea on a sunny day.

The morning crawled by while very little of the work on my desk got done. The inappropriate titles heading half of my emails didn't help. But I did manage to at least read the important messages. I even responded to a few. That was progress.

At lunchtime, I considered a trip to a McDonalds across town; she'd implied that it was her regular place. But since I'd decided to give her some time, I ordered in.

After lunch I held my weekly staff conference. We had to prepare for a client meeting with Clautex Industries, about twenty-four hours away. Plus, I needed to be in court on Monday to file a motion. So, there was a lot to discuss, a lot to distract. Thankfully. The afternoon hours passed quickly.

I ordered a pizza for dinner, anchovy and black olive, my favorite. I spent the rest of the evening cleaning. My place stayed pretty tidy, since I was so rarely home. But I recycled the old newspapers, dusted the glass shelves, books and electronics in the living room and sealed the granite counters in the kitchen. I even wiped a vinegar and water solution over my stainless steel.

I opened all the blinds and took in my views of the city lights, silently thanking my King for being so generous with me.

I should have cleaned my bathroom; the one room that needed it. But I didn't like dealing with actual filth, so I usually let it accumulate until I couldn't stand it anymore. Eventually, I'd call a maid service. It hadn't reached that point, yet.

My Lord didn't speak to me that night, which left me feeling more lonely than usual. I ended up imagining Carly, sitting on my black, leather sofa with a book in her hand, smiling over the cover at me, while I worked at my computer, preparing for tomorrow's meeting.

It was a hollow fantasy.

I checked the phone book in the morning, scanning the 'Be' pages over strong, black coffee.

I hadn't slept well. Again. Early on, I'd dreamed of evil, of Trinity, lurking around street corners. Waiting for a body. Waiting for me. I'd woken up, maybe screaming, unable to get back to sleep. It was one of those nights when I wished for someone to hold.

I'd moved out to the sofa but couldn't sleep there, either. For the rest of the night, I'd lain there, fighting an overwhelming sense that I was failing: failing God, failing myself, worst of all, failing Carly.

I wondered why on earth I'd been so truthful with her. I should have just lied and taken the pain. It wouldn't have been the first time. There were worse things than lying.

For example: Carly thought I was crazy, maybe even homicidal. Definitely, a *worse* thing!

I sputtered coffee, which I'd accidentally inhaled. It burned down my throat, making my eyes water. Coughing, I poured out my mug in the sink.

When I'd recovered, I returned my attention to the phone book.

There were three Carly Bensons with city addresses listed, plus, a C. B. Benson for good measure. I remembered that she lived with her mother and might not be listed at all.

You're not making this easy, I thought at my Lord. *Does that mean it's too soon?*

These are your choices, He reminded me.

I didn't know if that meant He supported my choices or not, but since I knew He wouldn't stop me, I tore out the page and took it to work.

On my lunch hour, I looked over the addresses again. *I should have brought the number for Scheoff Publishing*, I realized, but I could call information if it came to that.

I randomly selected the second Carly Benson and dialed. While it rang, I leaned back into my tufted leather chair, swiveling to gaze through the plate glass window at the city spread below me and Lake Michigan sparkling beyond. I enjoyed the perks of being in the King's service, perhaps too much. But then, He could take them away anytime He wanted.

The last phrase of Luke 12:48 popped into my head, *"from the one who has been entrusted with much, much more will be asked."*

I didn't have time to contemplate the quote. There was no mistaking Carly's sultry voice, weak as it was, when she answered the call, "Hello?"

I sat up. "Carly? It's me. Jaden."

"Jaden?" It sounded more like an accusation than my name. "How did you get this number?"

"The phone book."

"But... I never told you my last name."

I've never cursed. Never. But at that moment, many expletives jumped to mind. I held them in and blew out the pain, which came anyway, just for thinking them.

When I could inhale again, I said, "No. He did."

"He being... Jesus?"

My eyes closed. "I know how it sounds, but...."

She interrupted, "I'm not comfortable with this, Jaden."

"I'm sorry," I told her earnestly. "It's just that.... I'm worried about you. I had to rescue you twice in two days, and then, going a whole day without knowing...."

Her reply sounded tight. "I'm fine."

"You're not safe," I began.

"I know!" she snapped. "Because either Jesus really *does* want me dead, or you've spent the last twenty-four hours calling every Carly in the phone book until you got lucky!"

"You can't possibly believe I'm a threat to you," I insisted.

"I honestly don't know what to believe, Jaden. You tell me I'm on J.C.'s hit-list and the very next thing I know, I'm choking on what's supposed to be pasta of love!"

The fact that she would joke gave me hope. "Can I tell you what I believe?" I didn't give her a chance to say no. "The Lord Jesus Christ wants you before His throne. He's allowed me to stall the moment, but it *is* coming, and you need to be prepared."

She was silent for a while. I could tell she was smoking. I heard the regular, deep in- and ex-hales. To my surprise, she didn't hang up on me, so I waited.

At last, she asked, "Why would Jesus want me 'before his throne?' Assuming he exists at all, I mean."

"I don't know," I replied truthfully. *Apparently, I don't even have a good guess.* "As I tried to explain last night…."

She interrupted again, "Yeah, I heard what you said."

"But you misinterpreted me."

She snorted.

"Just… try an experiment before you label me crazy, okay?"

Silence.

"I'll take that as a yes… Think about what you're longing for the most right now. Focus on what's missing in your life, where your greatest needs are, and open your heart. Do this, and I bet you'll hear Him, too."

Several quiet minutes passed while I prayed for Him to reveal Himself to her.

"I'm hanging up now," she announced, sounding annoyed.

"Meet with me," I implored. "Let me tell you about His love and sacrifice."

"Like I haven't heard it all before! And you know what? I'm not feeling all that loved by him." She sounded almost angry now. "So how 'bout we say, 'you gave it your best shot, Jaden,' and let this thing go."

"I cannot let you go," I insisted.

She cried, "You don't know me at all!"

That should have made sense. It didn't. "Hamburger," I whispered.

She paused. "Excuse me?"

I took a deep breath and sighed it back out, rubbing my temple with my free hand. "Most people who donate food to the homeless either just hand over their left-over lunch or, if there's a well adver- tised collection, they'll drop in a can of baked beans that's been sitting in their cupboard for years…. You not only bought that homeless man a burger, you made sure you got it to him hot."

I added, passionately, "I cannot *imagine* why Jesus called your name right now, but I'm not giving you to Him without a fight!"

For a long moment, there was silence, and then she said, "Look, Jaden, I've gotta go. Really."

"Meet with me," I pleaded again, unable not to sound desperate.

More silence.

I squeezed my eyes closed and waited.

"Only in a very public place," she said softly.

I couldn't believe it! My pulse raced. "Anywhere."

She thought for a moment. "How about the Art Institute? I kind of want to see that Halloween exhibit."

It was my turn to pause. Trinity probably wouldn't look for me downtown, but that exhibit.... *Is it safe, Lord?*

Make your choice quickly, Timon, He answered. *She's waiting.*

I heard myself say, "Perfect!" in a surprisingly eager voice. "I can be there in... three minutes." I could see it from my window.

"But aren't you at work? Because, unless your last name is 'Bethany, Fink and Jones,' you're calling from an office somewhere."

"Just Bethany," I answered. "Our offices are downtown."

Her shock was audible. "Wait. You're a partner? At *that* law firm?"

I couldn't help but grin, thrilled that she'd heard of us.

She added, "Isn't that a little... far-reaching for a crazy person?"

"Will you take my law license as proof that I'm not crazy?"

"You said you were a philanthropist!"

"I am." I didn't add that I was, among other things, a doctor, a social worker and an educator. "But that takes money. So, right now, I'm also a lawyer."

I heard the cigarette again.

"Criminal law?" she guessed. "Does God's man spend his days putting dangerous non-believers behind bars?"

"No, corporate law. I spend my days negotiating contracts. When can you get here?"

"God, I don't know…. I need a shower first."

I grimaced at her use of His name; glad she couldn't see my pain, relieved that she was still coming.

"I have a client meeting at two, anyway," I told her, glad that I'd remembered it. "How's four o'clock?"

A pause. Then she answered, "I think they close at five."

She was right. I should have realized that myself.

"Tomorrow morning, then?" I offered. "I'll meet you out front at ten o'clock."

She considered it, but only briefly. "Yeah. I'll be there."

There wasn't a lot of excitement in her voice, but my heart rate jumped anyway. "Thank you," I breathed, addressing both her and Him. "I'll see you then," I added before hanging up.

Chapter Six

The sound of frozen raindrops tapping at my window glass woke me on Saturday morning. I wondered if the weather would keep Carly from showing up for what I couldn't stop myself from labeling 'our second date.' I decided not to ask Him. It was sleeting for a reason, quite probably unrelated to me, and I'd find out if she was coming or not when I got to the museum.

My normal Saturday routine would have me leisurely reading through the newspaper over a pot of coffee, but today, I swept the thick publication from my threshold and frisbeed it onto the coffee table without so much as glancing at the headlines. I didn't even make coffee. For breakfast, I ate an untoasted sesame-seed bagel and a carton of raspberry yogurt, washing it down with a tall glass of orange juice.

In the shower, I deliberated over what to wear. Jeans might be too casual, especially given my position at the Institute, but my other options seemed too formal for a Saturday morning. I didn't have a lot in my closet. My money went to other causes than clothing me. Yet, clothes did matter to me, keeping up with styles and trends helped me to hide from my enemies, and today, would help Carly to see me as a normal guy and not a crazy man. I settled on dark jeans and a blue and gray, vertical-striped shirt.

I looked myself over in the full-length mirror glued to the back of my bedroom door. No one would mistake me for the most handsome man in the world, but I couldn't look much better than this, every line smooth and straight, every hair in place.

Does that make me look more crazy, or less? I wondered, and then mussed up my hair a little.

I sorted through my closet for my old wool coat, so old, in fact, it could be called vintage. Considering whether I should replace the green trench coat or just let it go, I grabbed an umbrella and headed for the door.

I arrived at the Art Institute five minutes early. A forest of black umbrellas crowded the steps, people waiting for the doors to open. Just beyond them, at the base of the north lion, a standout pink umbrella twirled, first clockwise, then counter and back. As I watched, a thin plume of smoke curled out from under its rim.

After steeling myself for an anxious wait to find out whether she'd actually show, Carly had, in fact, beaten me once again.

She tilted the umbrella back and smiled tentatively as she watched me approach. Her full length, camel-colored coat, cinched at the waist, covered everything but the tops of her boots. I couldn't tell what she'd worn underneath and hoped she wouldn't think I'd dressed too casually. Or worse: that my clothes indicated that I was lying about my career.

"Sorry," I said. "I thought I was early…. Have you been waiting long?"

"Only a couple minutes." She dropped her cigarette butt and stepped on it, then looked up at the verdigrisy, bronze statue. "I came early to spend some time with my buddy."

"Ah," I replied. "You must come here often."

She looked back at me and sighed, "Can't afford to."

I searched her eyes for any sign of discomfort, but she seemed fine. "I'm glad you agreed to meet with me," I said, "but I must admit, I'm a little surprised."

She shrugged. "I don't know. You asked me to focus on what I thought I needed most, and the short answer is, 'someone to fight for me.' So when you said you wouldn't give me to J.C. without a fight, I figured I should give you a second chance."

I smiled, unable to resist saying, "So, I'm the answer to your prayers, then."

She scoffed, "Don't push it, dude."

Fine. But I wasn't going to stop grinning about it, either.

She quickly changed the subject. "How was your meeting?"

It took me a minute to recall. Yesterday. I'd spent a great deal of time during that meeting daydreaming about today. Brittany had been forced to clear her throat at me a number of times. I thanked God, again, for my on-the-ball assistant.

Fortunately, the Clautex case was pretty straight-forward. I was using it more as a training session for my protégé, Madison, than anything. She would be ready to step into my shoes whenever my Lord needed me to move on from Chicago. I felt very confident in her abilities.

Suddenly, I realized that I hadn't answered Carly's question. "It went well." I said, but her eyes had left mine.

I turned to see what had caught her attention. The museum had opened. The crowd began folding their umbrellas and making their way inside.

"Shall we?" I motioned toward the steps.

As soon as she moved, I bent down to retrieve Carly's cigarette butt, dropping it into a trash bin on the way by. If she noticed, she didn't comment.

"I hadn't expected it to be so busy," she said as we waited in line to get inside.

I had, but I didn't say so.

In front of us, a mother was trying to herd her three young children through the door without losing any. The youngest, a curly-haired cherub of about three-years, was giving her a hard time. She couldn't manage to hang onto him long enough to get the door open. People were pushing between her and her other children.

"Let me get that for you," I offered, hauling the heavy door open and holding it there for the older children to enter while their mom scooped up the little one.

"Thank you," she wheezed in a harried voice as she slipped through the door ahead of us, but her words were sincere.

I held the door for some other people who seemed to be ahead of us and then motioned Carly inside.

She gave me an admiring glance before turning to her left to get in the already-long ticket line.

"This way," I said, guiding her with my arm, not quite touching her shoulder.

"Don't we need tickets?" she asked.

"I'm a member," I told her, reaching for my wallet as we approached a podium at the base of the grand staircase. I recognized the girl standing there, a perky, blond sophomore of the institute.

"Good morning, Jess," I said brightly, handing her my membership card.

She didn't even look at it. "Well, hey, Doctor Bethany." She beamed. "It's good to see you."

"You, too. Are you working weekends now?" I realized, peripherally, that Carly was staring at me, lips slightly parted, but I didn't break eye contact with Jessica.

"Leaves more time for my projects," she answered. "One guest today?"

I nodded. "Yes. This is Carly…. We'll be taking in the Saints and Demons exhibit."

Jessica didn't look at Carly. She handed me a pamphlet for the exhibit as she returned my card. "You'll have to take the Rice Elevator, but you won't have to wait in line. Jake's over there." She motioned in the general direction. "If you want, I can have somebody hang your coats and umbrellas for you."

"I don't want to trouble you," I answered.

She leaned toward me and whispered, "It's not like I'm gonna do it myself." Then she called over her shoulder. "Hey, Pete!"

I shrugged out of my coat and helped Carly, who still seemed somewhat stunned, out of hers as well. I didn't recognize Pete, but he very politely took our things and told us where to pick them up when we were ready to leave.

Jessica was greeting the next people in line. I leaned toward her and whispered, "Thanks, Jess."

"See ya later, Doctor B.," she replied.

Carly didn't speak as we glided up the stairs. Free of her coat, I could see she'd also worn jeans and a fluffy, baby-pink sweater. I wondered if it was as soft as it looked.

As I opened the door to Gunsaulus Hall for her, she prompted, "*Doctor* Bethany?"

"Ph. D." I replied nonchalantly, not mentioning how many of those I had actually accumulated.

"And how do you know the ticket girl?"

Is that a hint of jealousy? Aloud, I said, "Jess? She's getting her BFA. Ceramics." I tried not to grin too much, but it was hard.

"Okay, but how do you *know* her?"

Definitely a hint of jealousy. My heart skipped a beat while I shrugged as casually as I could under the circumstances. "I come here a lot. I've met quite a few of the students, actually."

We passed through Gunsaulus Hall and exited the far door without having stopped to look at anything displayed there. A kid wearing a dark blue vest over his white shirt stood slightly slumped at the top of the next flight of stairs. He looked bored. Or maybe half-asleep. I didn't have to read his nametag; here was another friend, Jacob Robertson.

"Hey there, Jake."

His eyes lit up as he straightened to his full height of about six-foot four. "Doctor Bethany! Haven't seen you in a while. Are you headed up?" His eyes strayed to Carly and took in every inch of her. When he looked back at me, he was grinning quite foolishly.

She had that effect. "Yes," I answered. "Is it any good?"

"The statues are pretty cool," he offered.

I nodded. Jake's interests lie in filmmaking, so 3D object would appeal to him above the others. He motioned Carly and I toward the hidden elevator. As we passed him, I heard him tell two women behind us, "Sorry. This line's for Fellows only." He directed them to the growing line of people, snaking around Gallery 150.

As we stepped into the elevator, Carly whispered, "Did that boy fail to notice; I'm not a fellow?"

I laughed and said, "Oh, I believe he noticed!" while thinking, '*Boy*?' Even if he was, Jake hardly looked like a boy. He was several years older than Carly.

I continued, "He meant membership level." I had to admit it now. "I'm a Sustaining Fellow of the Institute."

She stared at me. "You're a philanthropist, a corporate lawyer with a Ph.D. *and* a Sustaining Fellow of the Art Institute."

I shrugged. "Among other things.... Have I convinced you, yet, that I am *entirely* sane?"

She squinted. "Hardly!"

"I will," I promised.

As we made our way through the Rice Building, I paused to read some of the boards on the history of Halloween and All Saints Day, curious as to how historians had remembered these things. Carly grew impatient with me. She grabbed my hand and pulled me toward Regenstein Hall.

I gazed at our hands twined together as shock and adrenaline raced through my bloodstream. I had to remind myself of when and where I lived, that this meant next to nothing to Carly. She had, in fact, done far more intimate things with men she hadn't known half as well, and admitted to it freely.

But for me, holding hands was about as far as I'd ever let a physical relationship go with any woman. This was a big deal.

I was still thinking about it when we entered the hall and her hand slipped away. I let her go, disappointed, and made myself focus on the exhibit.

The space had been divided in half. Visitors had to choose, upon entry, whether to follow the path to the Saints or one to the Demons.

A marble statue of Saint Peter guarded the entrance to the Saints wing, holding his arms in open invitation with a look of peace on his smooth face. His hair and beard curled symmetrically around head. His features were perfect and angular. I stared at the intelligent, watchful eyes. The only part the sculptor got right, in my opinion. I would not have recognized him without the plaque at his feet.

I followed Carly, who'd wandered in the other direction, to a similarly sized carving at the Demons entrance labeled 'Lucifer.' It wasn't Lucifer, however. Although I'd never seen him, Lucifer was known for his intense beauty.

This creature had a beautiful face, certainly, but a contorted and elongated one. Its mouth was warped into an expression that mixed ecstasy with agony. Its eyes were wide and wild, the body completely obscured by billowing robes. Its white hands were lifted to the height of its head, the fingers bent and twisted into unnatural positions. Looking closely, I could see swirls forming eyes in the knuckles, ears in the outer folds of skin and mouths in the lines between the fingers. These were not hands, in fact, but other heads.

This was Trinity. Mistaken for Lucifer and matched to Saint Peter! No wonder the demon had come to town.

I shivered.

Carly looked at me, her bright, Mediterranean eyes shining. "Scared, Jaden?" she teased.

She didn't know the half of it. "I'm more comfortable with the Saints," I whispered, stepping back toward Peter.

She went with me, but I'm pretty sure I would have kept going even if she hadn't.

Inside, the Saints' space was bright and open. We paused before a copy of Leonardo da Vinci's 'The Last Supper.'

I knew who each person in the painting was supposed to be, although they were all painted as much more beautiful, more fluid, and in fact, cleaner than they existed in my memory. I had not been there that Passover. Christ had chosen only the eleven plus Judas.

"Can you imagine it?" I asked Carly. "Look at Him." I indicted Jesus in the painting, who didn't look at all like the man I remembered except for the expression, which was flawlessly done.

I continued, "So peaceful, even though He knows what's about to happen. Da Vinci intended to capture the moment following Christ's revelation that one of them is about to betray Him…. See how they all react?"

She stared intently. "Which one's Judas?"

"Fourth from the left."

"That black guy?"

"Not 'black;' he's in shadow. It's supposed to represent that he's fallen."

She studied the painting for a moment longer and then asked, "Which one's Mary Magdalene?"

I snorted. "None of them."

"But the book!" Carly protested.

"Hate to ruin it for you," I scoffed, "but da Vinci's own notebooks give their names." I pointed down the row. "Bartholomew, James, Andrew, Judas, Peter and John. Jesus, of course. Then Thomas, the other

James and Phillip. On the right side are Matthew, Jude and Simon."

Carly frowned, disappointed. "So, there really weren't any women?"

"There were lots of women," I assured her, "just none at the last supper."

I decided to guide this conversation back to the one I wanted to have. "Have you ever thought about it?" I asked.

"About… this painting?"

"About what this painting is about, the sacrifice that Jesus made for His friends. For *all* of us, in fact.

"Do you realize that this," I motioned to the painting, "really was His last meal? Hours later, He was arrested. Within days, He'd been tried and crucified. Not for any crime that He'd committed, but as atonement for us. He chose to be the bridge, reuniting all people with God our Creator.

"There's an old word I like. Lenity. It means kindness and gentleness, love and mercy, charitableness and self-sacrifice, all of those things that Jesus stands for." I turned my attention from the painting to Carly. "And when I think of lenity, I think of you as well, Carly. I think you would like Jesus very much."

She shrugged. "J.C.'s cool. But I think of him more as an ideal than an actual person."

"But He *is* an actual person," I insisted, "the King of the Universe, in fact!"

"Is that what you believe?"

"It's the truth," I told her.

She hummed at me and then said, "I didn't realize it was Sunday morning."

I blinked. "What, am I preaching?"

"Uh, *yeah.*"

I shrugged. "You're the one who wanted to come here. You should have known I'd want to talk about the paintings."

"Yes, I should have," she sighed. "Are you going to give a sermon on each one? Should I prepare myself?"

I raised my hands in defeat. "Let's just look."

We moved on, scanning a few more paintings. True to my word, I kept my mouth shut. I moved slowly through the gallery, lost in my thoughts and memories. Impatient with me, Carly wandered away, looking on her own.

"Hey, Jaden," she called. "This one looks like you with a bad haircut."

I spun toward her, my eyes catching on the surprisingly accurate portrait of Saint Stephen before her. His hair had never looked like that, either, though.

Stephen, my heart whispered. My fingers reached out to the painting involuntarily before I forced my hand to my side.

He'd been my dearest friend, close to me in age and temperament. We were from the same part of Palestine, from the same Greek-speaking synagogue. We'd joined Jesus at about the same time and after Christ's ascension, we'd begun our ministry together, distributing food to widows and children in Jerusalem.

He'd been the first of us to die, stoned for speaking the truth to the Sanhedrin. That had been the second of many black, confusing days in my life. Forgiving Saul ranked high among the hardest things I'd ever done.

Looking back now, of course, I could see how God had taken that single choice of Saul's and used it to His glory a thousand-fold. Yes, I'd thoroughly forgiven Saul, as Stephen had wisely done in the moment. My friend had understood, better than I did at the time, Christ's message of love and self-sacrifice. It had taken me centuries to catch up.

After Stephen's death, the rest of us had disbanded. I'd wound up in Syria, preaching in Bostra... where my first, fiery death was recorded.

"Jaden?" Carly's voice called me to the present.

Blinking, I tore my eyes away from the painting to focus on her.

"You look like you're about to cry," she said.

"Saint Stephen," I whispered, unable to say anything more.

"Do you talk to him, too?" she asked, joking, I think.

I glared at her and then turned and walked away.

She trotted after me. "Hey! Wait!" she called.

I felt her take my hand. It didn't mean the same thing now.

"I'm sorry, Jaden," she said as gently as her deep voice would allow. "I really am."

I stopped walking and gazed into her eyes. She really was.

"It's fine," I told her, letting her lace our fingers together.

"Do you want to tell me about Stephen?" she asked, leaning against my arm. "I've never even heard the name, but obviously, he means a lot to you."

I shook my head. "I get too emotional around Saint Stephen. He's my... " I settled for, "inspiration."

She nodded. "All right then..." She cast her eyes around the room. "Tell me what that pretty little thing is."

Chapter Seven

Carly guided me to a display case holding what looked like the base of a lamp. Instead of a light bulb, it supported an ornate gold and silver box topped with a tiny cross-shaped finial.

"That's a reliquary," I answered.

Her brow furrowed. "Which is..?"

"A shrine for encasing holy relics."

Nodding thoughtfully, Carly leaned closer to the display and read the card inside. "John the Baptist's… tooth!" she exclaimed. "Dude! That's so gross!"

I couldn't argue.

"Do you think it's really in there?" she posed conspiratorially.

I hesitated, remembering how many 'sacred' objects had been marketed in the middle ages. Every church wanted to have something holy to display. Authenticity, however, was difficult to prove in those days. "I'm sure there's a tooth. It could be John the Baptist's," I conceded, "but I tend to doubt it."

She shuddered. "I think I'm ready for the demons," she told me, straightening.

I didn't want to go. I didn't want to leave the Saints, particularly Stephen, and I really didn't want to walk past that statue of Trinity. But Carly was still holding my hand, so I let her lead me.

The Demons' wing was darker, more dramatic than the Saints'. On display were a few small Japanese statues in glass cases and a familiar painting of Michael fighting a satanic-looking beast. The rest were an odd assortment of monsters, movie posters and erotica.

I heard myself sigh loudly.

"You bored?" Carly asked.

I looked at her. "Actually, I'm really uncomfortable."

She motioned to a smirking devil, red-faced and be-horned. "This upsets you?" She tentatively lifted our hands, fingers still twined together. "Or this?"

I placed my free hand over our linked ones. "*This* is wonderful," I assured her. "I just don't get *that*." I inclined my head toward the devil print. "Would it make you terribly unhappy if I stepped out for a minute? I should call my office."

"We can go if you want," she offered quickly.

"No. You don't have to miss anything," I insisted. "I'll just trot around the corner to the member's lounge, and you can meet me there when you're ready."

"I'm not a member," she reminded me.

"I'll watch for you," I promised. "Jake can point you in the right direction."

I felt her hand release mine, and I let her go. "See ya later, then," she said. I thought she sounded a little sad. But she'd already turned away from me, so I couldn't be sure.

I slipped out, ducking past the statue of Trinity without looking back and took the stairs down, two at a time.

Jacob still stood outside the elevator, directing the ever-growing crowd.

"Jake!" I called to get his attention as I closed the distance between us. When he turned to me, I asked, "Will my cell phone work from the member's lounge?"

"Should," he answered, looking past me. "What happened to your girlfriend?"

I chose not to correct the terminology. "I didn't want to bore her with office talk. But when she's finished up there, will you send her down the hall?"

He nodded.

"You'll recognize her, won't you?" I asked.

He smiled and said, "She's really pretty," kind of sheepishly.

"She is," I agreed, adding, "Thanks," as I patted his shoulder.

Calling the office on Saturdays wasn't required, but I usually checked in when big cases, like Clautex, were looming. I'd needed a truthful reason for my escape from the exhibit. This seemed like the sensible thing to do.

Brittany answered on the first ring.

"Why are you at work?" I teased her without even saying hello.

She laughed. "I'm trying to impress you. Somehow, I knew you'd call…. That and I wanted to download Gaines' PowerPoint presentation before Monday. Also, I'm getting a head start on research for the Phillips-Meyers case…. Oh, and Adam needed copies of the Bowden file this morning."

I wondered why Brittany would have that task when Adam had his own legal aid, but I didn't ask. "Sounds like you've got it under control as always," I told her. "Need me for anything?"

"You're not coming in?" She sounded disappointed.

I hesitated. Brittany tried to hide her crush on me, and I hated to hurt her in any way. But, there was no point in withholding the truth. "I think I'm on a date."

She hesitated for the briefest second before quipping, "Then you shouldn't be ignoring her like this."

She was right, of course. "I know, but I thought you might…."

"We're good," she sang over the rest of my sentence. "Have a great date, Jaden."

She hung up before I could sort out whether she'd actually said, 'date' or just 'day.'

I was alone in the Member's Lounge as I put my phone away. Still, it surprised me to hear my Lord's voice shout, "Usher!" so loudly. He added, "It has one of my little ones!"

Usher, I repeated. Not nearly as powerful as Trinity, the demon, Usher, was dangerous, nonetheless. Usher usually didn't possess humans itself, but rather, acted as a lure, finding individuals at risk for believing its lies. Once Usher hooked a person, it then 'ushered' him or her to a more powerful demon.

However, if Usher was feeling emboldened, perhaps by this exhibit or the holiday in general, it wasn't too surprising that it might pick a small victim of its own.

There were, no doubt, dozens of children at the museum today. I couldn't imagine driving a demon from one, especially not publicly, but I'd do it if the Lord would allow me the use of His Spirit's power this time.

"Where, my Lord?" I asked. "Show me."

He did, but it wasn't an image of the chubby, curly-haired three-year-old from the front steps that He formed in my mind. It was a nasty, silvery-yellow centipede, flitting along the edge of the wall under the sinks in the Member's Lounge restroom. I was both relieved and disgusted. So much so, that I grimaced.

My little one, He reminded me, which probably also meant that He'd be unhappy if I just walked in there and squished the insect. That really wouldn't solve the problem, anyway. Usher would simply move to a new host.

May I use the power of Your Spirit to 'usher' it to Your throne? I asked Him.

Instantly, I felt the cool-but-not-cold electricity of His Spirit's power awakening within me. Starting at the center of my chest, the power spread toward my fingertips with every beat of my heart.

I shouldered my way into the attached bathroom, my eyes searching for the bug. Fortunately, there were no patrons of the museum in the restroom. I wouldn't have to explain myself to anyone unless they happened to walk in. The insect was there, exactly where I'd expected to find it.

Centipedes normally sleep during the day. This one, however, was racing in circles around the tiled floor. It lifted and turned its head in order to see into my eyes, which is what the demon inside would need to do in order to view my soul. Normally, this was the moment when humans were most vulnerable. A demon could know all of a person's weaknesses with one glance at that person's soul. And once a person's weaknesses were known, the demons had no trouble exploiting them.

In my case, Usher could see not only my weaknesses, but also the power of the King that I wielded in His name.

The demon jerked the insect up, unnaturally, onto its rear sets of legs and arched it in my direction. It looked almost… cute. As if it wanted me to pick it up.

I wasn't fooled. "Usher, in the King's name, I command you to come out!" I drove the power of the Holy Spirit through my fingertips. It jumped across the space between us and entered the centipede.

The little body shook, but only for the briefest second, as Usher tried to hold on. Unable to resist the Lord's command, the demon rose like a veil of black fog, drifting out of the centipede's body.

Free, the insect dashed to the crease created where tiled wall met tiled floor and disappeared from sight.

As for Usher, it lacked the strength to stand against me. With my Lord's power, I compressed the fog into a ball, shrinking it smaller and smaller until it disappeared in a bright flash of red light.

The Spirit's power faded away. Usher was now on whatever passed for its knees before the throne of the Most High where it would receive fair judgment… and punishment.

I let out a long-held breath, but I wasn't in the clear yet.

My Lord's voice echoed through the room, "Raiser knows what you've just done and has alerted Trinity as well. Don't expect them to rest until they've searched every living being within this museum."

Trinity may or may not have recognized me when it chased me around campus, but now that I'd disposed of Usher, none of the demons could have any doubts about my identity. I reached for my Lord's power again, but He withheld it.

"Not at this time," He told me.

I didn't have time to argue. Raiser *and* Trinity were in pursuit. *How long will it take them to find me?* I couldn't wait for that answer either. I simply reacted, racing back into the Member's Lounge, bolting through the door, bursting into the crowded hall. I ignored the enraged shouts from two men I nearly ran over. I didn't even pause to apologize.

My Lord spoke into my thoughts before I'd regained my stride. *Raiser has entered the building.*

Does it have a host? I asked, dodging people as I sprinted for the Rice elevator.

Not yet, He replied. But before I could even begin to prepare for a face-off against a disembodied Raiser, my Lord continued, *Trinity is close.*

On my best day, I could never take Trinity and Raiser together. Raiser and something of Usher's caliber, maybe, but Trinity alone.... I stopped that thought and skidded to a halt in the middle of Gallery 150.

I'd found Carly. She stood close to Jake, her hand on his arm, laughing at whatever he'd just said. His head was bent low to talk to her, his eyes fixed on hers. I didn't have time to acknowledge my own moment of jealousy.

"I'm very sorry to interrupt," I said, approaching them, "but, Carly, we have to go. Right now."

She stepped away from Jake, asking me, "Trouble at the office?"

"Not exactly," I answered stiffly. "See you, Jake."

I hooked my hand under Carly's elbow and led her down the stairs, moving as fast as she could comfortably walk.

"You won't believe what he just asked me!" she began excitedly as we re-entered Gunsaulus Hall.

I replied with a distracted grunt as my eyes scanned the dark corners of the room. I worried about what might be lurking there unseen, even though the lights were still bright, and I felt no immediate threat.

"He wants me to star in his next movie!" Carly exclaimed. "He's making a documentary about volunteers who work with poor kids, and I told him I was a HOPES camp counselor last summer. So, he thought we'd be a perfect match!"

Normally, nothing could blur my focus when evil was closing in, but Carly's words sliced through my concentration. A bolt of electricity shot through me. "You were a HOPES counselor?" All I knew of the organization was that they provided after-school tutoring for homeless kids. I didn't know they offered a summer camp program. The image that came to my mind was of Carly in one of the medical camps where I'd worked. I knew it wasn't the same, but the picture stayed with me.

Carly responded, "Yeah. It got me out of the house for a couple weeks, and the kids were great... most the time." She added, "I had to use up every minute of vacation time I had, but it was worth it."

I wanted to pursue this conversation, badly, but I couldn't get excited about philanthropy now with danger imminent. I heard myself humming noncommittally in response to Carly's words.

A moment later, she asked, "Jaden, what's going on? You're not acting like yourself."

"I know. I'm sorry." What else could I say?

"Is everything all right with your case?"

I nodded.

She lowered her voice to an even more seductive level. "Are you upset because I'm attracted to Jake?"

I glanced at her. "I would be, if you actually were. But you're not, so I'm not."

She shook her head and exhaled a soft expletive. My shoulders stiffened, but I kept walking as she continued, "So it's a J.C. thing then?"

That sounded like an accusation. I didn't answer.

I held open the door at the far end of the hall for Carly. As I slipped through behind her, I felt Trinity advancing toward me on the grand staircase. Instantly, I dropped to one knee, pretending to tie my shoelace.

Trinity wouldn't know me if it didn't look me in the eye. I felt it pass quickly, rushing, no doubt, to the scene of Usher's departure. I waited until it had entered Gunsaulus Hall before rising. I took a deep, shuddering breath and noticed that Carly was already halfway down the stairs. I scrambled to catch up with her.

Unfortunately, Jessica still stood at the bottom of the stairs, and she'd seen me racing down.

"Leaving already, Doctor Bethany?" she asked.

I had to pause, at least long enough to acknowledge her question. Carly kept walking, but not headed for the front doors. Instead, she wandered off toward the gift shop.

"Something came up," I told Jessica. "I'll see you next time."

"Don't forget your coats!" Jess called.

Coats didn't matter. I skipped around an old man in my way and caught up to Carly just as she entered the museum shop.

I bowed my head to the level of her ear and hissed, "What are you doing?"

"Getting a post card," she answered, "to commemorate the day."

I put my hands on her shoulders and turned her to face me, fixing my eyes on hers. "I know you won't believe me, but we need to get out of this museum *right now*."

"Dude, we're no longer in the museum," she stated, stepping back from me. "And I want a postcard."

At war internally over whether to draw attention to myself by throwing her over my shoulder and carrying her out or to risk our safety by staying here in the hopes of sustaining our relationship, I clenched my teeth but didn't argue further. I just hoped that her technicality was correct.

I hated taking chances. Raiser and Trinity were somewhere in the building, attempting to scan the eyes of every patron, beginning in the members' washroom. When they didn't find me upstairs, they'd try down here. It was only a matter of time.

Still, I assured myself, *they can't complete their task too quickly.*

I followed Carly closely as we wove our way toward the postcards in the back, my senses trained on discerning any sign of Trinity or Raiser, my gaze lowered, just in case.

"Oh look!" Carly exclaimed, stopping at a glass display case filled with jewelry.

"I thought you wanted a postcard," I reminded her impatiently.

"But they're perfect!"

I finally looked at what she'd spotted, a pair of earrings, little dangling replicas of the lion statues out front. They were even the right shade of green.

"Cute," I said.

She turned her beautiful, sea-colored eyes on me. "Any chance you'd buy them for me?"

I didn't need to think about it. "In a heartbeat. *If* you promise that as soon as I pay for them, we're out of here."

She grinned. "Deal!"

As if on cue, a salesclerk appeared. She was older than most of the students, with orange-red hair piled high on her head, streaks of pink on her cheeks and bright lipstick. "Can I help you folks with anything today?" she asked in a heavy, mid-western accent.

"We'd like to purchase the lion earrings," I told her.

"These little jade ones, here?" she clarified.

Carly gasped, "Oh! They're jade?" She put her hand on my arm. "Jaden, that makes them even more perfect!"

I couldn't help but be charmed by the enthusiasm in her voice. I relaxed and even smiled at the clerk. "Those are the ones," I told her.

The woman slid the case open from behind the counter and brought the earrings out. Surreptitiously, she glanced at the price as she offered them to Carly who danced the little lions on her fingertips.

"They're one-hundred and thirty-five dollars," the clerk said to me, half-apologetically.

Carly inhaled sharply. "Oh," she said weakly, setting them back on the counter. "I didn't know they'd be so much…."

I shrugged and told the clerk, "That will be cash."

She beamed at me and picked up the earrings.

Carly turned to me, wide-eyed. "You can't spend that kind of money on me!"

"Ah! Ah!" I snapped. "You made a deal." I turned my attention to the clerk. "That's everything, and we're in a bit of a hurry, I'm afraid."

She didn't even pause to close the case. "I can ring them up for you right over here," she said, indicating that I would need to go around the counter's corner.

"I'll be right back," I said to Carly. "Stay here." It took me a moment to break away from her expression, mixing disbelief with gratitude, pleasure and anticipation.

I followed the clerk, pulling my wallet out as I went. It felt amazing to see Carly so happy. I was thrilled that I could give her a real gift, something she would treasure for the rest of her life. I wouldn't let myself think that that might not be the seventy-odd years I envisioned.

As the clerk worked, I planned the remainder of my day with Carly, walking over to the park or window-shopping the Miracle Mile, finding a café with a fireplace if we got too cold. There was still time to grab our coats and umbrellas, surely. Trinity and Raiser couldn't be half done upstairs, could they?

I was waiting for my change when the lights dimmed slightly. I felt a death-like chill brush the back of my neck. I shuddered. My euphoria evaporated. I instinctively squeezed my eyes closed, even as the clerk placed bills and coins into my outstretched palm.

Trinity, my Lord whispered.

We can still get out of here, I almost convinced myself.

I heard the woman say, "Thank you, and have a nice day." I felt the demon moving behind the counter, but it didn't enter the clerk, as I'd half-expected it to.

What's it doing? I asked my Lord. I didn't dare open my eyes, and He didn't answer me. I felt my change in one hand, the tiny, packet of earrings in the other. I turned back toward Carly, but I knew we were out of time. I had failed.

KA-BASH

I felt the explosion more than I heard it. It knocked me backward, off my feet. Shards of broken glass bit into my cheeks, my forehead, my fists raised for cover.

I landed hard, groaned and rolled over. Sensing Trinity high above me now, no doubt thrilling over the damage it had done, I kept my head down and pushed myself up on hands and knees.

When I finally opened my eyes and saw her, Carly was flat on her back. She had taken the full force of the demon's revenge. Apparently, the evil spirit had climbed inside the jewelry case and blown itself outward. As the broken glass had flown past Carly, a piece had sliced open the right side of her neck, just above her collar bone. Blood pulsed erratically from her wounded throat, soaking her pale sweater.

"Carly!" I cried, scrambling to her side. I checked her vitals. She was already losing consciousness.

Lord, may I save her? I begged within my mind.

You may use my power to keep her alive, He answered.

Even as I was thanking Him, His Spirit's power flooded through my hands. I pressed my fingers against the deep cut and prayed aloud in my native Greek as His spirit worked to mend her carotid artery. It didn't take long. The power left me before her skin closed.

I grabbed a T-shirt from a rack nearby and used it to apply pressure to the still bleeding wound. From the activity around me, I knew that others had been hurt as well. I prayed for them but stayed with Carly.

Where is Trinity? I asked my Lord. I could no longer feel it anywhere in the room.

When my power came into you, it fled, He replied.

Good. For once my Lord had given me use of His power in Trinity's presence. For once, the demon feared me. That didn't make me feel as relieved as it should have. Trinity would connect with Raiser and come looking for me. I knew Trinity well enough to know that it wouldn't rest now until one of us knelt before Christ's throne, and I was currently unarmed.

Will you ask me to face them without your power? I asked.

My power is not your only protection, Timon, He reminded me, adding, *Other choices have been made. You will not fight again today.*

Relief flooded through me. I wouldn't have to battle demons while Carly needed me, and for that I was profoundly grateful.

She roused, whispering, "Jaden?"

"I'm here," I assured her, stroking her hair. I could hear sirens outside. "You're going to be okay. The ambulance is on its way."

"Your face," she said weakly. "You're bleeding."

"It's superficial," I assured her, wiping my face with my own shirtsleeve. I winced. The cuts still stung.

"What happened?" she asked.

"I'm not sure." I wasn't exactly lying, but it hurt to say it anyway. A little. The pain of my physical wounds was worse. The thought that I'd almost lost her again because of my own stupidity was *much* worse. "The glass case shattered. You've been cut."

"I know," she whispered. "I meant, what did *you* do?"

Chapter Eight

Before I could answer Carly's question, a swarm of emergency workers flowed into the room, seeking out the injured, quickly determining that both Carly and I needed advanced medical attention. We rode to the hospital together, but were separated in the emergency room. By that time, the worst of my injuries had already healed. Fortunately, the E.R. doctor just assumed a mistake had been made on the report that accompanied me. He removed several small shards of glass from my hands and face, and placed stitches in the gash below my collarbone. I knew they would fall out, unnecessary, by the end of the day.

A short time later, I found myself sitting in a very warm waiting room, being interviewed by a surprisingly burly, female police officer.

I was able to answer her straightforward questions quite truthfully: Did I shatter the display case? No. Did I see the display case shatter? No. Did I see anyone with a weapon? No. Did I notice any unusual behavior from the other customers or the clerk? No. Prior to the explosion, did I hear or see anything unusual at all? Only that I noticed the lights dim a little.

I reviewed the actions of the clerk, Carly and myself with the officer. She didn't ask if there'd been a big, nasty, fog-like demon in the room, and so, I didn't tell her.

"What do you think happened?" I asked when we were nearly done.

She looked me over for a good three heartbeats before answering, "The clerk said someone fired a shot into the display case."

Good luck finding that bullet, I thought. "A robbery?" I pressed.

She shrugged and thanked me for my time.

I waited, praying, quite a while longer until I was finally allowed to see Carly.

The head of her bed was raised so she could sit up. A light blanket covered her legs. They had dressed her in a hospital gown. She had a big gauze patch taped to her neck, but aside from that, she looked better than I did.

"Are you okay?" she whispered, reaching for me. I could tell her eyes were taking in the amount of blood on my clothing. I didn't tell her that most of it was hers.

"Just some scratches," I assured her, taking her hand. "Are you okay?"

"The doctor said I was lucky, that the glass nearly nicked my carotid artery. I guess I lost a lot of blood anyway, so they're going to keep me overnight. I can probably go home tomorrow."

"Did you need stitches?" I asked, knowing the answer.

She nodded. "I have to see my regular doctor in a week to get them out."

"How's the pain? Did they give you anything?"

"Yeah, a shot before the stitches."

I grimaced.

"I'm okay," she assured me.

I let go of her hand just long enough to pull up a chair. I sat close to her head and laced our fingers together once more. "What can I do?"

She hesitated. "I'm pretty sure, you've already done... something."

I couldn't fuel her suspicions. I waited, my expression frozen in what I hoped passed for innocent concern.

"Tell me what happened," she pressed. "I was just standing there, thinking about how awesome you are. *Crazy*. But awesome.... Then the lights dimmed and there was a loud noise, and a lot of pain... And I heard your voice, but the words didn't make sense." She looked at me, willing me to fill in the blanks.

These were my choices. Tell Carly about Trinity and let her think I was even more insane than she already did. Lie, and take the pain. Or redirect. Admitting who I am was completely out of the question.

I picked option three. "The police say someone fired a gun into the display case."

She considered that for a moment. "Why?"

I shrugged, shaking my head.

"When you were talking, why couldn't I under-stand you?"

"Sorry. I didn't think you could hear me. I revert to my native language when I'm worried." *Like right now.* Realizing that my words had increased in both pace and pitch, I inhaled to slow myself down. I didn't have to lie, yet. "I was praying in Greek, asking God to help you."

"You're Greek? I would have sworn you'd said you were Jewish."

"My family was both," I admitted. "I don't con-sider myself either."

She was quiet for a moment and then asked, "So… Does this mean Jesus doesn't want me to die after all?"

"I'm not sure," I whispered.

My Lord remained silent on the subject, but I'd never known Him to change His mind about these things.

A nurse hauling a wheelchair backed into the room before I could say any more. She was young, though older than Carly, and heavy-set. Her dark brown hair was swept up and pinned back with kitty-shaped barrettes.

"Here we go, Carly," she announced. "Time to get you settled upstairs." She swung the wheelchair around and noticed me. "Oh, hi there. I'm Nicole," she extended her hand. She had a friendly smile. I could see His Spirit sparkling in her blue eyes.

I shook her hand. "Nice to meet you. I'm Jaden."

Carly glared at the chair. "I can walk," she told the nurse.

"Why walk when you can ride?" Nicole asked, winking at me.

"Can't argue with that logic," I said to Carly. "Up you go."

I hooked a hand under her arm and helped her from the bed to the wheelchair. She groaned as she settled onto the seat.

Nicole knelt beside her. "Is that shot wearing off already, Hon?" she asked, concerned.

Carly looked away.

Nicole moved into position behind the chair. "We'll get you some pain meds once we settle you in upstairs." She looked over her shoulder at me. "Could you grab her things, Sweetie?"

I located the bag containing Carly's purse, boots, jeans and undergarments. The sweater wasn't there. *Ruined*, I assumed and also realized that I'd have to go back to the Art Institute for our coats. I didn't have another one outside of my winter parka.

I put my hand in the front pocket of my jeans, relieved to find the small paper sack with the earrings there. I hadn't remembered what I'd done with them.

Nicole stayed for a while in the dim, upstairs room, making sure Carly's bed was adjusted to the right height, getting her water and a little cup of high-powered Ibuprofen pills, bringing the phone within reach. "She needs her rest," she told me on her way out.

I thanked her and promised I wouldn't stay long.

"I should go home and clean up," I said to Carly, pulling the paper sack from my pocket. I took her hand and dropped the earrings onto her palm.

She smiled weakly, petting one of the tiny lions. "Thank you," she whispered.

"Will you be okay until I get back?" I asked.

Her eyes shot up. "You're coming back?"

I hesitated. "Unless you don't want me to."

"No, I just…."

I never found out how she planned to finish that sentence. Instead, she said, "I'll be fine. I'm gonna call my mom, and then… probably watch TV all day."

"Excellent," I grinned. "I'll be back in time for the Bulls game." I'd always enjoyed sports, following various games and teams over the years. In this country and in this century, my favorite was basketball. I loved watching, even in the pre-season. It seemed like a nice way to relax after the day we'd had. "It starts at four."

She grimaced and then said, "Well, if the game's on, at least I'll get some sleep."

I went straight home from the hospital, spending a very long time in a very hot shower. After that, I threw away my blood-soaked clothes. I briefly considered tossing my wingtips on top of that garbage bag before I sent it down the chute.

Your bathroom is filthy, Timon, my Lord told me.

He hadn't spoken since the Art Institute, so this seemed like an extra-odd statement. I guessed that He expected me to clean it, though, and I obeyed without question. Perhaps this meant I would host a visitor. Carly, hopefully. But it might also mean that He wanted me out of the way for a while. It really could go either way.

It took me almost an hour, but my bathroom was spotless in the end. I finished off the leftover pizza before heading down to the garage. Normally, I didn't drive my very special car if I knew I'd have to leave it in public parking. But I had a lot to do in a short time period. It just didn't make sense to try getting around by bus, train or taxi.

The museum had been closed so police could investigate the accident, but plenty of people were milling around on the sidewalk anyway. Fortunately, the freezing rain had stopped. The sky remained heavy and overcast, and a cold wind blew in from the north.

I found one of the directors, a friend, who was relieved to see me. News had gotten around that I'd been in the museum shop when the explosion occurred. After I explained my situation to her, she found someone to retrieve my coat, Carly's, and our umbrellas. I stayed and answered a few more questions from police officers and from people I knew. I assured them all that Carly would be just fine. That came as a relief, especially for the director. No one had the first clue what had actually happened in the museum shop that morning.

Concentrating hard, I felt around, as far as my mind would reach, but found no evidence of Trinity or Raiser or any other demon in the area. My Lord offered no new information on them. Relieved nonetheless, I returned to my car and drove to Water Tower Place to do my shopping.

I picked out a simple, light pink, cashmere sweater for Carly. It was very similar to the one she'd had, and I knew exactly how soft this one was. I had it boxed for her.

For myself, I found another gray and blue vertical-striped shirt. It was displayed with matching gray chinos, so I bought those and a replacement pair of dark jeans as well. I passed by a shoe display with only a flickering thought toward finding comfortable dress shoes, but I was running low on time and not certain such a thing existed anyway.

I had to walk a few blocks to the nearest drug store where I picked up a hairbrush, a toothbrush, and some other essentials for Carly. I also grabbed a couple of popular magazines, although I had no idea what might interest her.

I got back to the hospital just after four o'clock and found Carly as I'd left her, sitting up in bed, watching the door. Her TV wasn't on, neither was her radio, neither was the overhead light, just a small side-table lamp. The cup of pills and glass of water sat, untouched, on her table. I wondered if they'd brought her anything to eat, yet.

I forced an encouraging smile as I hung up her coat and umbrella. "How are you feeling?" I asked, gliding to her bedside and dropping my bags. I noticed the lion earrings, still in her hand.

She shrugged and then grimaced at the pain it caused.

"Hey, don't do that," I said gently, brushing the hair away from her face, using the excuse to stroke her cheek.

She took my hand, firmly, and moved it to the bedrail.

Wondering what that meant, I folded my hands together and sat down in the chair beside her. "Has your mother been by?" I asked.

Carly replied stiffly, "Couldn't reach her.... I guess she's out."

"We'll try again later," I offered reassuringly. *Is she mad at her mother? Or at me? Why is she avoiding eye contact?* "So, I got you something," I offered tentatively as I handed over the plastic bag from the drug store.

She cautiously peeked inside and then smiled slightly. "Thanks, Jaden. It was really sweet of you to think of this."

I relaxed, relieved to see her mood lighten, if only a little. "That's not all." I reached into the bag at my feet and brought out the box with the sweater. I set it on her tray table.

"What's that?" she asked.

"Something to match the earrings."

"Can you open it for me?"

"Sure." I lifted the lid, pulled back the tissue paper and placed the box on her lap. "It's not exactly like the one you had...." I began, but she cut me off as she brushed her fingertips across the material.

"It's beautiful, Jaden. My favorite color.... But you shouldn't have."

"Why not?"

She set the box back on her tray table and finally met my eye. "Well.... I've been thinking a lot over the last couple of hours. About you and me and 'you and me.' I've figured out that you have a lot of money, which is normally the first thing that attracts me to a guy, but…"

I'd been waiting to look into her eyes, but now, I had to glance away. "It's not enough to make *me* attractive to you," I finished for her.

"Oh…. No. It's not that."

No? I looked back at her. "You're worried that I'm trying to buy your affection?"

She blinked as though that thought had never occurred to her. "No…. What I'm trying to say is… that it's not about the money with you, even though with other guys, it has been."

I raised an eyebrow. "Well, that's good… isn't it?"

She sighed. "Jaden, you're a kind, caring person, and I literally could listen to your accent all day long, but…."

"But you still think I'm crazy." I had it right this time; I could read it in her eyes.

So it surprised me when she said, "Not exactly. It's hard to put this into words…. I've noticed that… that the world operates differently when you're around… in a… a dangerous kind of way."

She paused, inhaling deeply, as if gathering courage. "I'm pretty good at hiding it, Jaden; I've had years to practice, but, I've gotta tell you… I'm dealing with a lot of crap in my life. And today's been the craziest rollercoaster of emotions that I've ever ridden. I just don't think I can do… this," she motioned back and forth between us, "right now."

My gaze lowered as my heart sank. I should have asked her what was going wrong in her life, but, in the moment, I couldn't be that selfless. "You're saying goodbye?" I asked sadly.

"Well, see… I can't. All my life I've been wishing for somebody to protect me, and here you've gone and saved my life three times in five days! …I'm kinda convinced that I need you."

I felt so confused. *Where does that leave us?* I wondered and figured I'd ask, even though I couldn't bring myself to look at her as I spoke. "So, what are you saying?"

She took another deep breath. "That we should just be friends…. And maybe see each other a lot less often."

I nodded, staring at my hands. *So this is what the old 'let's just be friends' line feels like.* I'd offered it often enough without ever realizing that it could actually hurt.

She was right, of course. Friendship was, by far, the best plan for both of us. Really, it was. Yet, I didn't want to give up what I'd discovered with her today. This hand-holding-inability-to-control-my-thoughts-about-her relationship was new. *New!* After two thousand years, it was a word I never thought I'd use again, except as it applied to electronics.

With Carly, I nearly had what I'd been missing in Africa, what I've been missing my whole life, in fact: someone to remind me that, even though I live on the edge between life and death, I am still very much alive. I loved these feelings!

Now, she was asking me to relinquish them. And she was right. I needed to. I just didn't know if I could.

"You okay?" she asked.

I forced myself to meet her eyes, but kept myself from falling into them for once. "Yeah," I said and admitted, "It's actually, *probably*, best for me right now as well, if we don't take our relationship beyond friendship."

She looked relieved.

"Do you...?" I almost stopped myself from asking, but then pressed on. "Is there anything you want to talk about? With a friend?"

She looked away with a brisk, decisive shake of her head.

I didn't want to pressure her. "So, I should go, I suppose," I said, rising.

"You don't have to," she insisted.

"But I should."

She nodded and asked hesitantly, "Do you want these back?" She held out the earrings.

I smiled. "That's okay. They really don't go with anything I own."

Her lips twitched and then she laughed. "Jaden Bethany, I didn't know you had a sense of humor!"

"I reserve it for my friends," I replied with a wink.

Plucking a notepad from beside her telephone, I jotted down all of my phone numbers. "Call me if you need anything, and I mean anything at all," I told her. "I'm leaving you my home, cell and office numbers, so no excuses."

"Thank you," she said seriously. "Really, Jaden, I...."

I interrupted, "Don't worry about it. It's why I'm here.... To take care of people, I mean.... You will call, won't you? Sometime? To let me know you're doing okay after all of this."

"I promise. Even if I don't need anything."

I smiled at her, wanting desperately to lean over and kiss the top of her head. I stepped backward, toward the door instead. "Feel better, okay?"

She nodded, weakly.

Chapter Nine

At home once more, I knelt on my prayer rug in a patch of late-afternoon sun.

"Your kingdom come, my Lord."

I felt His presence, His peace, His love, but He didn't speak. "Thank you," I whispered. I meant for so many things, but I didn't have to enumerate. I felt His hand on my shoulder, His love in my heart. "Forgive me, for not listening to You," I added.

"I always will," He assured me.

"Carly doesn't want to see me," I told Him, "except as a friend and not anytime soon."

"Yes, I know."

"Does that mean I've run out of time?"

He answered, "There is time."

After a silent moment, I asked, "Is this some kind of… test?"

"Timon!" He laughed. "I shouldn't expect such words from you."

Shouldn't, but probably did. "I know," I said. "I'm just having trouble making sense of… this."

"Perhaps that is because you're not looking at it from the right angle."

"So, turn me around, please!"

He laughed more loudly and replied, "I'm trying, Timon. I'm trying."

I finished my prayers but felt restless. Wandering into my living room, I flipped on the game. But it wasn't exciting enough hold my attention. At half-time, the Bulls were already up by twenty-three.

The newspaper rested on the coffee table where I'd tossed it in my rush to get to the museum on time. I picked up the front section and flipped past the headlines, looking for the more pertinent-to-me stories that were usually buried further in. On page eight, I was surprised by a grainy image from Tuesday afternoon.

Is that us?

I stared. So much had happened since then.

The photographer had caught Carly and me in mid-air, her head against my shoulder, my arms flung out around her, bracing for impact with the black Audi. In the background, I could see the fleeing gunman, the pursing uniformed officers, the panic-stricken pedestrians.

My eyes returned to the center of the frame. I tried to remember the moment, but could only recall the instant my feet left the ground, before this photo, and when I crushed Carly against the car, just after this photo.

That memory, inevitably, brought to mind the feeling of her body beneath mine and a flood of physical desire.

Stop it! I ordered myself.

Sighing, I folded the paper, turning the photo to the back so I could read the article without distraction. It wasn't high-quality reporting. I guessed that an amateur on the street had snapped the image with his cell phone; the paper had bought it and assigned someone to dig up the story.

I read it through carefully twice. This was just the sort of thing I had to be wary of, the kind of article that could draw unwanted attention to me. Fortunately, my name wasn't given. Apparently, the police had honored my request to remain anonymous. *Either that, or…* I glanced at the author's name… *Rupert Culvert hadn't tried very hard to get it.*

Rupert hadn't sought out accurate details of any kind. Carly's name was given as 'Carlie Branson,' and the location of the accident was off by two blocks. I wondered if Rupert would keep his job for long.

I flipped the paper over to look at the picture again. The photo was unfocused; my turned-away face couldn't possibly be recognized. Still, Trinity and Raiser would be scanning the papers, and Trinity, at least, was smart enough to connect 'Carlie Branson' with 'Carly Benson' when today's accident at the museum finally got reported. It wouldn't hurt for me to lie low for a few days.

All evening long, I hoped for the phone to ring. It didn't. I ate a simple meal of pita wedges with hummus and tomato, a handful of olives and half a bottle of red wine. It reminded me of home, which reminded me of Carly, and, in the end, only served to make me more miserable.

I woke up very early the next day, having tossed and turned all night. I stayed in bed for a while, hoping sleep would return. I finally gave up and got dressed.

Although I didn't consider myself a member of any denomination, I did attend services every Sunday morning with various congregations around town. For me, church was about the people, the body of Christ, and not any specific doctrine that governed them. In fact, I'd stopped seeding churches after the First Council of Nicaea had met to define Christianity. Not that I disagreed with them, but to me, it's all very simple: through Jesus, the Son of God's sacrifice, *all* people have immediate and direct access to God, and all who call Christ their King will join Him in His eternal kingdom. Everything else is secondary, pertinent to each individual person's faith.

On this particular Sunday, I had the time and my mood seemed to require an anonymous congregation and a praise-themed service. Easy choice, as I lived close to what was probably the largest sanctuary in the United States.

I headed out to sprawling Willow Creek Community Church in the suburbs. The weather was cold and cloudy, but not raining, so I didn't mind driving my car. I made it in time for the nine o'clock service.

The auditorium, which can seat well over 7,000 people, was already three-quarters full when I arrived. I couldn't see the balconies very well from my seat, but I assumed they were filling up as well. Reluctantly, I switched off my phone to give my full attention to the service.

On stage, a lone acoustic guitarist was leading the congregation in a song with a single lyric, 'Hallelujah,' one of my favorite words, meaning 'God be praised.' I lifted my hands, like the people around me, and joined in.

I enjoyed the Willow Creek presentation on Sunday mornings, and the first half of the service did its job of lifting my spirit significantly. The sermon, however, was one in a series on family, and when the pastor made the casual comment, "We're all connected to a family," I felt my heart sink. It was possible that I still had nieces and nephews, generations-removed, living somewhere on the planet. But if I did, I did not know them. I had no family. I had to make due with short-lived friendships. Even those were hard to make, knowing that I'd have to say goodbye forever within a few months.

I wished, again, that things had gone differently with Carly, even as I prayed for the strength to live the life I'd been chosen and blessed to live.

As soon as worship ended, before I'd even made my way out of the auditorium, I switched my phone back on. The screen read, 'One new message.' And it was from Carly! I flew out the nearest door, oblivious to the fact that my car was parked on the other side of the building.

I couldn't tell anything from Carly's message. Her deep, smoky voice politely asked me to call if I got the chance. She'd also left a number for her hospital room.

My hands were shaking so hard as I dialed, I hit the three instead of the six and had to start over.

She answered on the second ring.

"I'm so sorry I missed your call!" I told her.

"I knew I was calling too early," she said. "Did I wake you?"

"Oh, no. I'm at church, actually."

Silence, and then she said very apologetically, "I should've known that. I'm sorry. You should go."

"No!" I realized how anxious I sounded and tried to tone it down. "I mean, the service is over. I was just about to head home…. Unless you'd like me to stop by?" I added hopefully.

"Yeah, um. That's actually why I called."

"You want me to come by?" I had to be sure I wasn't imagining it.

"Could you?"

"Of course! But I'm pretty far out. It might take me a while to get there."

"Where are you?"

"Willow Creek."

"Where's that?"

"South Barrington."

She sounded stunned. "You go to church all the way out in South Barrington?"

"Sometimes. I'm coming right now, though, okay? I'll be there as soon as I can."

"Don't rush. I'll see you soon."

It was Sunday, so the roads weren't too busy. My home was on the way to the hospital, and since I didn't want to risk parking my car there, and also because she'd told me not to rush, I stopped by my building long enough to drop off the car and change my shoes. The new chinos were fine for Willow Creek, but I'd opted for the wingtips to dress them up a bit. Now, I could be comfortable again.

A cab dropped me off at Saint Joseph's a few minutes before noon.

It took all the control I could muster not to run to Carly's room. I restrained myself, though, strolling through the lobby and waiting patiently for the elevator. When I arrived at the right floor and stepped off, my eyes caught on an elderly woman seated on a bench across the hall. She held her head bent low, sniffling into a tissue. She was alone.

My heart broke for her. I wanted to go to Carly so badly, but I couldn't walk away from someone so obviously in pain.

I approached the woman slowly and knelt at her side. "My name's Jaden," I told her. "It's my job to help people who are hurting. Is there anything I can do for you?"

She lifted her golden-brown eyes. They were red-rimmed from crying, but as clear as a young woman's would be. I saw the Lord's Spirit there, and I hoped that, eventually, she would find comfort in her faith.

She spoke in a shaky whisper, "They just told us; my husband's lung cancer is terminal…. We've been married for fifty-three years…. How are we supposed to tell our children we won't get a fifty-fourth?"

A fresh tear ran down her cheek. She didn't even try to wipe it away.

I placed my open palm in her lap. She clasped my offered hand.

I stayed with Theresa for nearly half an hour. She told me, not only her name, but about her children and grandchildren, and what she would miss most about her husband, Kennedy. When she said that she didn't know how she'd be able to sleep in their bed without him, I cried with her. I told her that, while I'd never been married, I knew exactly what she meant.

At last, one of her daughters arrived. I left so they could talk and grieve in private.

I finally reached Carly's room. I took a deep breath before knocking on the open door.

She looked over, smiled and motioned for me to enter.

"There you are," she said as I approached. I noticed that she'd recently had a shower, and that the gauze patch had been replaced with a surprisingly small bandage. She looked tired but pretty.

"I'm sorry," I sighed.

Her expression changed into worry. "Something happened," she guessed.

"I uh… met someone out in the corridor who needed me to pray with her."

Carly tilted her head. "You pray with complete strangers in hospital hallways? Or was it someone you know?"

"I just met her, and yes, I pray with anyone who asks me to."

"Will she be okay?"

I nodded. "But I am sorry that it's taken me so long to get here."

"No, I…. I shouldn't have even called you… except…."

I couldn't wait for her to finish. "What is it?" I asked nervously. "Are you okay?"

"I'm fine," she assured me. "They're actually releasing me at two o'clock."

I grinned, relieved. "Well, that's great news!"

She nodded half-heartedly. "Only I *still* haven't been able to reach my mom. Can you give me a ride home?"

Suddenly, I wished I'd brought my car. *You're such an idiot! Why else would she have called?*

"Of course," I answered aloud, "but I don't really like the idea of you going home to an empty house right now."

Her eyes shifted away from mine. "My doctor doesn't either."

I wasn't quite sure how to make my offer, but maybe she wanted me to. Maybe that's why she'd called me and not Jen. It was worth a try. "You could stay with me." I rushed to add, "Until you can contact your mother, I mean."

She considered it for a while and finally said, "Yeah, I don't wanna impose."

"There's no imposition," I assured her. "I was just going to watch the Bears game."

Her brow wrinkled. "I thought that was yesterday."

"Bulls yesterday. Bears today."

"Ugh," she grunted, but at least she was smiling again. "Are you sure it's okay? I mean, after my big speech yesterday... and now I'm asking you to take me in."

"It's fine, Carly. Your not-so-big speech ended with wanting to be friends, right? This is what friends do. The only issue I have is...."

I didn't get to finish. Nurse Nicole bustled into the room. She smiled at me. "Hello again," she said and then turned to Carly.

"Good news, Sweetie. I ran into Doctor Phelps in the hall and got him to sign your release early!" She patted her clipboard.

Carly asked hopefully, "So I can go?"

"Just as soon as I go over some paperwork with you," Nicole replied.

"I'll wait outside," I told them, excusing myself.

Pacing the corridor, I considered my options for getting Carly back to my place. I didn't want to bring her home in a taxi, but I didn't have time to get my car. She might catch a cab on her own to her mom's house and decide that she was fine there after all.

On a whim, I flipped open my phone and dialed Adam, one of my law partners.

"'S'up, Jaden?" he answered.

I decided not to beat around the bush. "I need a favor. Any chance you're at the office?"

He sniggered. "I live here, don't I?"

"Could I talk you into leaving for a few minutes?"

He hesitated. "Maybe."

I sighed. "Here's the deal, Adam. I'm at Saint Joe's. My friend is being released but can't go home. I offered to take her back to my place for a while, but I don't have my car...."

"Hold up; hold up! Did you say *her*?"

I rolled my eyes. "Yes."

He laughed and then, away from the phone, called out, "Hey, Brittany, I owe ya ten bucks!" Back on the line, he asked, "How'd you put your girlfriend in the hospital, Jay?"

"Are you coming?" I asked impatiently.

"Sure, bud. I'll be there in fifteen."

Nurse Nicole came out of Carly's room. She gave me another winning smile and told me that Carly could leave whenever she was ready, adding that she was getting dressed and that, perhaps, I should continue to wait in the hall.

Within two minutes, Carly appeared, wearing the sweater I'd bought for her. Its collar completely covered her bandage. Two little green lions dangled from her ears.

"You look beautiful," I told her.

She glanced down, said, "Thanks," and then fixed her eyes on me again. "What's your only issue?"

I shook my head. "I don't...."

She prompted, "Before the nurse came in, you were saying your only issue was...?"

"Oh! Well, I don't have my car here. But my partner, Adam, just agreed to pick us up, so we're good."

She squinted. "Define 'partner.'"

"Oh honestly! You two are going to get along great." I motioned her toward the elevators. "Are you all clear, then? Free to go?" I asked as we started walking.

She nodded. "I just need to figure out how to pay the fifteen hundred dollar deductible."

"No problem. I can write a check before we…"

She cut me off, "No, Jaden! I've taken advantage of you enough already."

I shrugged. "It's nothing. I'm happy to help."

"I'm sure you are," she told me, "but I'll manage this one on my own, okay?"

I didn't answer.

"Jaden?"

I conceded, "Okay."

Outside the doors, I saw Adam's berry-red Porsche 911 parked illegally, facing the wrong direction in the circle reserved for ambulances. I'd been planting seeds of selflessness in that young man for a year, but not one had sprouted.

I leaned toward Carly. "I'm afraid that's him."

"What, that Porsche?"

"Over the top, I know," I told her. "I'll ride in back."

"Is there a back?"

Adam got out of his car as we approached. I wondered what Carly thought, seeing him for the first time. He'd been a basketball player in college at the university down in Champaign. That put him over six-foot-five, with dark blond hair and an athletic build. Add in the confidence of an outstanding lawyer, and most women went crazy for him. Fortunately, he was fifteen years older than I looked. Carly was young enough, that might matter.

"You're not supposed to park here," I told him.

He grinned at me like I was the idiot and then turned a more-winning smile on Carly. "Hi, there. I'm Adam Fink, attorney-at-law."

Her response had me cringing. "Damn! You're really law partners?"

He put his arm around her shoulder and turned her toward the passenger door. "Now, now," he chided. "Don't cuss around, Jay. You'll give him apoplexy." I heard him add, "At least we're already at the hospital, should that happen."

I threw open the driver's door and crawled into what Porsche called a back seat. There wasn't much space, as Adam needed the driver's seat pushed back as far as it would go. I sat crosswise, with my feet behind Carly.

As soon as we were all in, Adam gunned the engine and peeled away.

"Nice," I said sardonically.

He grinned at me in the rearview mirror and then turned to Carly. "You're too pretty to be Jaden's girl-friend," he told her.

"We're just friends," she assured him.

I frowned. I'd agreed to that definition, but still, it hurt to hear her say it, especially to Adam.

"Hoo Ha!" Adam exclaimed. "I'm gettin' my money back!" From there, he launched into a memorized list of his own best qualities. For some reason, Carly appeared to find him amusing.

"Next time, I'm calling Jasper," I said, apparently to myself, since neither of them was listening to me.

"Sweet ride," Carly mentioned, stroking the dashboard.

"Well," Adam replied, "it isn't Jaden's car, but it's something."

She threw a glance over the seat at me. I shrugged innocently. Fortunately, Adam didn't notice.

My building wasn't far from the hospital, just about eight blocks up the road on the opposite side of the street. Adam had been over at least a dozen times. He nearly flew past it, anyway. "Whoops!" he hollered, pressing the brake pedal to the floor. "Hold on!" he added. The tires squealed as he cranked the wheel around, trying to make the u-turn too late.

"We just got *out* of the hospital!" I shouted, bracing myself against the roof.

Carly giggled.

Adam 'parked' with the passenger-side tires on the sidewalk and didn't pay the meter. My doorman-slash-security-guard glared at us with wide eyes, which grew even wider when I finally clambered out of the back.

"Hello, Ed," I said to him as we walked by.

"Doctor Bethany," he replied coolly. I'd have to make this up to him somehow. I preferred to be friendly with my doorman.

Adam guided Carly to the residents-only, south side elevators as if it was his place and not mine.

"Thanks for the ride, Fink," I told him. "See you tomorrow."

"No. No," he answered. "You got me out of the office; now at least invite me up to watch the game."

"Only if you go park your car properly.... And apologize to my doorman."

"What for?"

"I said, *only.*"

He thought for a moment. "Got any beer?" he asked.

I shook my head.

"'kay," he sighed as the elevator doors opened. "I'll be back."

Carly and I entered the elevator alone. It was possible that Adam would go back to the office, more possible that he'd find a nearby bar in which to watch the game. But I doubted either would happen. Most likely, he would go buy beer, re-park his car, forget to apologize to Ed and be at my door in less than twenty minutes.

Oh well, I concluded. *Carly would probably prefer not be alone with me anyway.*

"What floor?" she asked, staring at the panel of lit-up circles.

"Top," I said, "but you need my card." I slid it through the reader and pressed the button.

Carly leaned against the walnut paneling as we started up.

"Swanky place," she commented.

"A gift," I replied.

Chapter Ten

Carly peeked out through the narrow window at the end of the hall while I unlocked my door. "Wow, dude, do you have these views?" she asked.

"Better," I answered as the door popped open. "Please, come in."

Beyond my entry hall, the floor plan opened up, with the living area to the south along the wall of windows, the dining area on the north end where I had my computer set up, and the kitchen in the northwest corner. The only closed-off room was the single bedroom in the southwest corner, behind the living room. My corner bedroom had two walls of windows, which was great, and the only bathroom in the whole apartment, which was not so great.

I tried to show Carly around, but she wouldn't come away from the windows.

"The best view is from my bedroom," I told her, motioning to its open door.

I'd made the comment innocently. So, it took me a moment to interpret the look she shot me. I decided not to acknowledge it. Instead, I asked, "Do you want to try calling your mom again?"

She turned back to the window. "Not yet."

"Then do you mind if I make a quick call to my office assistant?"

She shook her head, so I plucked my landline off its cradle and dialed the office.

"Brittany?" I began when she answered. "I don't pay you to work on Sundays."

"Adam's paying," she answered.

"You don't work for Adam."

She sighed at me. "But he asked me to…."

I interrupted, "My staff does not work seven days a week, and I know you've already been there six."

Behind me, Carly chided, "Don't be mean, Jaden."

"I'm not…" I turned away from the phone. "I'm not being mean, Carly."

Brittany asked, "Is your girlfriend there?"

"Yes. No." I exhaled. "Look, Brittany, I appreciate the extra effort that you always seem eager to make, but go home now, okay? You need some time off."

"It's just that Adam…"

I cut her off again, "Adam is also finished working for today."

"He's there, too?" she guessed.

"Been and gone," I confirmed, "and likely on his way back."

"Invite her over," Carly whispered. She'd approached without me noticing, and now stood right next to me.

"Excuse me a second," I said to Brittany, then covered the receiver. "What's that?" I asked Carly.

"Does your assistant like football?" she asked.

The game! We'd already missed kick-off. I answered, "I don't know. I don't think so."

"Then, for my sake, invite her over!"

I paused to figure out what she meant by that. "Don't you need to rest?"

"It'll be fun. A party."

I stared at her, finally concluding that she absolutely did not want to be alone with me. I told myself not to be hurt.

"I insist," she added.

That cinched it for me. I returned my attention to the phone. "Sorry about that, Brittany... I was saying that it would mean a lot to me if you would stop working for today. If you want, you can come and watch the game with me and Adam and my friend, Carly."

Brittany was quiet for a moment, and then she said, "You don't do anything spur of the moment."

She knew me well. "Apparently that's not true," I answered. *Good thing my bathroom's clean.* I offered a quick prayer of thanks.

"Okay," said Brittany slowly, "I'll be there in about an hour."

"Stop working!" I insisted.

"I am," she answered. "I just need to run a quick errand on the way."

"Oh." *Oops.* "Sorry. Really, Brittany, I am. I'll see you in a little while."

I hung up the phone and handed it to Carly. "You should try your mom again. She's probably worried."

"Ha!" she barked, but snatched the phone out of my hand anyway. She sat on a bar stool on the dining room side of the kitchen counter to dial, drumming her fingers while she listened.

"Machine again," she announced, and then talked to it. "Hey, Ma. Thought you'd want to know I'm out of the hospital. I'm at a friend's house. If you want, call me back at this number." She pressed the 'end' button and handed the phone to me.

I opened my mouth to ask if her mother was often gone over the weekends, but before I could speak, the doorbell buzzed.

"Excuse me," I said to Carly. I pressed the intercom button, knowing who it was.

"Let me up," Adam demanded before I'd even spoken. I considered the alternative, even as I pressed the button to admit him.

A few minutes later, Adam burst through my door with two six-packs of Sam Adams.

He pointed one of them at my plasma screen. "Where's the game?" he asked.

I countered with, "Why was Brittany working for you today?"

"Oh. Sorry, buddy." He crossed the room and set his beer on the counter next to Carly. "I had to borrow her."

"Why?" I asked. "Is Louise sick?"

He shook his head. "Just not smart enough. I had to let her go." He used the edge of my granite counter to pop the cap off a beer and handed the bottle to Carly.

"Carly shouldn't drink," I told him.

"Sure I should," she replied and tipped the bottle to her lips.

Adam grinned and opened another bottle for himself. "What kind of work do you do, Carly?"

"Ah…" she hesitated, "receptionist."

"Close enough!" he whooped. "Want a paralegal job?"

"Well…" she said, setting her beer on the counter, "I might need one. I missed two days of work last week, and now I can't go back until after I see my doctor on Tuesday. I might not have a job anymore by then."

"They can't fire you for being injured," I assured her.

"Oh, but let them try!" cried Adam. "Carly'd love to see the best da-a-a… dang Chicago lawyer in action." He threw his arm around my shoulder and chugged a few swallows of beer.

Carly looked at me skeptically. "You said you dealt with contracts."

Adam answered for me, "He usually does 'cause contracts are a logistical bi… I mean, nightmare. Wrongful termination, however, that's just plain fun. Believe me, Jay'd take them to the cleaners."

"Okay," I said, stepping away from him. "Carly doesn't want to hear it."

"Actually, I do," she answered.

Adam grinned and sat on the stool next to hers. "Here's a story. A year ago, I was working for

Sandresen and Smith. Remember when that big garbage collectors' strike was looming?"

Carly nodded.

"We were working on that case," he continued. "Getting nowhere, I might add. An absolute impasse."

"Right," she replied. "It was all over the evening news… how stinky it was going to be when just one day's worth of trash didn't get picked up in the morning."

Adam pointed at her with a nod. "Exactly. We were burning the midnight oil, completely deadlocked, with a five a.m. deadline. When in walks," he motioned toward me with his beer bottle, "some… upstart, foreign kid, uninvited, who says he's just settled a similar case in Paris." He'd pronounced the word poorly, mimicking a French accent, rolling the 'r,' adding a hard 'e' sound at the end.

"Paris," I corrected in perfect French.

Adam ignored me. "He said he'd come to offer us a resolution. Somehow, he convinced my boss to call some guy in France and sure enough, Jaden wasn't lying."

Carly's eyes fixed on me. "Uh-huh," she said. I couldn't tell if she was impressed or if she thought Adam was making it up.

"I never lie," I put in.

"Never," Adam confirmed. "And you plopped your solution on the table and they all went nuts!"

"They liked it?" Carly clarified.

"My God!" Adam swore. "You've never seen such a thing."

I gripped the edge of the counter and growled at him.

"Sorry, buddy." He didn't seem to be; he was already moving on. "Jay was brilliant, Carly. He got the workers the benefits they'd demanded plus a three percent wage increase per year for the next five years and paid for it by selling thirty-five thousand tons of waste a year to W-2 Energy for their waste conversion program."

Skeptically, Carly asked, "Nobody else thought of that?"

"Sure we did!" Adam cried. "But when we approached them, W2E wasn't interested." He turned to me. "I still don't know how you got them to change their minds."

I chuckled. "I'm not sharing my trade secrets. I have to keep some edge on you, my friend."

Adam lifted his beer again. "Touché." He took a swallow. "So, after all the dots and crosses, Sandresen offered Jaden a job, but our young man decided to hang his own shingle and brought me along for the ride. Jasper Jones joined us after our first case, and we've been makin' history in this town ever since."

After a thoughtful moment, Carly asked him, "So all this cringing and stuff he does... it doesn't bother you?"

Adam shrugged. "You learn not to swear."

"You haven't," I pointed out.

He ignored me. "It's no big deal... better for business, in fact."

"What about...." She glanced at me.

"Adam knows I talk to Jesus," I told her.

"All the time," Adam confirmed with a dramatic eye roll. "He prays before he accepts a case, before and after every meeting, every court appearance.... Oh, and there's the Monday morning prayer-break-fast-slash-Bible-study he hosts, but I usually skip out on that one."

"You shouldn't," I told him.

"I know!" He turned back to Carly. "Jasper and I do better than average for guys in our field, but this boy has *never*, to my knowledge, lost or failed to settle a case."

I had, in fact, but too long ago to mention now.

"Wow," she said, possibly truly impressed at last.

I headed into the kitchen, snatching the beer she'd left on the counter as I went by.

"Hey," she complained. "I'm not done with that."

"Adam just told you that I'm the best lawyer in town. That's because I respect the law."

I got her a glass of water. "Besides, you lost a lot of blood yesterday. You need this right now, not alcohol."

Adam finally put it all together. "You're not twenty-one?" he asked her. "I would never have guessed that."

"He really, truly, doesn't drive you nuts?" she asked him.

Adam laughed. "Of course he drives me nuts! But he makes a ton of money, which means, I make a ton of money, so I force myself to ignore any... quirks he might have."

"We're missing the game," I reminded him.

"Right!" he cried, jumping up. In two strides he'd made it to the living room and plopped down in the middle of my black leather sofa, his beer in one hand, my remote in the other.

Carly sat beside him, on the end closest to the windows. Leaving me the choice of sitting on the other side of Adam or on a separate chair. I chose the chair closest to Carly.

She gave it a good effort, but Carly couldn't manage to watch football. She leaned forward after a couple of plays and plucked today's newspaper from the coffee table. The explosion at the Art Institute Museum Shop had made the front page.

I hadn't noticed it when I'd brought the paper in this morning. Now, I tried not to read it over her shoulder.

Adam had no such reservations. "Oh hey, did you hear about that?" he asked. "They're trying to figure out how a glass case could explode spontaneously, but it looks like that's what happened."

Carly's eyes shot to mine. "You said somebody fired a gun."

"That was what the police thought," I amended.

"You two know about this?" Adam asked.

"We were there," I told him. "That's how Carly got injured."

"And you," she added.

Adam snorted. "And I thought you were just reckless with your razor this morning."

My hands flew to my face, brushing the small scratches, which were healing rapidly, as Adam continued, "Neither of you saw anything?"

Carly shook her head. I was lucky in the way Adam had phrased his question. My eyes had been closed. "No, nothing," I confirmed.

A short while later, my doorbell buzzed again. I jumped up to press the intercom. "That you, Britt?" I asked.

"Yep."

"Come on up." I pressed the button to allow her entry to the guest elevators and then cracked my door open so she wouldn't have to knock.

I returned to my chair, but watched the door. I knew about how long it would take Brittany to arrive.

"Hey everybody," she announced, pushing through the door at the exact moment I expected her, carrying a bag of groceries in either hand, which I should have expected, and wearing a Bears sweatshirt, which I'd never have expected in another thousand years.

She normally wore her dark hair twisted up on her head, but today, it fell in waves around her shoulders. Her nearly-black eyes scanned the room, stalling briefly on Carly.

I jumped up again. "Let me get those for you," I offered, taking her bags.

She gaped at me. "What happened to you?"

"You heard about that accident at the art museum?" Adam offered. "Jaden and Carly were there."

"Are you okay?" Brittany pressed.

"I'm fine. Just some minor scratches. And Carly will be fine, too, which brings me to introductions."

Nodding toward Carly, I said, "My friend, Carly Benson, meet my legal assistant, Brittany DeWitt."

The girls shook hands.

Adam stood up long enough to greet Brittany with a peck on each cheek. "Hello, sexy Bear's fan" he crooned.

"Stop harassing my employee," I snapped.

"We'll file charges tomorrow," Brittany said, turning me toward the kitchen, pressing against my side in a gesture that felt a bit too intimate for me. "Right now, let's eat," she added.

"What did you bring?" I asked, creating space between us.

"Just some munchies," she answered. "I figured you wouldn't have any."

She was right, of course. "I have hummus," I said in defense.

"To eat with…?"

I'd finished the pitas. "Olives."

My friends let out a collective, "Ew!"

Brittany knew my kitchen, perhaps as well as I did. So I stood back against the counter and watched as she efficiently set up a buffet of chips, dips, fruit, cheese and veggies.

"I really am sorry that I was so demanding on the phone today," I told her.

She glanced at me and then returned her attention to slicing a cucumber. "It's okay, Jaden. I know how you are."

Carly silently slid onto a barstool to watch. Brittany noticed her and asked, "So, how did you meet Jaden?"

Carly smiled. "He rescued me from certain death."

Brittany didn't even look up. "He does that a lot," she said.

"I'm starting to get that picture," Carly replied. "Guess I'm not so special after all."

That drew my attention, but I didn't know what to say.

Brittany spoke for me, "Oh, you're special. He's never brought anyone home before."

"How do you know that?" I asked, defensively.

She smiled, chidingly. "A well-educated guess."

"And Brittany has four degrees," Adam offered, rising from the sofa, drawn by the snacks, apparently, as the game hadn't gone to a commercial. Rather than using the pretty stone plates Brittany had set out, Adam pushed his fist into the nearest bag of chips and drew out a handful.

"Wait," I commanded. "I haven't blessed those yet."

Adam sighed and looked at Carly. "That's one I forgot. He prays before eating."

"I've noticed."

"Indulge me, please; it's my house." I waited for their heads to bow, and prayed, "Father, King and Creator, we thank you for the fellowship of friends and the pleasure of sports. We thank you for the people who raised these foods and those who handled and prepared them for us. Bless them now, to nourish our bodies. In the name of our Savior and Lord, Jesus Christ, Amen."

"Can God really nourish your body with potato chips?" asked Adam, popping one into his mouth.

"God can do anything," I assured him.

Brittany stared at Adam for a moment and then looked at me. "Can I use your bathroom?"

"Of course. You know where it is."

She rinsed her hands in the sink and excused herself.

Carly leaned toward Adam and whispered, "My God, she's beautiful!"

I white-knuckled the counter.

"And brilliant," Adam added to Carly's assessment, "and a little unhappy that her boss," he tipped his head in my direction, "hasn't noticed either of those traits."

"Her boss has noticed," I said. "I hired her because she's so intelligent. As for the other thing... I'm *her boss*."

Adam looked at me. "So, let me take her off your hands. I'll get the best paralegal in the county, and you won't have any conflicts of interest."

My eyes slid to Carly and then to my shoes.

"Oh," quipped Adam. "Well, that's different then."

I wished I could excuse myself to the bathroom. There was no place else to hide. Instead, I filled a plate with some fruit and headed for my computer.

"You can't work if we can't," said Adam.

"I'm not working; I'm checking email. You're not my only friends, you know."

Adam turned to Carly. "He's mad."

Brittany picked that exact moment to reappear. "Who's mad?" she asked.

I headed off Adam's response, "I'm not mad. I'm checking my email."

"I thought you didn't work on Sundays," said Brittany.

"I'm not working!" I cried.

"Ooh," said Brittany, "he is mad."

They all laughed. But ignoring them was easy. Unfortunately, I had no personal email in my inbox. I pretended for a moment longer and then put the computer back to sleep.

My friends all sat on the sofa. Adam, in the center, was reabsorbed in the game. Carly sat on his left near the windows, reading today's paper. Brittany sat on the right, reading the article I'd left open from Saturday. Both she and Adam had beers sitting on my coffee table.

I dropped my plate in the sink and mixed a couple of glasses of pomegranate juice with Sprite for Carly and me. I carried them into the living room and handed Carly a glass as I settled back into my chair.

"Thanks," she said absently.

I was about to apologize for my outburst when the phone rang. I groaned. I'd left it on the kitchen counter, so I had to get up again.

I glanced at the caller I.D., hoping I wouldn't have to answer, and recognized the number. "I think it's for you," I said, offering the phone to Carly without answering it myself.

She looked at the screen, rolled her eyes, and pressed the talk button.

"Hi, Mom," she began brightly, but then, her tone changed, serious and on alert. "Perry. Where's Mom?" She listened for a long time, her face growing more and more anxious. At last, she stated, "Well, *that's* not gonna happen!" and hung up.

Chapter Eleven

"Where's the bathroom?" Carly asked, her voice thick and even more husky than usual.

"Through that door and turn right," I told her.

She disappeared, taking my telephone with her.

Adam and Brittany both looked at me, but I didn't have any answers for them. I shrugged to ward off their questions and turned my attention to the game. I couldn't concentrate on it, though. I prayed, but heard nothing back. I listened to Brittany asking Adam about a referee's call. I couldn't follow his answer.

At last, Carly emerged. She held out the phone. "Jen wants to talk to you," she said softly.

Surprised, I pushed myself up. Carly passed me the phone and then took my chair.

"Hello?" I said, crossing into the privacy of my bedroom and closing the door so I could hear over the television.

"Jaden? Hey, thanks for talking with me…. I'm trying to find a safe place for Carly to stay… with her mom all… you know."

I didn't know. I didn't have the first clue, in fact. "Shall I bring her to you?" I offered.

"Well, that's the problem…. I'm not at home. I'm in Indianapolis until Wednesday."

"Oh," I tried not to sound delighted. "Well, she's welcome to stay here. I have plenty of space." *If I sleep on the sofa*, I added to myself.

"Are you sure? Because she seems to think it would be a serious imposition…. But honestly, I don't think she has anywhere else to go. Home is a… really bad idea."

"It's no imposition," I assured Jen. "I'll make sure she knows that."

Jen sounded relieved, "You're a doll, Jaden! Really. 'Bye."

I hung up the phone and knelt on my prayer rug. "Your kingdom come, my Lord…. Is it all right for Carly to stay with me?"

Safest for her, indeed, He replied in my head.

Maybe that meant 'not exactly safe' for me. I didn't ask.

"Will you tell me about her mother?"

Carly will do that herself, if and when she chooses.

I nodded, adding a few words of thanks and praise. I returned to the living room to find all three of my guests cheering madly as Chicago's star running back crossed the last few yards for a touchdown.

I picked up my juice and joined them, squeezing onto the sofa now that Carly had my chair.

"You told her no, didn't you?" Carly asked without looking at me.

"Who? Jen?" I clarified. "Of course not. I never say no unless I have to."

"Well, you have to."

Adam asked, "What's up?"

"Carly needs a place to stay," I told him.

He grinned. "I'd take you in, Carly, but these two wouldn't let me. I'm not half the gentleman Jaden is."

Brittany drank her beer and said nothing.

"So it's settled," I concluded. "You can have my room, and I'll sleep here on the sofa. What's the score?"

Adam and Brittany left as soon as the game ended, both in a cheery mood as the Bears had won by two touchdowns and a field goal. Carly perched silently on a stool and watched me put away the snacks. I stared into the open refrigerator to see if I could scrape together a meal for dinner. *Nope.*

"Tomorrow night, I'm going to cook for you," I promised, "but tonight, I'm afraid we'll have to go out… or order in. Your choice."

"Didn't I see a sub shop across the street? Let's just bring home sandwiches."

"Sure. I'll go get them," I offered. "Tell me what you want."

Carly barely spoke after that. She didn't acknowledge me leaving the apartment or returning. She sat silently at the table while I prayed over the food. She spent a good, long time picking every last shred of lettuce off her sandwich, making a mound of it on her paper wrapper.

I would have sworn before a judge that she'd requested it. "Why order it that way if you didn't want lettuce?" I asked.

She shrugged without looking at me.

I was still sitting at the table when she got up, tossed the lettuce-filled-wrapper in the trash and returned to the chair in the living room, unfolding the newspaper once more.

I swallowed a few more bites, while quickly clearing the table. After that, I wandered over to the sofa. "If you're really so uncomfortable here, I can get you a hotel room," I offered, sitting near her, but not too close.

She sighed heavily. "I'm just waiting for the interrogation to start."

I shook my head at her. "What interrogation?"

"Oh, come on!" she snapped. "You're dying to know why I can't go home. What's up with my mom, and all that."

"Not *dying*," I answered, adding, "I mean, of course I'm curious, but that's because I care about you. If you want to tell me, I'm happy to listen, and to help you if I can. But I won't force you to talk if you don't want to.... I'm just glad you're here."

She rolled her beautiful eyes. "What I said yesterday still holds, dude," she warned.

"I know," I assured her. "We're friends. I would take in any friend who needed to crash." It wasn't a word I normally used. It sounded as awkward as it felt, leaving my lips. Afraid Carly would sense that and read something else into it, I rushed to add, "I'd also listen to any friend who needed to talk."

She glared at me skeptically.

"But only if you want to," I repeated.

"Frankly," she said, "I'm bushwhacked."

"In that case," I said, standing, "I'll go change the sheets for you."

She looked mortified. "You are not giving up your room for me. I'll be fine right here." She patted the arm of the sofa.

"I wouldn't feel right," I told her. "Besides, I sleep out here most of the time anyway."

"Why?" she asked.

I almost didn't answer. "Honestly, it's because that bed is too big for one person. I've never gotten used to it." I stopped myself from telling her that I got lonely at night, that I very badly wanted a wife and a family. She would *definitely* read too much into that.

She looked at me with sympathy and said, "I know you'll find someone to share it someday.... Just like I'll find the right person to protect me." She didn't offer any more.

I stripped off the bedding and took it out to the sofa while Carly remade the bed with clean sheets and blankets. I had to stand on a chair to reach the cupboard where I stored the extra pillows. Never before had I hosted an overnight guest in this penthouse. No doubt it showed.

"I love your bathroom," Carly told me as I reentered the room. "That tub is amazing!"

"You're welcome to use it while I'm at work tomorrow."

To my great surprise, she looked disappointed.

"I'd stay home," I explained, "except I have to be in court early. Maybe I can cut the day short."

"Oh. No, don't. I'll be fine."

It sounded like she meant it, so I didn't press the issue. "Is there anything else you need before I say goodnight?"

She looked down. "I'm kind of embarrassed to ask, but.... These are the only clothes I have right now and...."

"They're not exactly comfortable for sleeping?" I guessed.

She shrugged. "I don't want to ruin the sweater."

I opened the bottom dresser drawer. "I have some sweats," I told her, extracting them from the pile. "Maybe if you tighten the drawstring...." I let the sentence die. Nothing could make them fit her.

"They'll be perfect," she said, taking the folded gray fleece from my hands.

Appreciating her kind lie, I asked, "Anything else I can get you?"

She smiled. "I still have the toothbrush and stuff you bought for me, so I'm good."

I smiled back. "Then I'll just grab a few things myself and get out of your way."

My pajama bottoms were buried pretty deep in the drawer, as I normally slept in boxers. But I was glad to have something modest for tonight. I took them into the bathroom and used them to wrap up my toothbrush, shaving kit, and everything else I thought I'd need, either tonight or tomorrow morning.

I stepped back into the bedroom. Carly was still standing in the middle of the room with my sweats pressed against her chest. I hurried to my closet to get clothes for my court appearance.

"Well. Make yourself at home," I said, indicating the room was hers with a sweep of my free arm.

She nodded. "Hey, ah.... Don't be shy about coming in if you need to use the bathroom, okay?"

Ha! I'd use the facilities in the lobby downstairs before I'd walk in on her. Still, I heard myself say, "Sure." I added, "Sleep well."

Thoughts of Carly in my bed kept me from sleeping most of the night. It was just too tempting to imagine myself in there with her. In the morning, groggy and annoyed with myself, I realized there were two things I'd forgotten from the bedroom closet, my dreadful, black wingtips. And I had to be in court, so I needed them.

I spent a few minutes deliberating whether I should sneak quietly into my room to get them or just go out and buy a new pair. In the end, nothing seemed like a bigger waste of resources than owning two pairs of shoes I couldn't stand. So, finally, I crept into the bedroom.

Carly was curled up on one side of the bed, her straight, light-brown hair fanned out behind her. The much-too-large sweats were bunched around her arms and neck, obscuring her bandage. She appeared to be sleeping peacefully.

For the first time, I noticed how long her eyelashes were. The color of her eyes had always distracted me before.

I told myself not to stare, but how could I look away? She was there, in my bed, with space for me beside her, more lovely than any vision from my imagination.

If only.... I didn't let myself finish the thought. There was no sense in wishing for that kind of relationship. Even if Carly was interested, which she wasn't, it wouldn't be possible for me.

I'd had this conversation with myself centuries ago, concluding that I could not treat any woman so unfairly, let alone someone I loved. Marriage and children were not in my past or my future. I'd never expected to be tempted by the idea again.

And I won't be tempted now, I promised myself as I slipped silently around to the opposite side of the bed. I snuck my horrible shoes out of the closet and left without waking Carly.

Before heading to work, I wrote down my phone numbers again, just in case she'd lost them, and a list of possibilities for Carly to make herself breakfast and lunch, promising a Mediterranean meal for dinner.

I stopped in the lobby restroom to shave before leaving the building and noticed that my cuts were barely visible now; most of them had healed entirely. That was good for court; I wouldn't have to explain anything. I wondered what Carly would think, though. Maybe she hadn't noticed how deep some of them had been.

My court appearance went according to plan. Textbook, in fact. I could have given it to my protégé, Madison, or even to a junior staff member, but the client had wanted my name and face attached to the motion, and so I presented it. The judge wouldn't get back to me for ten days, however. So, I decided to free up my schedule and take the rest of the week off.

I was a little disappointed, when I got back to the office, to find that Carly hadn't called. She didn't call all day, but I did put in the time, getting a lot done, so that I could leave everything to Madison, without reservation, should Carly need to stay with me for a few more days.

Brittany wasn't surprised in the least when I told her my plans. She did, however, seem a little sad. I felt bad, although, I'd never consciously done anything to encourage Brittany's crush on me. She was as independent as they come. She didn't need me. Not for anything. Even her relationship with Christ was secure. Again, I prayed that He would lead her to her own special someone.

On the way home, I stopped by a favorite Middle Eastern market. I thought of myself as a good cook with a limited repertoire. If I wanted to impress someone, I went with Mediterranean dishes every time.

I picked out some beautiful lamb chops, an eggplant, fresh basil and mint, a small bag of shallots. I couldn't remember if I had green cardamom pods at home, so I bought those, too, along with Stone Pine nuts, golden sultanas, more olives, rice and a loaf of bread so fresh, it was still warm.

Carly sat wrapped in the blanket I'd used the night before, reading one of my many books when I walked through the door. I have to admit, I felt relieved to see that she was still there.

She smiled at me, folded up the novel and asked, "How was court?"

"It went well," I answered, making my way toward the kitchen. "Are you cold? You could have turned up the heat."

She left the blanket on the sofa and followed me, choosing not to answer my question.

"So... You're really gonna cook?" she asked.

"Of course."

"Can I help?"

I started unpacking my bags. "Sure. Here," I handed her the eggplant. "Wash this up and slice it up. There's a cutting board and knives over there." I nodded toward the knife block.

She turned the purple fruit in her hands. "I've never cooked an eggplant," she commented.

"You like it though?" I prompted.

She pouted. "I don't think I know."

"You will," I promised. "I'm a great cook."

She hummed skeptically, as if I'd have to prove it.

I decided not to push it any further. She'd find out soon enough. I measured out water for the rice and then moved out of her way so she could wash the eggplant.

"Did you have a good day?" I asked.

She didn't look at me when she replied, "I called my mother."

"She's home?"

Carly shook her head and placed the eggplant on the cutting board. It nearly rolled away before she stopped it. "I called her at the shop. Boy, was she ever peeved! Apparently, Perry, that's her 'boyfriend,'" she put the word in quotes with her fingers, "told her I'd been hospitalized but not for long, and that I'd found a friend to bunk with. So Mom didn't think there was any need for me to pull her off the line at work."

Nice, I thought, but didn't say it.

"She'll get over it," Carly added. "How do you want this sliced?"

"In rounds, about an inch thick…. Are you going home then?"

She laughed. "Not until after dinner!"

All I heard was that she'd be leaving me tonight, and that was disappointing. I told myself not to ruin the evening by dwelling on what I couldn't change.

As I crossed behind her to dig the food processor out of a cupboard, I accidentally brushed against her hip. "Sorry. Small kitchen," I said apologetically, hoping she wouldn't notice my blush.

She didn't seem to. "But nice," she said. "This place is amazing, in fact, and I love the furniture. Nothing at my house matches."

"Well, I can't take credit for it." I began peeling a shallot. "Etienne furnished the place."

"Etienne?"

"Etienne Ebert. He gave me this condo and everything in it."

"So... Yesterday, when you said it was a gift, you meant that literally?"

"I did." Sensing she needed some of my story, and since it was novel to have someone to talk with while I cooked, I started, "Etienne's a stock broker in Paris."

"A *rich* stock broker in Paris," Carly interjected.

I conceded with a nod. "A mutual acquaintance introduced us, and over time, we became great friends. Eventually, Etienne admitted to me that he admired the charity work I was involved in, and hoped, himself, to find a deeper meaning and purpose to his life."

"Deeper than money?" she clarified.

I nodded again.

"And you're the go-to guy for deep meaning and purpose?"

I decided to answer that indirectly. "I took him on a tour of orphanages in eastern Russia, a trip that both humbled him and restored his spirit."

"Whoa, wait... Dude, you just said that like it's nothing!"

"It's not nothing, it's everything," I replied. "But how can I convey the magnitude of another person's

transformation? Especially when he's not here....
If he *were* here, he'd tell you himself that that trip
changed his life."

I threw the shallot into the bowl of the food processor and added basil and mint leaves while I continued, "See, Etienne felt like he had lost his soul to
the pursuit of profits. He wanted to have hope again;
he wanted to hear Christ's message of charity and
love. He needed to see that 'salvation' isn't about
getting a free ticket into Heaven.

"We talked for weeks, driving thousands of miles.
I showed him how far just a little bit of his money
could go, helping children who had nothing except
for hope. He ended up giving them a lot of what he
had and the kids gave him all they had in return. And
so, Etienne learned how great a blessing it is to do
the work of Jesus Christ."

"He became a Christian?"

I nodded. "Maybe not by everyone's definition
of the word, but yes, he's become a very committed
follower of Jesus."

"But you don't have to be a Christian, by anyone's
definition, to be charitable," she said defensively.

"No, of course not," I agreed. "I'm just saying
that the message and the motive clicked for Etienne."

I added half of the pine nuts and some honey to my
food processor. "Sorry, but I have to run this, now."
The machine roared to life, tearing the ingredients
into tiny pieces. I streamed some olive oil through a
hole in the lid, until the mixture became pesto.

I switched the machine off, and picked up my
story. "So last year, when I told Etienne that I was

coming to Chicago, he offered me this penthouse. He'd been using it for rental income, but it was not occupied at the time. He turned over the key and the deed, and even paid to ship my car over from France."

"Wow, that is generous.... This is done, I think." She showed me the sliced eggplant, laid out nicely on the cutting board.

"Perfect," I said, meaning it. I leaned past her to pluck a lemon out of my fruit bowl. I offered it to her. "Now you can cut this in half and squeeze the juice over the eggplant." As she began, I motioned to the saltcellar. "When that's done sprinkle them with salt. Then they can sit for a while."

I rinsed off my hands and turned my attention to the boiling water. I stirred in the rice and cardamom pods, set the timer and then lit the grill. Etienne had purchased top appliances for this place, too, and even though I rarely used it, I really appreciated the grill feature of my gas range, especially since the condo had no outdoor living space.

I pulled out a small skillet to toast the remaining pine nuts.

Carly offered, "Anything else I can do?"

"Um...." I looked around. It really was coming together quickly. "All that's left is to salt and pepper the lamb chops."

"I can do that," she said, lifting the package off the counter.

A little while later, when the rice was almost done, I added a small handful of the sultanas.

"What were those?" Carly asked.

"Golden sultanas."

"Golden sultanas?" she repeated with a raised eyebrow.

I grinned. "If I say raisins, will you still eat them?"

"Raisins and rice," she said skeptically. "I don't know...."

"It's delicious," I promised as I began placing the lamb chops and eggplant slices on the grill. Once they were searing, I returned my attention to my rice, pulling out the cardamom pods. I showed Carly how to split them open and asked her to add a just few of the seeds back into the rice along with the toasted pine nuts and some salt and pepper.

I returned to the grill, but it only took a couple of minutes to finish there. I sliced the bread, dished out the olives and put the rice into a serving bowl while Carly set the table.

"Got any candles?" she called. "Because something tells me this meal is candlelight worthy."

I smiled, hoping that a candlelit dinner might lead our relationship back to the hand-holding stage. I didn't even reprimand myself for having the thought. "They're in the right side of the credenza," I told her as I carried a couple of the dishes into the dining room.

"Need help with that?" she asked.

I didn't want to distract her from the candles. "In a minute," I said, returning to the kitchen. I placed a layer of the grilled eggplant onto my serving platter, arranged the lamb chops over that and topped the whole thing with mint pesto.

"Wow! It looks like the cover of *Gourmet*," Carly commented as she arrived to help me carry the last of our meal out to the table. She added, "You know, this needs wine."

"I know," I told her. "When's your birthday?"

"Today! I forgot."

I poured pomegranate juice for us anyway and followed her to the table.

She waited while I prayed and then picked up her fork. "So, do I start with the rice or the meat?"

"It's all good," I said as I served her.

I watched while she took the first tentative bite of lamb. Her eyes widened. "Oh man!" she exclaimed, still chewing. "This is fabulous!"

"Admittedly, it's my best thing…. I'm glad you like it."

"Well, I haven't tried the raisin-rice yet." She winked at me.

Carly was loading the dishwasher while I did the hand washing when she said, "As much as I like your place, Jaden, something strikes me as odd."

I looked around. Only the kitchen lights were on, though the candles still burned in the dining room. Everything seemed okay to me. "What is that?" I asked.

"You said you've lived here for a year, and yet, there isn't a single personal photograph anywhere in this entire apartment."

I scrubbed at the bottom of the rice pot without looking at her or responding.

"It's just unbelievable," she continued, "given all you say you've done, that you haven't documented any of it."

Oh, it's all documented. Well documented. "Just because I don't have framed photos on the walls…" I began, but she interrupted.

"I even checked your underwear drawer. There isn't a single picture in this entire apartment. None of the places you've been, or the work you've done, or your family, or your… ex-girlfriends. Nada."

I cleared my throat. Even so, my voice broke as I asked, "You went through my drawers?"

"Yeah, but I planned to tell you all along. That way, it didn't feel too invasive."

"Uh…."

"I didn't find anything you need to worry about," she said quickly. "I didn't find anything at all. That's what's so weird. It's like you barely live here."

I returned my attention to the pot with a heavy sigh. "I never stay in one place for very long. There's no point in personalizing."

"But you could take pictures with you… I saw that you have a camera, by the way."

Yes. If she went through my drawers, it wasn't exactly hidden. I decided to tell her, "I send all of my photographs home."

"To your parents?"

I shook my head. "No, they're deceased."

I felt her eyes suddenly on me, but I didn't look at her. She said gently, "Oh, I didn't know. I'm so sorry."

"It was a long time ago," I told her, and for a while, we both went back to work.

Then she asked, "So, who's at home to get your photographs?"

I looked at her, then, wondering exactly how much I should share, but I couldn't resist her interest in me, and I couldn't lie. "I've been, sort of, adopted by a group of monks in Greece."

She blinked. "Now, you're a monk?"

"No... But they've become my family."

She seemed willing to accept that statement. "Do they visit?"

I wanted to laugh at the image of Brother Dimitrius dressed in his rough, rust-colored habit, sleeping on my sofa, but I kept that to myself. "No. I go to them once a year. They don't leave the monastery. Ever. But I don't think you can change the world if you're not out in it."

She chided, "You don't honestly believe you can change the world, do you, Jaden?"

"I already have," I assured her.

"So, your life's been pretty perfect after all," Carly commented. The dishes were done, and now, we were sitting on the sofa, listening to Rachmaninov. I'd been sharing stories about the charity I'd worked for in Paris.

"Blessed, yes. Perfect, no."

"Mine hasn't been either of those," she offered.

"Want to talk about it?"

"Not really."

"You still don't trust me?"

She reached out and took my hand. I'd been waiting for it for so long, my breath caught. She probably heard it, but she pretended not to.

"It's not about you," she answered. "It's just that... there's stuff I don't talk about."

I stared at our hands, locked together. "I understand."

"No, you don't," she insisted.

"Yes, I do." I looked up again and held her eyes with mine. "I *really* do."

She raised her eyebrow at me. "*You* have a secret?"

"As a matter of fact. And it's big."

She scoffed, "You do not."

When I looked away again, she prompted sincerely, "What is it?"

Sure, I'd been drawn into this exact conversation before. And I certainly wasn't forbidden from speaking the truth about my life. I just found it easier to do my work and to avoid creatures like Trinity and Raiser if I kept quiet. So in the past, I'd made it my policy not to answer that particular question, not to reveal my secret.

But this time, the situation was different. Carly was holding my hand, and despite the tenor of our preceding conversation, I felt that her interest was genuine. And besides, what she really wanted to know was whether or not I trusted her.

I thought I did, or maybe, I just wanted to.

Is it worth the risk? I asked Him quickly. *Should I tell her?*

It is your choice, He replied.

I knew you were going to say that.

Carly interrupted our internal dialogue, noting, "You've been quiet for a long time, Jaden."

"I was praying over whether or not to tell you my secret."

"And what does Jesus have to say?"

I looked her in the eye. "He says it's my choice."

She remained quiet for a long minute and then asked, "What do you choose?"

I took a deep breath, but kept hold of her hand and her eyes. "I choose to trust you," I said softly, "with one of the most significant secrets the world has ever known."

Chapter Twelve

Carly's eyes narrowed, but she didn't scoff or mock me.

So, I began, "My parents are deceased because I was born over two thousand years ago. I am one of Christ's original Disciples. I've walked with Jesus; I've heard his teachings from His own lips; I was there when He died; I saw him after He rose from the grave, and I watched him ascend into Heaven."

Even though I could have quoted Him from memory, I let go of Carly's hand to open a drawer in my coffee table and pull out one of my Bibles. It fell open to the page I wanted.

"Are you familiar with the Bible?" I asked.

She snorted and crossed her arms over her chest. Never a good sign.

I pressed on, "This is from Matthew. It's Jesus speaking, 'For the Son of Man is going to come in his Father's glory with his angels...'" I skipped ahead. "'I tell you the truth, some who are standing here will not taste death before they see the Son of Man coming in his kingdom.'

"Carly," I continued, fixing on her sea-blue eyes again, "He was speaking to me and about me. When He said those words, I was standing before Him. I felt His breath as the words left His lips. I felt the power of His Spirit rest on me, and I knew; I was destined to wait here and proclaim Him when He returns!"

The silence that followed was nearly unbearable, but not half as bad as what she said next.

"Jesus, Jaden."

I was caught so far off guard that I crumpled up and nearly cried out in pain, even though she'd barely whispered the words.

She stood up without looking at me and disappeared into my bedroom. When she returned a moment later, she carried her plastic bag of meager belongings in hand. She walked purposefully to the front door, turned to look at me with sadness in her eyes, and then looked away again. "So…. Thanks for dinner and for letting me crash here." She twisted the knob. "I'm gonna catch a cab home."

"Carly…."

The door closed behind her before I could even decide on what words to say next.

I crawled to my prayer mat. "Your kingdom come, Lord." I didn't wait for Him to acknowledge me. "The truth didn't go over so well."

"You expected it to?" He asked.

"I'd hoped for some discussion at least…. What do I do now?"

"Now, *we* wait for Carly to make her next choice."

I was glad for the reminder that we were in this together, but waiting wasn't the plan I wanted to follow, and it wasn't easy to do.

I slept on the sofa again, tossing all night long. I couldn't eat breakfast in the morning or read the paper. It might have helped to go for a run, but I feared another encounter with Trinity, especially while I was this distracted. Finally, I put on a suit and went to the office.

Brittany was surprised to see me but didn't press for details. She brought me some coffee, which I waved away. She set it on my desk anyway, and gave me reassuring pat on the shoulder on her way out.

I hid behind closed doors all morning with no real work to do. I scanned some documents and made a couple of phone calls, but I couldn't concentrate. I didn't want to involve myself in anything significant.

I was staring out the window, charting the path of the sun by its reflection off neighboring buildings, figuring that it was probably past noon, when Brittany buzzed me.

"Carly's on line three," she said.

I'd swear my heart stopped. I barely registered the melancholy in Brittany's voice. "Thank you," I croaked, reaching for the receiver so quickly, I knocked it off the cradle. I pulled myself together and pressed the button to connect line three.

"Hello? Carly?"

"Yeah," answered her deep, smooth voice. "Hey, Jaden."

I closed my eyes and listened as she continued, "I just wanted to apologize for running out on you last night. You've been so good to me, and I...."

I didn't hear how she finished the sentence. None of that mattered. "Did you get home okay? Was everything all right with your mom? Are you all right?"

"Fine."

There was silence for a while, and then I realized that she was trying to give me a chance to explain things. "Carly," I began, "I can only imagine what you must be thinking right now. But thank you for calling me." I inhaled, trying to slow my racing thoughts. "I feel such a strong connection between us, but I never should have burdened you with the truth. Call it a lapse in judgment. I've never told anybody before. *Ever.* Because I know how impossible it seems. If it's too much for you... If I've ruined our friendship, I'll never forgive myself." I pressed my palm against my forehead and whispered, "Carly, I'm so sorry."

Carly remained silent. I thought I heard her smoking again. I also heard her flipping pages over the line.

"What are you doing?" I asked.

She started babbling, "Getting a number for you. Because I shouldn't even be... be talking to you! But I don't have that many friends. And I *am* grateful that you were there when I needed you. But I need a *sane* friend right now, so I'm thinking if... if you just get some medication, Jaden, then...."

She interrupted herself, "Here it is: Mental Health Chicago. Seriously, they can help.... Got a pen? The number's three-one-two seven-eight...."

"Carly?"

She cried, "You *need* medication, Jaden!"

"I'm certain, I don't."

"Certain?" she echoed.

I sighed. "I know the truth sounds... well, completely nuts, I admit. But is there anything I've done that would lead you to believe I need medicine?"

She thought for a long time, and then said softly, "I guess not."

"So we're friends again?" I asked hopefully.

"Honestly," she replied softly, "I don't know if we can be."

"Of course we can. It's easy. Let's start this conversation over.... Hi Carly. Did you get home okay last night?"

"Yeah," she began tentatively, but then played along. "I called to thank you for putting me up... and for dinner."

"No problem. Did you see your doctor today?"

"Uh... yeah. She says I'm healing just fine, no infection. I can go back to work tomorrow."

"Then we have today," I said, a bit too excitedly. "It's nice outside. Meet me in Millennium Park."

"Hold up," she said. "Are you asking for real?"

"Yes."

"Don't you have to work?"

"No. I'm just wasting time here. Meet me at the park."

She didn't answer for the longest time. I held my breath and worried.

Finally, she mumbled, "I cannot believe I'm agreeing to this…. Okay. Under the jellybean. I'll be there in an hour."

I could contain neither my relief nor my excitement. "Excellent! See you then."

I abandoned work, the office and Brittany in favor of the park, arriving ridiculously early. After wandering around for a while, I bought a cup of coffee from a vendor and gave my change to a very talented, trumpet-playing street musician. At last, I settled onto the grass under the Jay Pritzer Pavilion's skeletal sound system.

It was a gorgeous day, one of Chicago's most appealing: warm and sunny, a gentle breeze coming off the lake, the scent of autumn in the air. After the cold weather of the past few days, it felt wonderful. I knew there wouldn't be many more days like this before winter.

I balanced my coffee on my briefcase and slipped off my suit coat. I rolled the sleeves of my starchy, white shirt and kicked off those awful wingtips, vowing to leave them where they landed. *Why did I wear them today?* I wondered. Perhaps I'd been subconsciously punishing myself.

I checked my watch. *Fifteen more minutes, and then I can hike over to the jellybean.* Time enough to remove my tie and undo a couple of buttons. I leaned back on my palms, tipping my face to the sky. With my eyes closed, I enjoyed the stillness, the sunshine.

Thank you, Lord, for this exquisite day, I thought to Him, *and for second chances… or fifth chances, or whatever number I'm on now*. It didn't really feel like praying. At times like this, I was just talking with my friend, a man I knew well… and not at all.

Carly's voice cut across my thoughts, "You don't look Biblical."

I opened my eyes and smiled up at her.

"*And* you're not at the jellybean, either," she reminded me. "This particular spot's pretty isolated."

I looked around. There were hundreds of people enjoying their Tuesday afternoon in the park, just none nearby. "Private," I corrected, "not isolated, and you're early." I motioned to the jellybean. "We can walk over if you want."

She dropped to the grass instead. "I'll take my chances." She smiled cautiously at me and then focused on removing her strappy, complicated sandals. It took some time and concentration.

I enjoyed watching. She had small feet with high arches and long toes. I noticed that her toenails had been polished to match her fingernails before she buried them in the grass.

If I thought her feet were pretty, then her ankles were very pretty. Above them, she wore a peasant skirt and a lightweight, v-neck sweater. Neither was pink. It was the first time I'd seen her in another color. These shades of brown and tan were not quite as flattering against her skin, and she still wore a bandage at the base of her neck, but to me, she looked perfect.

The wind blew her hair around, causing my heart to flutter. I thanked God, yet again, for introducing us.

"Are you feeling okay?" I asked.

"Super."

"Want some coffee?" I held out my cup.

She reared back, shaking her head.

"I'll buy you your own," I offered.

"No, thanks."

"You look beautiful," I couldn't help myself. The truth just slipped out. Her makeup was natural now, just a little blush on her cheeks, her eyelashes darkened, her lips coated in shiny, cotton-candy-colored lip-gloss. I couldn't keep myself from wondering if that's what it tasted like.

"You, too," she quipped, adding, "but honestly, shouldn't you be dressed in a toga and thongs?"

I tried to play along. "My original outfit disintegrated, forcing me into Armani."

I was rewarded for my pathetic effort with a crooked smile. She picked some grass. "Seriously, why don't you look like...?"

"A mummy?" I finished for her. "I don't know. God can do anything. I haven't aged a day since... that day."

"Sick?"

"Never."

"Broken bones?"

"Yes, and, while you're asking, I do feel pain from injuries like that as well, but I also heal quickly."

Nodding, she said, "I noticed. There isn't a mark on you today."

"That was actually a slow recovery for me," I told her. "The more serious the injury, the more quickly I recover."

She hummed at that and then asked, "What about scars?"

"None."

She raised an eyebrow and playfully questioned, "Tattoos?"

I laughed, loudly, knowing that was reply enough.

She continued, "Wherefore doest thou not talketh funny?"

I kept laughing. "Because I didn't travel through time to get here."

After a silent moment, she sighed, "It would be easier to believe if you'd said you were an angel."

I spread my hands. "Just a man."

"Right," she said slowly. "Then shouldn't you be famous, Immortal Man? Some kind of medical wonder?"

"It makes more sense to keep silent until Jesus comes back."

"But... you told me."

"You're the first." That was a true statement. The sect of monks had formed from a congregation I'd preached to in Corinth, in the year 96 C.E. They continued to function in the Pelopónnisos region, passing down my secret to incoming generations, but I'd never had to 'tell' them; they knew from experience.

Carly spoke slowly over my thoughts, "Uh-huh. You've said that before. ...Why me?"

I looked down and softly replied, "I don't know."

"Are you in trouble for telling me?"

I shook my head. "God lets me make my own choices. He lets all people make their own choices."

She thought about that, but only for a moment. "Are you stuck wandering the Earth forever?"

"Just until Christ returns."

"Right. When's that, then?"

"I don't know."

"It's been, like, two thousand years."

I sighed, nodding. *Not quite*, I thought, but didn't say it.

She continued, suggesting, "Maybe he's not coming back."

I replied firmly, "He's coming back."

She hummed, not convinced. "So, is that why you're so lonely? Because you don't think you can tell anyone the truth?"

Exasperated, I replied, "Well, I told you the truth and look where it got me." I softened my tone to continue, "It's not so much that I'm lonely, really. I have lots of relationships with people, and Jesus is always with me. What I'm lacking in my life is physical intimacy."

"You mean sex?" she asked.

I started. "No! I mean... because I can't stay in any one place for very long, I can't develop deep friendships, the kind where you can just go to a person when you need support, or if you want to sit holding someone's hand, without having to explain why you need it."

She considered that for a long time, and then asked, "How long have you been in Chicago?"

I wasn't expecting that one. In fact, I'd been rather hoping she'd take my hand. But she didn't. So, I answered, "You already know, just under a year... this time," I conceded.

She picked more grass. "When was the last time?"

I didn't even have to think about it. "Eighteen Sixty-Nine to Seventy-Two."

Her breath caught. The blades of grass fluttered from her fingers to the ground as her eyes found mine again. "The fire?"

I nodded.

"Were you ferrying souls to the other side?"

I scoffed, "That's Davy Jones' job."

"Chicago is not at sea," she said authoritatively. "So, what were you doing?"

I shrugged. "Helping people get through it, mostly; mourning their losses with them; rebuilding.... Lots of building, actually."

"So, you're an architect, too?"

"No. I can't draw."

She shook her head and sat silently for a moment.

I interjected, "Other questions?"

"Yeah, as a matter of fact.... I got out a Bible. Don't go into shock, dude, but I have one. Well, Mom does.... Anyway, I was looking for that bit you read to me. I had to read most of Matthew, but I found it."

I nodded, not wanting to break her flow.

"I really appreciated that stuff Jesus said, earlier, about giving to the needy and doing it humbly. I thought it was great that he called people 'hypocrites' for drawing attention to their acts of generosity. I never knew he said anything like that."

"I told you, you'd like Him," I reminded her.

She ignored that comment. "And all the healing and casting out demons and stuff... was that for real?"

"Very real," I answered.

She seemed disturbed by that, but quickly moved on. "So, anyway, I reread the part you said was about you. The word 'some' caught my eye. Are there others... like you?"

I nodded. "Two others."

"Who?"

I couldn't tell her. It wasn't my place. They were keeping quiet, like I should have. "What difference does it make?" I asked.

"I don't know. It would make this all more... real. Especially if their names are Matthew and Mark."

I smiled, but said seriously, "I can't speak their names. Or my own, my real name, I mean. It's too dangerous. I haven't seen them since we all fled Jerusalem. We are... hunted."

She sat up straighter. "By invisible things that cause glass display cases to shatter?"

I nodded.

She seemed disturbed by that but asked only, "Why are they hunting you?"

"They think if they kill us, they can stop Jesus from returning.... He said we'd be here when He comes again."

"That's kinda lame.... So Jaden's a pseudonym?"

"It's my current name, but I've had others."

"Tell me your real name. Just whisper it."

I shook my head.

She let it go. "Okay.... Who are 'they?'"

I thought about telling her. Coming forward with the names of the things we'd faced in the museum. I decided against it. "You don't want to know."

"Do you have *any* proof of all this?" she asked hopefully.

"Yes, tons, in fact. But it's all with the monks in Greece. Their sect has been following me from the beginning. I've sent them detailed letters describing my adventures. Ever since the invention of photography, I have sent pictures. I've been sending video as well, lately. They even have a lock of my hair that I sealed inside a clay jar about nineteen hundred years ago. The jar can be carbon dated, and the hair inside matched to my DNA."

"That does sound like proof," she replied. "Can they send it?"

"It's for proving myself when Jesus returns, not before."

"So you've got nothing to show me." She actually sounded disappointed.

"No, but I do have an ardent wish that you'd believe me without proof...." In my head, my Lord hummed in agreement. "That's what faith is all about," I added. "Can I ask a question, now?"

Hesitantly, she said, "Sure."

"Have you had any near-death experiences today?"

I'd meant it as a serious question, but she smiled slowly as she replied, "No, not one... but then, you haven't been around. I'm starting to put two and two together."

I couldn't help but react to her smile. "Right. It was great seeing you, then, but I guess you'd better go." I hoped she'd see that I was kidding.

She did. Or at least, she didn't leave. Instead, she stretched out on her back with one arm crooked over her face, shielding her eyes from the sun. Her skirt rode up to her knees, exposing satin-smooth shins. I couldn't help but stare.

"Promise me that if one of those beams inexplicably decides to come down," she indicated the aluminum bars crisscrossed overhead, "you'll jump on top of me and take one for the team."

Was that a joke? Was it an offer? Did she know I would've used any excuse to do that very thing? "I promise," I replied hoarsely.

I asked my Lord to refocus my mind, breathing deeply while that happened. I couldn't tell if Carly was awake when I looked back at her, until she unexpectedly slurred, "What're ya thinkin'?"

"I'm wondering... Do you believe me? Or do you still just think I'm...?" I couldn't bring myself to finish the sentence.

"I believe that you believe you," she answered warily, "that your conviction is real, even if you're delusional.... At the moment, the only thing *I* believe is that you're really not a danger to me."

I felt my shoulders slump. "Well, that's progress, I suppose.... Will you promise me something, though?"

She considered her answer for a very long time and finally said, "If I can."

"Will you read more of the Bible? Will you let God talk to you?"

Beneath her arm, she nodded. "I can do that.... In fact, I think I'd like to. But for now, I'm going to enjoy my last few moments on Earth."

Her words gripped my soul. I couldn't tell if she was kidding. I thought she meant to torture me, in fact. I watched her for a long time, memorizing every angle, line and curve of her, but she didn't say anything more.

Certain that she'd fallen asleep this time, I sipped my quite-cold coffee and watched the gulls looping through the sky.

But she hadn't fallen asleep. Out of the blue, she said, "Days just don't get any better than this, do they?"

"And no matter how many of them you have, the perfect day is still perfect," I added. "Days like this remind me of my childhood."

She teased, "You can remember that far back?"

I smirked. "Surprisingly."

"And what do you remember?" she prompted.

I shrugged, knowing she wasn't looking at me to see it. "Running," I replied. "I loved to run through the hills around my hometown, even on really hot days, but in the fall I could reach top speed." I laughed at my memories. "I wasn't a pretty runner, though. I'd careen around rocks, slipping and sliding with my arms flapping for balance. My father called me *Ciconia*, which is the word for 'Stork,' in our native language. He said I'd fly right off the hillside one day."

I noticed that beneath the crook of her arm, Carly was grinning.

"What?" I asked.

She laughed out loud. "I just can't believe it…." She waved her arms around. "I'm diggin' a Bible guy! And not just any Bible guy, but a Bible guy who *thinks* he's a Bible guy!"

I should have focused on the 'Bible' portions of her comment, but my human ears heard only that she was 'digging' me.

"So, ah…" I began, "what does that mean for us?"

"I can't seem to decide, can I?" she offered, clasping her hands behind her head.

I chuckled, uncomfortably. "Nope."

"It's your own fault for being so darn unbelievable on every level. How can I fall for someone who's convinced that he was born two thousand years ago? Who thinks he's hunted by something evil? Who talks to Jesus and hears a reply *out loud*?

"And yet, how can I *not* fall for a man who's smart and successful, yet humble and generous? Who shares my desire to help people in need and is actually able to do that? …And let's face it, you're incredibly hot and that accent melts my soul whenever you speak to me."

Really? I couldn't think of anything to say in reply.

A stronger, colder breeze blew in from the lake. Carly sat up, shivering. "Time to go, I think," she announced.

I protested, "But… we haven't resolved anything."

"I think we'll just have to see how it plays out."

I felt disappointed, but couldn't argue, so I offered her my suit coat. She put it on gratefully, while I finished my coffee.

After quite reluctantly stepping into my shoes, I offered my hand to help her rise. She'd just finished tying the last strap of her sandals. "Can I walk you to the 'L?'" I asked.

She nodded. "But first, to the jellybean."

Along the way, I tossed my empty cup in the trash. As we crossed the pavement, approaching the sculpture, I watched its silvery, convex contours for our reflection. I found us before she did.

We stopped a few yards away, keeping the rest of the fascinated crowd at a distance.

"You have a reflection," she mused.

I scoffed. "I'm not a vampire, Carly. Or any other undead creature." I turned her to face me. "I'm a man. An ordinary man." I took her hand and placed it against my chest, knowing she could feel my heart pounding, that she could probably hear it, too.

"You are anything but ordinary," she replied, stepping closer. Her sandals added an inch to her height. Even so, her head came to just below my chin. She rested her cheek near my heart and didn't resist when I wrapped my arms around her.

I held her that way, maybe for a minute, maybe for half of eternity.

Chapter Thirteen

"**M**y Lord?" I called, from the prayer rug I'd placed on the floor between my bed and the setting sun out my wall of windows. I knew I did not deserve these awe-inspiring views. I hadn't done my duty. I'd spent the afternoon with Carly, talking about myself but not saying nearly enough about my King.

I felt his warmth before he replied, "My son."

"Your kingdom come, Lord," I began. "I barely felt you with me... out in the park today."

"I did not leave you. Your attentions were focused elsewhere."

How true. "I'm not myself with Carly."

He knew. "Because you are choosing not to be."

"Am I?"

"Aren't you?"

I let myself feel his long fingers wrap my shoulders. It was comforting, but not in the way it had been when He'd held me in His physical form. He continued, "I remember what you've chosen every other time a woman caught your eye."

"To run away," I confirmed, "because I was afraid to get distracted from my purpose…. But all those times," it really wasn't *that* many, "I was certain of the woman's soul, absolutely sure I would be with her one day. Carly could be lost to me, forever."

I thought of her eyes and her heart and the endlessness of the sea, and how lost I would feel without those things. I barely heard Him continue, "Thus, she is more appealing?"

"That seems backward, doesn't it?" I asked, wishing that I could see him. I turned my face toward his voice.

"May I help you think it through?" He offered.

"Please, Majesty."

"You were emotionally drained by our work in Africa. Unlike those around you, you had no one of your own to lean on to help you through it."

"Yes," I replied. "I remember that all too well."

He continued, "We went to Iran where you had many close calls with the thing that calls itself Trinity and the thing that calls itself Eifer. We ran, but those demons followed you to Europe, where your soul was soon exhausted, your body as well…. Do you remember?"

I nodded. There was no point in reminding Him that if He hadn't withheld His Spirit's power, things might have played out differently.

"And so, you chose to come to Chicago and take a less stressful job. Now that your mind and body can rest, you are hearing your heart again, and we are back to where we left things in Africa. We will keep coming back here, until you resolve your longing for a partner."

I nodded at that, too. "I thought I *had* resolved it, but Carly is...." I changed my mind and instead whispered, "I've never met anyone like her."

"There has never *been* anyone like her," He answered, obviously pleased.

"She's so complicated," I said.

He answered, "*All* of my children are complicated."

I returned to my original thought, "She reminds me of the sea.... No. It's more than that. She *is* the sea. When I'm with her, I feel like I'm home." I smiled, sadly. "I think I love her."

"Why is that so distressing?"

He knew why. I'd always preferred to find more work when my heart led me in this direction. My job for Him involved loving everyone, not one specifically. I answered him anyway, "Because I *can't*! Where would it lead? Marriage is...."

He finished for me, "a choice you could make."

"A choice to create intricate and painful lies to explain our relationship while she grows old and I don't," I raged, "to have her resent me for staying young, to be left alone after she dies!" The truth struck me, hard in the chest. My heart missed a beat.

I swallowed hard and continued quietly, "Not even those things, Majesty, not with Carly, anyway; you've already called her name."

He held me in silence.

"Can't you… make her… like you've made me?" I begged. "Or undo this… *thing* that's been done to me? Let me be twenty-nine next year!"

He gently replied, "Timon, don't you know? You are as you are because you heard my words and believed them. No one who has truly believed can un-believe, no matter his or her future choices."

"Then speak in Carly's hearing, so she might believe!" I pressed my fingers against my stinging eyes. "Please, Lord. I don't think I can live without her."

"Do your job, my son, and you won't have to try."

His strength pulsed through me. I dove for the phone, quickly chanting, "All praise, glory and honor to the King!"

I dialed Carly's number, determined to get her away from Chicago, Raiser, Trinity, and whatever she was hiding from me so that I could do my job, undistracted.

An answering machine picked up. I cleared my throat. "It's me, Carly…. I guess you're not home yet." I couldn't stop the next phrase, "Or else there's been a train wreck." I rushed to add, "Sorry, that wasn't funny.

"Hey, I've decided to blow-off work tomorrow… for the rest of the week, actually. It's supposed to be unseasonably warm, so I thought I'd head out for a long weekend. Camping. Up at Devil's Lake…. So, I was wondering if…?"

There was a click. She'd picked up the phone.

"Jaden?"

"Yeah."

"I just walked in the door."

"Sorry. I was inviting your answering machine to go camping with me this weekend."

"At Devil's Lake, I heard…. Isn't that place off-limits for you?"

Confusing. "Should it be?"

"Well, yeah. I thought the devil was after you, so why would you go to his lake?"

I chuckled at her joke. "Okay, I'll pick a different lake…. So, do you want to come along?"

"I don't know… I mean, didn't we just decide to see where things go? A camping trip seems like… rushing it."

"Well, that wasn't my intention. I just want to get out of the city for a while, after the week we've had, and I hoped that maybe you felt the same."

She thought it over. "I guess I could tell my boss that the doctor wants me to take the rest of the week off."

"Don't lie," I ordered.

"Dude! Some of us aren't blessed with cushy jobs where we can decide not to show up, and yet, earn tons of cash."

"Tell them the most irresistible man you've ever met wants to take you away for a long weekend."

"Ah," she mused. "Hit 'em with the truth…. But that's not on the list of approved absences, and I can't afford to lose pay, not with this fifteen hundred dollar deductible hangin' over my head."

"Say the word, and I'll make that go away."

"No!"

"Just offering…. Okay, how about I forget the early weekend, and we leave together after work on Friday?"

She hesitated. "The truth is, I've never been camping."

"All you'll have to do is be there, I swear."

"You never swear, and it pisses you off when other people do." I could hear her smiling.

I corrected her, "You're wrong. It hurts me when other people do. Physical pain."

She sighed heavily. "See, now you're sounding crazy again."

"I only want you to have the facts…. So, will you come?"

She paused again, but only for a moment. "Sure. Why not? What do I pack?"

"A warm jacket, boots, clothes that can get dirty and a toothbrush."

"That's it?"

"That's it." I was grinning now, myself. "I guess that means I have nothing to do for the rest of the week."

"Poor baby," she replied, sounding a bit jealous.

"I'll pick you up for lunch tomorrow. Around noon, okay?"

"If you insist. Remember where the Scheoff building is?"

"No, actually." I had a vague idea, but I'd been wandering around so much that day; I hadn't paid attention to the intersection.

"Jesus knows the way," she quipped and hung up on me.

"I have a GPS!" I shouted at the dead receiver.

The drive to Scheoff Publishing the next morning took twice as long as the GPS predicted, mostly because of unexpected lane closures and a couple of inoperable lights. There were no open parking spaces in front of the building. I would have double-parked for the brief time I'd be there, but unfortunately, a florist's van had beaten me to it. I thought about waiting, even though it was already twelve-fifteen, but then I noticed a parking garage directly across the street and swung into its entrance instead.

I parked on the third level, between two small, red Hondas and ran for the stairwell, flying down the steps two at a time. The stairs let me out directly across from the entrance to the publishing house. I bolted across the street between cars and circled through the revolving doors.

Inside, it felt more like a library than a business. Every wall was filled, floor to ceiling, side to side, with shelves of books. Thick carpets covered the floors. The chairs were comfortably over-sized and over-stuffed. I could smell coffee brewing somewhere.

Carly sat behind the receptionist's desk straight ahead. She jumped up when she saw me, grinning as she came around the side of the desk. To my great surprise, she lifted onto her tiptoes and kissed me lightly on the cheek. My heart hammered.

"You really are pushing it!" she exclaimed, "But thank you; they're beautiful!"

I smiled back at her, completely lost. "What are?"

"Duh, the flowers?" She motioned to a huge pot of bright yellow mums, obscuring roughly a third of her workspace.

"They are very beautiful," I agreed. "But I'm sorry to say, they aren't from me."

She pouted. "But they have to be!" she insisted. "Who else would send me flowers?"

And why didn't I? I thought to myself. "Isn't there a card?" I asked.

She shook her head.

"Perhaps it fell off. The van is still out front." I turned toward it, just as it began to pull away.

Carly sighed. "Well… maybe Jen sent them. It would be like her. I guess. I'll ask when she gets back."

"I thought she was back," I mused.

"She's stuck in traffic on the south end…. This whole day sucks!"

Uh-oh, I thought. "Why? What's going on?"

"Nothing…. I had a horrible night. I'm behind on all my work. The office temp is ridiculously incompetent. One of the authors tore into me for no reason. Jen's not here. Those flowers…." She grunted instead of completing the sentence. "Can we just go?"

"Sure," I replied. I'd only understood half of what she'd just said, but she still managed to convey quite clearly that I had let her down. "My car's right across the street."

Carly didn't say a word as we walked down the block and waited on the corner for the light to change. An older man approaching us tried to dash across the street without waiting for a 'walk' signal. He stumbled over uneven pavement just as he reached our side of the street.

I jumped forward and caught him before he fell. "Easy there," I said, helping him to straighten up. "You okay?"

He nodded, embarrassed.

I smiled supportively as I released him and said, "We all need someone to keep us from falling on occasion, don't we?"

Clearly still embarrassed, he mumbled his thanks and moved on.

We had our walk sign now, but Carly didn't move. She just looked at me and said, "You…."

When she didn't finish the sentence, I prompted, "I what?"

She shook her head as if to clear it. "You say things to other people, but I feel like you're talking to me."

I took her hand. "Carly, if there's any way, literally or figuratively, that I can keep you from falling, believe me, I want to do it."

"I know." She suddenly grinned at me and repeated, "I know! You make it impossible for me to stay mad at you."

Mad? I hadn't realized she'd been mad. I felt compelled to say, "I'm sorry I let you down today."

"It's okay. Really, it is. Let's get lunch."

We hurried to cross the street before the light changed again. Carly began talking about the girl who was covering her lunch hour, a temporary employee who had trouble pronouncing the company's name and hung up on as many people as she managed to put on hold. Carly wasn't making fun of her, just sharing a frustrating struggle of her day, one she felt safe sharing with me.

It felt good that we were back on track. I happily listened to her vent.

She was still sharing stories about the temp when we reached level three of the parking garage, so I pointed to my car.

Without hesitation, she approached the first Honda.

"No, this one," I said, using the remote to unlock my lustrously-black Jaguar XKR-S. Its lights flashed in greeting.

Carly stood aghast for a moment. Then she exclaimed, "Dude, this is *not* your car!"

"This is my car," I confirmed.

"You called Adam's car over the top!"

"That custom Porsche? It is over the top. And he drives like a maniac. This is...."

She interrupted, "An idol." She ran her hand along the shiny fender and then inhaled a mock-shocked breath. "Jesus shouldn't let you drive this car."

"I do not worship my car, or He wouldn't," I assured her.

I opened the passenger door as she said, "Others worship your car. I'd bow down to it, myself."

My mood shifted. "Do, and, believe me, I will leave you in this garage."

"Sorry," she purred, sliding in. "I'll be good."

I raised a doubtful eyebrow and closed the door.

By the time I'd settled into the driver's seat, she'd fastened her seatbelt and was grinning at me with anticipation. I pressed the red ignition button on the console between us. Four hundred and twenty horses hummed to life. I gunned it a couple of times, but then backed slowly out of the parking space.

Carly shook her head at me and then put her window down.

"Ah, it's still pretty cold out to have the window open," I said.

She responded lightly, "Doesn't it have heat?"

"Yes, but I'm not going to waste energy just so you can feel the wind in your hair…. If you want that, you'll have to stick with me until summer." I prayed that we'd have that long, but my Lord did not answer.

Carly hummed and said, "We'll have to see if it's worth it." She rolled the window up then leaned into me to look at the dashboard. "How fast does it go?"

"Depends on the speed limit," I told her, keeping a straight face.

She stared at me. "You're pathetic. You know that don't you?"

When I didn't respond, she rolled her eyes. "What's the stereo like?"

"Pretty hot," I replied.

She glanced at me skeptically then tapped the power button. The pulse-pounding beat of hip-hop vibrated through our seats. She turned to me, wide-eyed. "I was expecting Gregorian chant!" she shouted.

I grinned at her, nudging the volume down a tad. "Don't you know me at all?" I shouted back.

I did, in fact, prefer sacred music, but I'd wanted the sound system to impress her, and this was a Christian band in the disc player, even if they didn't sound like it. No swear words, at least.

She turned the music off on her own.

"Seriously," she began, "I'm kind of relieved to discover that you're a hypocrite after all."

My eyes widened, but I didn't take them from the tight bend down to street level. "Excuse me?"

"Well, as far as I can tell, all Christians are hypocrites. Up until now, I was afraid that I might have to take you seriously."

"My choice of music makes me a hypocrite?" I asked, confused.

"No, your car."

I scanned the interior. "What about my car makes me a hypocrite?"

"Oh, come on, Jaden! You could open a homeless shelter on what you paid for this car.... Unless you're going to tell me it was a gift, too."

"It was a gift," I said defensively.

"Well then, shouldn't you sell it and give the money away? Isn't that what Jesus would want?"

I thought about that for a minute, remembering how this car had helped me to outrun the demon, Eifer, in Germany. If I hadn't had a fast car.... "No," I said decisively. "I'm pretty sure He wants me to have this car. He gave it to me, and when He decides I shouldn't have it any longer, I won't.... How many Christians do you know, anyway?"

"Including you? One. Personally. But you can't miss those guys on T.V."

"Those 'guys' don't represent the majority of Christians."

"They think they do."

"Well... I don't know any of them, either, so rather than judging them, I'm going to change the topic." We were third in line to pay at the booth. "Where do you want to go for lunch?"

She considered it. "Something fast but nice.... I can probably be away for an hour and a half and make up the extra time tomorrow.... My boss will be flexible. She *thinks* you sent me flowers."

"I should have," I admitted. "There's a French Bistro over on Dearborn, isn't there?"

"That sounds good. But I think it's on Darrow."

"Let's ask the GPS," I said brightly, handing my ticket to the garage attendant.

"How ya doin'?" he asked.

Before I could answer, there was a bright, orange flash from across the street, accompanied by an earth-shaking boom.

Chapter Fourteen

"My God!" cried the garage attendant. "Did you see that?"

He wasn't really asking; of course we had. The blast wave had blown charred debris directly at my windshield. I wondered if I'd felt the heat; it was over too quickly to know for sure.

Across the street, the Scheoff Publishing building was burning.

As usual for me in these situations, time stopped for a moment and then began to roll slowly forward. Flames licked through the blown-out windows of the ground floor. Slivers of glass and chunks of blackened debris littered the sidewalk and street. Two human figures, dressed in fire, it seemed, stumbled through the mangled door. They fell to the ground, one trying to roll; the other lying perfectly still.

Carly shrieked, a sound that jolted time back to normal speed.

"Call 9-1-1!" I shouted to the man in the booth, scrambling out of my car before I was even sure I'd cut the engine.

I raced across the street, sensing Carly at my heels, but I didn't speak to her; I was focused on my frantic prayers. *May we save them, Lord?*

You may, He replied as I felt the power of His Spirit flood my body.

"Beat out the flames!" I shouted toward Carly. Shrugging out of my own jacket, I ran for the still body. She went to the person still rolling.

As soon as I'd smothered the flames, I gently rolled the victim over to check his vitals and discovered that it was a woman, very badly burned and not breathing. I began C.P.R., letting God's healing power flow through my hands and into her chest.

Over the roar and crackle of the building fire, I became aware of sirens in the distance. Behind me, the other victim coughed and moaned. I heard Carly cry, "Hang on, Len! Help's coming!"

Not a second later, an authoritative voice announced, "I'll take over, now." The man speaking placed his hand on my shoulder. "I need you folks to move back across the street."

I spared a glance at the surprisingly calm police officer who had spoken. "I cannot leave her; I'm a doctor," I informed him, returning my attention to the unconscious woman. I continued rescue breathing without waiting for his permission.

The officer didn't challenge me. Instead, he removed his hand and spoke to Carly, "Are you a doctor, too, Miss?"

I didn't hear her reply, but I did hear the officer continue, "There could be another explosion...."

"Help Len!" she pleaded, loudly, over his words.

"We will," the officer assured her, "but we don't want any other injuries. Were you involved in the accident or a witness to it?"

"Witness," she snapped. I could tell by her tone that she wasn't interested in talk. She wanted to help her coworker and was frustrated that she couldn't.

The officer sensed this, too. "I'll get Len to a hospital," he promised. "I want you to cross the street. Do you see that woman over there? That's Detective Shultz. She'll take your statement, okay?"

I didn't hear Carly argue further, so I assumed that she had gone. My focus returned to the power in my hands, which allowed me to diagnose the woman's injuries. She must have been standing close to the detonation. Several of her ribs were broken; both lungs had been punctured. I continued C.P.R. while the Spirit healed those injuries first.

Able to receive oxygen again, her heart started to beat on its own. Even I couldn't tell if there would be brain damage, but I felt certain that she would survive. Still, many of the burns were third degree, especially on her face, neck and scalp. I repaired what nerve and deep-tissue damage I could, leaving the surface damage, including the disfiguration of her face, for the doctors of this day and age to manage.

She started to come around, whimpering expressions of pain. I felt the Spirit's power retreat. Emergency crews had arrived and were rushing to us now with a gurney for this woman and another for Len. What had felt to me like hours of surgery had only taken the Spirit a few minutes.

I turned her care over to the emergency crew and straightened. Now that this person's life was no longer my primary focus, my own repressed memories flooded back. The sight of flames, often, even the smell of wood smoke, took me back. The heat coming from this building in twenty-first century Chicago suddenly felt exactly like a furnace in first century Bostra. I'd expected to die that day, as so many of my colleagues had, my life sacrificed so that the Gospel of Jesus Christ could spread.

It didn't happen that way, though. I'd stood amid flames that reached higher than my head. I'd felt pain as if my flesh were searing off the bone. I'd endured it for hours. But, in the end, once the fire had died down and the governor's slaves came to open the furnace, I'd walked out alive, unscathed, a promise fulfilled.

Fearful of and awed by my God, those slaves had put their faith in Christ Jesus that day and had smuggled me out of the city, hiding from their master the true outcome of his vile edict.

Yes, I'd lived through an undeserved sentence of death, but the event haunted me to this day. With a shudder, I cast my gaze across the street. Carly stood huddled with a soot-stained group of office workers, all of them wringing their hands, many of them crying.

Next to me, the E.M.T.'s had loaded Len onto a gurney and started him on oxygen. He caught my eye and struggled up onto his elbows, putting his caregivers on alert.

"Lucy?" he croaked, the word muffled by his mask.

My Lord confirmed that this was the name of the woman I had saved.

I placed my hand on Len's foot, the only place I could reach from my position. I noticed the rubber sole of his shoe had melted slightly. "She's awake," I answered. "They're taking good care of her."

He collapsed in relief.

"Doctor?"

I didn't recognize the face of the man who'd spoken, but I did recognize his voice. It was the officer from before. Apparently, he'd stayed with Len until help arrived. He'd also witnessed the miracle of Lucy's revival. He motioned for me to join him, and together, we walked down the street, away from the burning building and toward the jumble of emergency vehicles now on the scene.

He'd barely introduced himself as Alex Cindry, when his two-way radio crackled. He pressed it to his ear but didn't speak into it. He motioned for me to follow him.

It was a relief to walk away from the relentless heat. Sweat dripped off my face and rolled like a tiny river down my spine. I shivered and tried again to shut down the flood of memories.

Officer Cindry and I jumped back as a firefighting crew rushed by. We stepped cautiously through the web of pipe-like hoses crisscrossing the wet sidewalk. When he finally lowered the radio, I introduced myself and then asked, "Any idea what happened?"

He shrugged. "A bomb of some sort. In the lobby. That's all I caught." He added, "Seems like the two you pulled out were the only ones on that level. Everyone else got out through neighboring buildings, connections on other floors. We think they're all accounted for, anyway."

I didn't correct him about pulling Len and Lucy out. "A bomb in the lobby?" I repeated.

"Most likely."

I stopped walking. "Could it have been concealed in a potted plant?" I didn't like where this was going, what might be confirmed, but it suddenly seemed terrifyingly apparent that either Raiser or Trinity had found Carly.

The officer had stopped when I had. Now, he studied me with great intensity and interest. "You know something?" he asked. Quickly, he held up a finger to keep me from answering. He turned away and shouted urgently, "Captain!"

The police captain broke off his conversation with the fire chief and a few others to join us. He approached with a focus so fierce it was nearly frightening.

"Yeah?" he barked.

"This witness, Doctor Bethany, might have some information," Officer Cindry explained.

I began immediately, "I'm a friend of the receptionist here, Carly Benson. When I picked her up for lunch today, I saw that she'd received a huge potted mum. She wasn't expecting flowers from anyone, and there wasn't a note or card with them. But she has been in the hospital recently; anyone who knew that could have sent them. We assumed that the card had gotten lost.

"Now, it seems very suspicious," I continued. "At the very least, it was something new in the lobby today, and definitely big enough to hide an incendiary device inside."

"Did you see such a device?" the captain asked.

"No. In all honesty, I was running late and didn't look closely at the flowers at all. They were yellow, in a big pot." I held out my hands to indicate the size, about the width of a beach ball.

"Do you know who delivered them?" he pressed.

I closed my eyes, visualizing the van. "Someone from Flautis Family Florists." I met his gaze again. "Their van pulled away about five minutes before the explosion."

"I'm on it," announced Cindry, waiting for only the barest of nods from his captain before darting off.

The captain asked me, "Did you see the person who made the delivery?"

I shook my head and said, "Sorry," at the same moment as the fire chief called out to him. He held up a finger toward the other man.

I dug into my wallet. "Here's my card, if I can help your investigation further." I made sure it was an M.D. card before handing it over.

The captain glanced at it, nodding, and excused himself.

I hurried across the street.

"Jaden!" Carly gasped as I approached. She threw herself into my arms, but my brain was spinning too fast to enjoy it. If a demon had bombed this building, it would be nearby watching the outcome.

"We've got to get out of here," I told Carly quietly, directing her to where we'd abandoned my car.

She didn't protest. "What happened?" she asked.

I shook my head sadly but didn't answer. Any answer I could give would terrify her. Any answer I could give had already terrified me.

We reached the car in silence. Someone had moved it out of the exit lane and parked it in an 'employees only' space behind the attendant's booth. My keys were inside.

No one manned the booth now, but I felt guilty leaving without paying my parking fees. So, I tossed five dollars through the booth's open window before pulling out onto the empty street. I drove cautiously, careful to avoid the larger chunks of charred debris. The police captain saw me as I approached the intersection and waved me through the barricade without stopping me.

Carly asked anxiously, "Where are we going?"

I glanced at her while silently asking, *Lord, is her home safe?*

I am with you, Timon, He responded.

That wasn't much help, but I knew He meant that He would stay with me, no matter what. "I... thought you'd want to go home," I told Carly.

For some reason, that statement caused Carly to shiver. "Um... could we go to your place instead?"

I remembered her saying that she'd had a bad night and wondered if she wanted to avoid something at home. Or was her fear solely a response to the trauma of today?

"Absolutely," I answered. Realizing, belatedly, that if Trinity knew where she worked, it stood to reason that it also knew where she lived. Maybe Carly had simply felt an intuition about that.

We crawled our way through traffic congested by the incident until I turned south onto LaSalle Street, and our speed finally picked up.

"Are you really a medical doctor in addition to all the rest?" Carly asked, but before I could answer, she blurted out, "Forget I asked; I know you don't lie."

I flashed her a grateful smile before returning my attention to the road.

"Who was that with Len? The person you were trying to save?"

"Lucy," I answered, "and I did save her."

Carly inhaled sharply. "She'll be okay?"

"She's been badly burned, Carly, so we'll have to see, but I do expect her to survive."

Carly nodded then moaned, "Oh God, I feel so awful!"

I squeezed the steering wheel. "Why?" I asked tightly.

She didn't seem to notice my reaction. "Because I've been complaining about her all day!"

Only then did I realize that 'Lucy' was the name of the temp who was supposed to cover the phones while I took Carly out for lunch. There was no doubt, then, if the explosion had come from the flowers on Carly's desk, Lucy had taken the full force.

"Well," I said, "fortunately, there will be time for you to seek her forgiveness."

"It's not like she heard me," she mumbled.

"Does that matter?" I asked.

She didn't reply.

I rolled to a stop at a red light and glanced over to see her staring contemplatively out the window.

She sensed my eyes on her. "It's just like the Art Institute all over again," she said, changing the subject. "Only this time, the injuries were worse, and the building was totaled. I'm scared, Jaden! It feels like someone's out to get me. I can't help remembering what you said before. Jesus..."

"Is *not* behind these attacks!" I finished adamantly. "He wants you for His kingdom, but He doesn't work through terror." I placed my right hand on top of her left, causing her to look at me. I held her phenomenal eyes and assured her, "You're safe for now."

"For now?" she repeated, snatching her hand away and crossing her arms over her chest.

The light turned green. I returned my attention to the road and back-peddled, "I didn't mean it that way.... I meant, you *are* safe. With me, you're safe."

"You *meant* that Jesus *is* trying to kill me," she challenged. "So, I'm right."

"No. You're wrong," I insisted. "Jesus' life is about love and compassion and forgiveness. Does that sound like someone who could bomb a building?"

After a pause, she admitted, "No." Adding with frustration, "So explain it then. You've said that I'm going to die soon because Jesus wants me to. So how can you also say that he isn't trying to kill me?"

It was difficult to explain. I did my best. "He uses the choices of people, along with the natural processes of the world, to work out His divine plan. I can't imagine how He does it, but I trust Him."

"Easy for you to say; you think you're immortal."

"I'm not immortal," I corrected. "I'm… on hold." I continued, "But my faith was formed long before that, in the moment I opened my heart to His love. Once I'd experienced that, it was easy to trust Him."

"Trust is a hard thing for me," she confessed.

"I thought you trusted me," I said.

She shook her head. "It's a roller coaster. I'm in a valley right now."

I didn't know how to reply. Ahead on the right side of the street I saw a gyro shop with an empty parking space out front. I took that as a sign and pulled over. Maybe some food would make us both feel better.

"What are we doing?" Carly asked suspiciously.

"Getting lunch," I replied. "Aren't you hungry?"

She shrugged.

I let her go through the line ahead of me, noting that she ordered her gyro with extra shredded lettuce. I remembered her removing it from her sandwich with surgical precision, just a few days ago. *Odd*, I thought.

She didn't speak to me in the shop or on the way back to the car or even when I settled into the driver's seat beside her. She didn't look angry; she looked numb.

When she still hadn't spoken, or even looked my way, by the time the next traffic light stopped us, I asked, "Would it restore your trust if I apologized?" I didn't wait for her answer. "I'm sorry for upsetting you with my poor choice of words. Can you forgive me?"

She shrugged at me again.

"Know what will help?" I offered brightly to offset her mood. "Something to eat followed by a nice, warm bubble bath."

She looked at me then, at first suspiciously but then, well... seductively.

The car behind me honked. I hadn't noticed the light change. I tapped the gas, thankful for an excuse to break eye contact. This was absolutely the wrong time for my humanity to sneak up on me.

You only imagined it, I assured to myself, clearing my throat and concentrating on the drive.

Carly's phone rang just as we were pulling into the underground parking lot at my building. She lost the signal before she could answer. She swore, whacking the phone against her palm as if that could bring back some bars. "God, I hate this new phone!"

I winced, recovered from her choice of language and told her, "You won't get a signal down here. Wait until we're upstairs."

Outside of the car, she clung to my arm, pressing close, nearly tripping me as we made our way to the elevator. She didn't speak, but hung on to me that way, to the top of the building, until my door closed behind us and locked us safely inside my penthouse. Only then did she let go.

I felt better here, too. My walls had been consecrated. This place was as holy as a church. The vilest of evil could not force its way in.

"Go ahead and return that call," I told Carly, handing her the sack with our lunch inside. "You can eat, too, if you want. I'll be right back." I quickly crossed to my bedroom, closing the door tightly behind me. I couldn't remember the last time I'd felt such an urgent need to prostrate myself on my prayer rug.

"Your kingdom come, my Lord," I breathed. "Right now would be a great time, in fact."

"I will come... in my time," He answered.

"Trinity found us," I guessed.

"Trinity and Raiser, working together. They found Carly, not you," He corrected.

That didn't make sense. "Why would they care about Carly?"

"For the same reason you do, I expect."

Yes. Trinity valued beauty and vulnerability. It's victims were, without exception, both. I didn't know enough about Raiser to understand that one's interest, though. "Will you, please, let me keep her safe?" I begged.

"For now," He agreed. "But you must hear me, Timon. Your time is short."

"Yes, my Lord, I understand," I replied, "and I'm tired of feeling helpless when I know that, with You, I am anything but! May I hunt them?"

"Is that what you choose to do?"

"Yes," I replied vehemently. "And if I track them down, I ask for the use of your power to destroy them this time." I needed to fight these creatures head-on, but that required not only His help but also His blessing.

"Granted. Where would you like to start?" He asked.

Granted! I could hardly think beyond that word. At last, I could wipe a great evil from the world, two great evils, in fact.

Heady with anticipation, I considered my Lord's question. I had no idea where to start, no leads to follow, unless I put Carly in danger again, and that wasn't going to happen. I knew a fair amount about Trinity, but next to nothing about Raiser, and I'd never faced such a strong pairing before. I'd have to find out all I could about their weaknesses.

"I'd like to start with Dimitrius," I answered at last.

Chapter Fifteen

I returned to the living room where Carly sat, perched on the windowsill, chewing her nails. "Did you eat?" I asked.

She jumped up and threw herself into my arms. "Oh, God, I'm so scared!"

Alarmed, I held her tightly, resting my chin against the top of her head, and asked, "What happened?"

She shook her head, her whole body in fact. "When you didn't come 'right back,' I started freaking out! I kept thinking something terrible must have happened to you. I mean, so much other terrible stuff has happened this week! I was afraid to go in there."

Stroking her hair, I assured her, "Nothing terrible can happen to me. Especially not in my home."

"All the same," she said against my chest, tightening her grip around my waist, "I'm not letting go."

I smiled. "That's fine with me." It made it hard to think about what I had to do; it made it hard to think about anything at all except for her perfect little body; but I'd make the sacrifice if she needed me to.

I couldn't fool myself for long. I'd held women who were upset before, but this time was different. She was in my arms because she needed comforting, but I was holding her purely out of desire to hold her. And that wasn't fair. I knew what I had to do, but it took me several minutes to force myself.

Gently, I pulled back from her. "Better?" I asked.

She nodded. "Just don't leave me alone again, okay?"

"Okay." I guided her toward the dining table where her uneaten gyro waited, unwrapped. A pile of shredded lettuce was mounded on the paper beside it.

I couldn't keep from asking, "Why do you do this?"

She shrugged.

"Aren't you hungry?"

She shrugged again.

"What about that bath, then?" I offered.

Her lips curled into a surprised, quirky smile. "I'm up for that." She took my hand and started back toward the bedroom.

"Um," I said, stopping. "I'll just... stay out here and make a phone call."

She looked at me like I was crazy. "But... I'm going to be in there." She pointed toward my bedroom and added, "naked."

I closed my eyes, willing my body to stop reacting to the thought, but all that did was give my imagination a blank slate to play with. I sighed and looked at her again. "I… didn't think that you, ah… felt that way about me."

"Maybe I'm starting to." She snuggled against my arm. "Or maybe it would just make me feel a whole lot better right now…. Wouldn't it make you feel better right now?" She glanced at my belt, maybe lower.

I'd guessed correctly. She was no closer to loving me than she'd ever been. "No," I whispered, "It wouldn't."

She raised an eyebrow.

I sidestepped to the sofa, plucking the phone from its cradle as I sat down. "I have to make a phone call," I repeated.

She crossed her arms at me. "Right now?"

"Yes," I answered. "Before it gets any later."

She glanced at her watch. "It's not even three o'clock!"

I started to dial. "Well, my friend lives in Greece and that's eight hours ahead. He'll be going to bed soon."

She huffed at me then stalked through my bedroom door, slamming it closed behind her.

Well, if she's mad, then at least she won't be frightened, I thought as I finished the eleven-digit phone number. Another thought tried to sneak in, something about the possibility that Carly had never actually been frightened, but had only been playing me. I wouldn't let that one fully form.

In Greece, the phone rang just once. "Hello, Timon!" Brother Dimitrius greeted. He may have been a recluse monk, but he had caller I.D., and he preferred to practice his English rather than to speak in our native language.

"Dimitrius, did I wake you?"

"I may be an old man," he replied, "but not so old as to fall asleep before I'm expecting a phone call!"

Okay, his English wasn't perfect. Good, but not perfect. Of course, he had not been with me at Pentecost, so he'd had to learn the traditional way. "You were expecting me?" I asked.

"Of course, my child... What? You think our Lord wouldn't tell me?"

I had to smile at the word 'child.' Dimitrius knew how old I was, but considered himself my father-figure all the same. "Then you know why I'm calling," I assumed.

"Well, no," he admitted. "Are you sending something?"

I heard, tried to tune out, but failed to fully ignore the sounds of Carly running water for her bath. "No," I said to Dimitrius, "and it's not a social call, either, I'm afraid.... I've had a few run-ins with demons in Chicago. Specifically, Trinity and Raiser."

"Odd." Dimitrius sounded concerned. "Those two don't often... interact together."

"There is a Saints and Demons art exhibition in town, " I offered.

"Ah, that would explain it."

I went on, "I've faced Trinity numerous times, but Raiser is a complete mystery to me."

Taking his cue, my old friend said, "Raiser is not so powerful as Trinity, thanks be to God. But that is not to say it lacks strength. Raiser usually looks for a specific personality, a man or a woman who feels entailed, I mean, *entitled* to… power, let's say. The victim comes from a family of power, but lacks the drive or the intelligence to earn power of his own. That's when Raiser enters in. It loans its intelligence and drive, raising the victim in power but guiding the use of that power toward evil."

We were silent as I considered his words. It didn't seem that Carly was a likely candidate for Raiser.

Dimitrius read my thoughts. "Timon, what I've just said may not be of use to you. If they are working together, Trinity outranks Raiser. Raiser would be compelled to do Trinity's bidding in that case…. Can you explain your situation?"

The noise from the bathroom changed. I heard the water turn off and the tub jets come on. I tried to ignore them as I told Dimitrius everything. I began with the police chase that led to me rescuing Carly on Russell Street and ended with Carly slamming the bedroom door, just as I sat down to make this phone call. I left nothing out, not my own emotional conflict, not Carly's mixed messages. It was cathartic, like confessing to a priest.

Dimitrius listened intently, occasionally asking a clarifying question, but in general, allowing me to tell the tale unbroken until my words ran out.

"Well," sighed my old friend, "you've gotten yourself into a mess, haven't you?"

I chose not to answer.

"I'm not certain when it happened," he continued, "but Trinity is into you."

I grinned. I couldn't help it. "I think you meant, 'onto.'"

"Yes," he said, "onto you. It is using this girl, Carly, to draw you out. No doubt it wants to pick up from where you left things in Paris and finish you off."

"Trinity is the one who's finished," I insisted. "I have permission to track it down and destroy it."

Dimitrius cried, "Praise be to God!"

"But where do I start?" I pressed him.

He considered that for a moment. "Are there other demons in Chicago?"

"Not that I've felt," I answered, "but that doesn't mean much. Usher was here. I sent that one to judgment a few days ago."

"Again, praise be to God!" He continued, "So, they know the Spirit is with you in this…. Trinity will use Raiser to draw you out, rather than risk facing you itself. You must destroy Raiser, first, and then Trinity will have to come to you."

I nodded. "Sounds good. How do I find Raiser?"

Dimitrius thought about that for a long time. So long and so silently, in fact, that I started to wonder if I'd lost the connection. He must have been praying about it, because suddenly and authoritatively, he said, "Raiser will not get a choice of its next victim; Trinity will assign one. However, Raiser will possess that victim in its usual way, with a promise of raising that person above his or her station…. I'd imagine the victim will be someone close to Carly, a parent or sibling, since that is the best way to weaken you."

His last words caught me by surprise. "Why would you say that?"

He chuckled. "Because you love her, Timon! It's evident after a few minutes' conversation. And the effects of love are exponential. If these demons go after Carly, whom you love, through someone *she* loves, that will weaken you threefold over attacking you directly."

Huh? I didn't ask for more explanation. I'd figure it out eventually.

He continued, "Now, tell me about Carly's family."

I was still pondering his previous words as I replied, "As far as I can tell, she has no family except for a mother, but they are not close."

"What about friends? Who is most at risk?"

I thought back to when Carly had gotten out of the hospital and needed a place to stay. Jen was out of town then, which had left only my place. There hadn't been anyone else to call.

"Jen," I said aloud, "and she may have called Carly a few minutes ago."

"Find out," Dimitrius advised.

"Yes," I agreed. "Right now. Thank you for your help, Dimitrius. May God bless you."

"God bless you and your endeavor, Timon," he replied. "I will pray for you."

After hanging up the phone, I went to the bedroom door and knocked. There was no answer. I could tell that the jets had been turned off in the tub, but I couldn't tell if Carly was still in the bath.

I cracked the door open. "Carly?"

She didn't answer. I braced myself and stuck my head in. She wasn't in the bedroom. I exhaled and approached the closed bathroom door.

"Carly?" I called through it.

"Yeah?" she called back.

"Who called you?"

She was quiet for a second before shouting, "What?"

I raised my voice, "Who was it that called when…?"

She shouted over me, "I can't understand you. Open the stupid door!"

I stared at the doorknob, watched my fingers wrap around it, not by my control at all, it seemed. I closed my eyes and prayed for strength to keep them closed as I twisted the knob. When the catch sprung, I opened the door a quarter of an inch and asked, "Was that Jen who called you?"

"Jaden, you're ridiculous! Open the door and talk to me."

"Are you decent?"

She crooned, "Most men think I'm more than."

"Apparently, you can hear me just fine…. I need to know if you've talked to Jen."

"Why?"

"I'd like her to come over," I said, truthfully. If Raiser had possessed her already, I could drive it out here, on my own turf. If Raiser was still looking for her, I could protect her along with Carly.

I heard water sloshing as she, apparently, adjusted her position. Then she said, "I doubt she'd be into it, but you can ask."

I leaned my head against the doorframe. "Have you talked to her?" I asked again.

"Yeah," Carly sounded defeated.

"How did she sound?"

"Like *Jen*."

I ignored that. "Had she heard about the fire?"

"Yep."

I had one more important question. "Did she send you those flowers?"

"Yes. Jen cares about me… Unlike the person I'm talking to *right now*."

That was all the confirmation I needed. Either Raiser had possession of Jen, or the demon was using her in some other way. I sighed loudly, but not at Carly's attitude. "Does she want to see you?"

"Of course! She'll be here at seven. I gave her the address."

"Good," I said. "Thank you."

I started to close the door again, but stopped when she called, "Jaden?"

"Yes?"

She splashed the water. "You haven't changed your mind about joining me in here, have you." It wasn't a question; it was an accusation.

"No." I closed the door tightly and then checked my watch, even though I knew approximately what time it was. I had to draw up a plan for driving out Raiser without harming Jen, without her awareness, if possible… just in case I needed one.

Chapter Sixteen

"I'm going to the lobby to meet Jen," I announced. I'd been on the Internet all afternoon, looking for information I could use against Raiser, unable to turn up much.

Carly had eaten her gyro-sans-lettuce and spent the rest of her time flipping through television channels, wishing for an update on the building fire, which got mentioned and dismissed as 'under investigation.' I could tell she was getting frustrated by the way she huffed at every news anchor who moved on to sports scores or celebrity gossip.

She hadn't spoken to me since our conversation through the bathroom door, but now she snapped, "You might as well, since you don't give a damn about me anymore."

"How can you say that?" I asked.

Her eyes widened. "Let's start with the fact that you know I don't want to be left alone! You could just buzz Jen in. But no. You have to go to the lobby."

I fixed my eyes on her. "Truthfully, Carly, you're very safe here, and I need to talk to Jen in private before she comes up."

She glared back. "About me? Wanna tell her what a slut I am? That I'm a threat to your precious celibacy?"

"No." I started closing windows on my computer.

"Well, if you're thinking about asking her to take me off your hands, you can do that in front of me. I'm going to ask her myself!"

I sighed and stood up. "I don't want you to leave, Carly. As for the other thing…. I only want to make love with a woman who actually loves me back, which you don't, so you've no right to be hostile about it, okay?"

I walked through my front door, hoping she wouldn't follow me. She didn't.

I hated that she was angry with me, but it would have to wait. If Raiser was about to come through the lobby door, it needed my full attention. I just hoped that Carly would allow me to make it up to her later.

Downstairs, Ed, my doorman and security guard, sat at his post, reading a letter. He looked up and greeted me as soon as I'd stepped off the elevator. He'd apparently forgiven me for allowing Adam onto the premises.

I described Jen to him and asked if he'd seen her.

"No," he answered, "but I'll let her up when she gets here so you don't have to wait around."

"I appreciate that, Ed, but I'll wait. I just wanted to be sure I hadn't missed her." *And that Raiser isn't waiting to ambush me.*

He nodded and returned his attention to the piece of paper he'd been reading.

I paced around the room, wondering how I'd explain things to Ed if he happened to witness me driving a demon out of the woman I'd just described as my friend.

As always, God provided a plan where I could not. A brown-uniformed deliveryman carried an enormous package through the revolving front door. He left it on Ed's station, and the two exchanged pleasantries while Ed signed the man's clipboard.

The man nodded toward me as he made his way back outside. Ed had already dialed his phone. I heard him say, "Ms. Phelps? It's Ed. We just received a delivery for you down front."

He listened and then replied, "Well, yes, it is rather large.... Heavy?" He lifted a corner of the cardboard box. "I guess, maybe." He listened again. "Well, it's taking up most of my wo...." That last word morphed into, "Oh, okay." He sounded resigned when he added, "I'll bring it up." He hung up with a loud sigh.

I smiled supportively as he lifted the big awkward box with a grunt. "Can I get the elevator for you?" I offered.

"Thanks," he wheezed.

We waited together for the doors to open, and then he stumbled inside.

"Floor?" I asked.

"Seventeenth."

I leaned inside to swipe my card and press the button, then I backed out again. I gave a friendly salute as the doors closed between us.

When I turned around, Jen was pushing through the revolving door from outside. Her blond hair was down, cut in a bob at her chin. She hadn't seen me, yet, but I prayed for, and received, the power of the Holy Spirit anyway.

"You!" she exclaimed as we made eye contact. The voice was Jen's, but the sneer belonged to Raiser.

"Come out of her!" I demanded, forcing the power of the Spirit to flow from my hands.

Raiser made Jen laugh. "Who are you to make demands of me?"

I'd forgotten to speak in the Lord's name. "A witness for Christ," I answered, maneuvering God's power, preparing to drive a wedge of it between this demon and its host, "and in His name…"

Raiser cut me off, "You're not as strong as you think you are!"

From the demon's mouth came a blinding flash of white light. When it cleared, I could see neither the lobby nor Jen. Instead, my vision was flooded with imagines of Carly, my memories and my fantasies of our week together. The images came randomly, distracting me as I tried to fight Raiser blindly.

Raiser forced me to relive my last conversation with Carly and then, the demon whispered, "But she does love you, and you know it. Denying your humanity won't add one moment to her life, not one breath more. Even if you save her soul, her body will never again be available to you.

"This body, the one I wear," it stroked Jen's stomach, "can talk to her, reason with her. I can tell her to open her heart to you. And she will listen. I can give you what you really want."

The memory dissolved, replaced by an earlier memory of Carly asleep in my bed with space for me at her side. My desire for her was suddenly overwhelming. Raiser's doing, I knew, but nearly impossible to resist.

I felt my Lord's power slipping. "God, give me strength!" I prayed aloud.

My only chance, I realized, was to turn Raiser's temptation around. I remembered Dimitrius' words, 'the effects of love are exponential.' I had to love Carly so completely, that my desires no longer mattered to me at all.

And it wasn't that hard to do, as it turned out. I'd made the decision hundreds of centuries ago that I would not tie any woman to this life of mine. All I had to do was renew that resolve.

Every new image Raiser placed before me, I augmented to a vision of Carly, happy and content without me, as I knew she would and could be. I remembered how Jesus had spoken her name to me and used that to fuel my passion for her happiness. I created images of my own: of Carly with a husband who wasn't me, who loved her in ways I could not; of her life with children and grandchildren, like Ingrid has had. And I found myself truly at peace with the idea that she could have a fulfilling life without me.

The visions cut off abruptly with a shriek from Jen. Failing at one tactic, Raiser had tried another. Torture.

I blinked, able to see again, but shocked by the sight. Raiser had twisted Jen's head until she was looking back over her shoulder. And then it twisted some more.

"You shall not hurt her!" I cried. "In Christ's name, come out!"

The Spirit exploded from my fingers, driving into the space between Jen's soul and the demon. I felt Raiser squirm, slip and scramble. It made one final effort to distract me. My ears seemed to hear Carly's deep, smoky voice say, "I love you, Jaden."

One simple sentence, not even really from her, but for a split second, both my resolve and my concentration faltered; the Spirit's power within me weakened. Instead of being forced from Jen's body straight to the throne of Jesus Christ, Raiser evaporated from my grasp and was gone.

Jen's body started to slump. I dashed across the room to catch her. To my surprise, she didn't completely pass out. Most people would have. "Jaden," she said weakly. "What happened?"

"I think you nearly fainted," I explained, wanting to know how much, if anything, she remembered.

Behind me the elevator chimed. I heard Ed's voice ask, "Is everything okay, Doctor Bethany?" Then, with more concern, "Shall I send for an ambulance?"

"How do you feel, Jen?" I asked.

"Dizzy," she answered, rubbing her neck as she regained her balance. I kept one hand under her arm

as she continued, "Something caught my eye outside. Startled me.... I guess I turned my head too
quickly...."

Ed asked, "What was it?" and I held my breath,
waiting to hear how she'd answer.

She laughed. "Just a little dog! Not worthy of a
trip to the hospital."

Ed raised his eyebrows at me. "What do you
think, Doc?"

I looked into Jen's eyes. Carly's friend looked
back, not Raiser. Her pupils seemed okay. "I'll take a
closer look upstairs," I answered, "but I think she'll
be all right." I added directly to her, "Can you walk?
The elevator's just over here."

She nodded, but I helped her anyway, steadying
her all the way to the top of the building and into
my penthouse. Carly was sitting on the back of my
sofa, watching the door. I didn't have time to interpret her expression before it changed into concern
for her friend.

"What happened?" she asked, jumping up. "Did
he hurt you?"

Jen looked at her like she was crazy. "No, you
idiot; he's *helping* me."

I led Jen to the sofa and asked her to lie down.
"I'm going to get a little light. Be right back, okay?"

As I entered my bedroom to dig out my medical
kit, I heard Jen's voice say, "I'd have sworn you said
he was a lawyer, but a doctor's even better."

Carly's response sounded less impressed. "He's
both."

"I like school!" I shouted to them.

I hadn't needed my kit for a long time. It was in the back of my closet along with my luggage. I checked that the penlight still worked before returning to the living room.

"Has anything like this ever happened to you before?" I asked Jen in my most-doctorly voice, shining the light in and out of her left eye, even though I knew there was nothing wrong with her now.

"No, never," she replied.

I checked her other eye. "Headaches?"

"Not lately. Although my neck feels really stiff."

"And are you feeling dizzy now?"

She shook her head.

I helped her sit up. "How about now?"

She frowned but said, "I feel perfectly normal."

I smiled. "Good! Slide over, and I'll work on your neck."

I sat beside Jen on the sofa and brushed her short hair back. My Lord allowed me to use some of his Spirit to diagnose the pulled muscle. As I massaged, the Spirit healed.

"Ah," Jen sighed, relaxing. "That feels good."

"Jaden has magic fingers," Carly interjected, bitterly, from the chair nearest Jen. "He brought Lucy back from the brink of death; he did something to me at the Art Institute; and if I'm not mistaken, he's been curing malaria in Africa without medication."

I continued working on Jen's neck and shoulder. But Carly's attitude frustrated me. "I could tell you that the Holy Spirit helps me to heal people," I snapped, "but you don't want to hear it."

"Wow, is there some tension between you two?" asked Jen.

Neither of us answered her.

"So, what happened downstairs?" Carly asked.

Again, I was curious how Jen would answer.

"It was so weird," she said. "I walked through the door, and saw Jaden waiting for me." She leaned into me and interjected, "Which I thought was really sweet, by the way," before continuing, "I don't remember if we even had a chance to say hello. I noticed movement out of the corner of my eye and thought someone was coming through the door behind me. Like, reflexively, I twisted my head around to see, but it was just this little dog trotting down the street."

Good, I thought. She'd not been aware of Raiser or of its influence on her.

She continued, "I guess I turned my head too quickly. The next thing I knew, my knees were buckling and your hero was dashing over to catch me before I fell."

Carly glowered at me. "Guess he's everybody's hero, now."

Jen's brow furrowed. "I feel like something else happened, like I'm missing some time somewhere. I can't quite grasp it."

"Oh, that's Jaden," Carly quipped. "He makes you feel like you are *losing your mind*."

Jen slipped out of my grasp and asked Carly, "Are you pissed that he's touching me?"

"No!" Carly snapped. "In fact, you're welcome to him. It's too much effort; *I'm* sick of pretending!"

She stood up and went into my bedroom, slamming the door behind her for the second time that afternoon.

I blew out my breath.

"What's up with her?" Jen asked.

How am I supposed to know? I wondered. I had no experience with twenty-first century women. Carly certainly expressed herself, but I had no idea how to interpret it.

"She's been through a lot in the last few days," I attempted to explain. "And apparently nothing I do is the right thing to do.... I wish she'd open up to me, but she won't."

"Well," said Jen, "you do know about her mom, at least."

I shook my head.

Her eyebrows went up. "Perry?"

"Her mom's boyfriend, right?"

Jen's eyes widened. "Oh my God! She hasn't told you anything?"

I wasn't sure how she'd interpret my wince of pain, but she didn't seem to notice. She pushed herself off the sofa and went to pound on the bedroom door. "Carly Bell Benson," she shouted, "get your butt out here. Now!"

Chapter Seventeen

To my surprise, the bedroom door opened.

Jen didn't give Carly a chance to speak. "Go sit with that boy on the couch and tell him about your mom *and* about Perry," she ordered.

Carly's eyes, filled with a tempestuous storm, found mine. She glanced away quickly, as if embarrassed. When she looked back, her expression had changed again, no longer angry or embarrassed, but fearful. "He doesn't want to hear it."

"He deserves to know," Jen said gently, placing her hand on Carly's back to force her in my direction. "Talk to him. You'll feel better."

Carly flopped onto the chair nearest me and proceeded to study her chewed up nails.

Jen turned to me. "I think I'm gonna get going." I started to protest, but she spoke over me, "I just wanted to make sure you were both okay, but you don't need me for this conversation." She turned to Carly. "Call me tomorrow, okay?"

Carly mouthed the words, 'Don't leave me.'

Jen patted her shoulder and then kissed her top of the head. "You need to do this, Carly. You'll be fine."

Is it safe to let Jen go? I prayed.

I will watch over her, the Lord replied.

I walked Jen to the door. "I need to talk to you," I whispered and guided her into the hallway.

"Now what?" she asked, suspiciously.

I didn't pause. "There's a chance that a bomb went off at Scheoff Publishing today, and it might have been planted in the flowers you sent to Carly."

"What?" she gasped.

"Did you order them in person?" I asked.

She shook her head. "No, over the phone. I was still in Indiana."

"Your cell?"

"Yeah."

"Good. There'll be a record.... The police will want to talk to you. Be honest with them. If you need a lawyer, I know a good one."

She forced a smile and then covered her face with her palms and groaned, "Oh God, I'm in trouble, aren't I?"

I felt the knife in my chest again. "I don't know," I said slowly, as soon as I could talk. "Did you bomb your office?"

"No!" she cried. "It's just.... I've been mouthing off about my boss being a jerk for not promoting me.... Doesn't that make me look guilty?"

Raiser. That's how it had found a way into Jen, by promising a promotion. I hated that demon more than ever. *How could I have let it escape*? I tried not to let my thoughts show. "Not at all, Jen. Everyone complains about the boss. Even *my* employees," I joked. "Just tell the police what you know, turn over your phone if they ask. Call me if you need me." I added the promise, "It will be fine."

She nodded. "Guess so. Thanks for everything, Jaden."

"You too…. Oh, and if you have any more dizzy spells, well… you should call me, then, too."

"Got it, Doctor Lawyer." She smiled weakly. "See ya."

"Tell Ed down there at the desk that I said he should call you a cab and pay for it. I'll reimburse him."

"Oh… I couldn't…."

"Trust me," I assured her. "He'll want to do it."

She nodded in reply. I watched until she'd gotten in the elevator, and then I returned to Carly.

She was still on the chair with her feet tucked up under her. Her eyes, huge round pools of the Mediterranean Sea, fixed on me as I reentered the room.

"What do you think you want to know?" she asked, her deep voice resigned.

I spread my hands. "Whatever you want to tell me."

She shook her head and averted her eyes as I approached. So instead of sitting down with her, I went to my stereo.

"How about some music?" I offered. "Would that help?"

"Not if it's that garbage you were playing in the car."

I ignored her and stretched out my fingers to select a disk of Italian arias, something I hoped would sooth us both. As the music started, I headed to the kitchen. I'd decided to make tea.

"What's she singing about?" Carly called from her chair.

"Love." I added apologetically, "Well, it *is* Italian."

She didn't say anything more. As I waited for the kettle, I began to sing along with the CD, unable to help myself as the song was a duet with a haunting tenor part.

I was still singing as I carried a steaming cup back to Carly.

"You have a nice voice," she said, taking the tea.

I finished the stanza before saying, "Thank you…. Want milk or sugar in that?"

She shook her head and made the comment, "Just when I think I'm getting to know you, something else surprises me."

I shrugged at that, settling onto the sofa near her chair. "Are you ready to talk now?"

She sipped her tea before answering, "I don't know where to start."

"How about with something easy?" I prompted. "Tell me why you order, but don't eat lettuce."

She looked at me and then her eyes slid away. "You think that's easy to explain?" She sighed out a big breath. "Jen thinks it's a control-thing. Since there's so much in my life that I hate, but can't control, I order something I hate and then control it by not eating it…. I don't know. That's the best answer I've got."

I'd heard of such things; they weren't that uncommon. "That makes sense," I said. "Want to tell me what it is that you can't control?"

She shook her head and whispered, "Not yet."

"That's okay," I replied and waited for her to look at me again. "Maybe you could tell me why you've been so angry with me today."

"I don't know," she mumbled.

After a minute, she continued, "I started out afraid. These last few days… " She let that thought die. "I started thinking that… maybe you *are* who you say you are, or maybe even something worse. I thought I'd feel better if I got you to prove that you're just a man. You know, in the way men usually like to prove themselves?"

She exhaled. "But you're not interested, and I refuse to be hurt by that fact. It's easier to be angry…. Beats feeling scared."

"I'm sorry," I said, reaching for her.

She leaned away. "Don't touch me."

I let my hand drop and repeated, "I'm sorry."

She pressed her cup to her lips and hid behind it.

Hesitantly, I asked, "Are you still afraid of me? Of what I am?"

"No," she answered softly. "You were so gentle with Jen…. You've been kind to everyone…. I even believe that, in rejecting me before, you were really trying to protect me."

"I'd do anything to protect you," I assured her. "Please, don't think I was rejecting you."

She almost smiled.

"Thank you for being so honest," I continued earnestly.

"I try to do what Jen tells me to; she's usually right," she answered.

"Would you tell me about you and Jen, now?"

She put down the teacup and crossed her arms over her lap. "Jen's family lives downstairs from us. They have, as far back as I can remember. She's six years older than I am, so we shouldn't be friends, except that she found me, once, out on the fire escape and listened when I had no one to talk to. She believed me when no one else would. Since that day, she's always been the one person I can talk to.

"The four years she was away at school were torture! We talked on the phone, but it wasn't the same. It made me really sad when she came back to Chicago but got an apartment downtown with her boyfriend instead of moving back in with her parents. I really can't blame her, though."

She paused and looked at me as if she expected me to say something, but I wasn't about to interject now. I just wanted her to talk.

She took a deep breath. "Jen got this great job, editing at Scheoff, at about the same time as I dropped out of high school. I worked retail for a couple of months and at a burger joint on the weekends. They hired me at a bar, and that would have been pretty good money, but the owner caught onto my fake I.D. before I could start.

"Jen understood that I wasn't making money fast enough to get out of my mom's house. So she pulled some strings, called in favors. Basically, she committed herself to indentured servitude in order to get me this receptionist job. If you think a publisher would willingly hire a kid without an English degree, let alone without a high school diploma, you're really wrong."

"Why did you drop out?" I asked gently.

She smiled sadly. "Can't believe it, can you, Doctor 'I Like School?'"

"I'm not judging you," I assured her. "I want to understand what's happened to you."

She bit her bottom lip and covered her face with her hands. She whispered, "My mother," and then exclaimed, "God, I need a cigarette!"

"Sorry," I wheezed. "I don't have any."

"Beer?" she asked hopefully, knowing I had some left over from the weekend. When I didn't answer, she peeked through her fingers at me. I shook my head.

"Fine," she sighed, dropping her hands. "No anesthetic. We'll just rip it wide open."

I waited while she glanced around the room. Her eyes finally settled on her teacup. She picked it up, but didn't drink any. "Mother," she sneered at the word, "insisted I get a full-time job instead of enrolling for my junior year. She threatened to move us in with Perry if I didn't.

"At the time, I took her seriously," she said, "although I've since come to realize that Perry doesn't have a home, and even if he did, neither of us would be welcome there. Mom's learned not to ask where he goes when he disappears 'cause he beats the crap out of her when she does."

Softly, I asked, "Does Perry beat you, too?"

She frowned and starting rocking, forward and back on the chair. "Sometimes. I prefer that to the usual, actually…. Mom started seeing him when I was twelve." After exhaling loudly, she added, "He ah…. He raped me the first night she brought him home… hasn't stopped since."

Her words were so shocking, so sad. No wonder she didn't want to go home. No wonder she didn't feel safe there. "Oh, Carly," I whispered sadly, trying to quell the rage rising within me. I didn't think it would help her if I got angry now. "Did you… tell your mom?" I asked as gently as I could.

"Yeah, I told her."

I prompted, "What did she say?"

"To quote her would require profuse use of foul language. I'm fairly certain you'd implode."

"Tell me anyway."

She sighed. "The gist of it was that I should get my own boyfriend and leave hers alone."

Even without certain words, I felt myself gag. My chest burned. I swallowed hard and forced out, "You were *twelve*?" I wanted to drive to her mother's house and rip the woman's head off, her boyfriend's, too. My feelings were so strong, I couldn't even acknowledge those desires as sinful.

Carly nodded, still rocking. "I tried to talk to her again a few years later, when I thought I was pregnant. That time she told me to get an abortion or move out."

I physically trembled from the fury I felt. "Were you?" I croaked.

"Pregnant? No. Thank God."

I couldn't help but ask, "Where was your father through all of this?"

She shook her head. "Took off before I was born, never to be heard from again. He hadn't wanted children, so when Mom got pregnant, he got lost...."

I looked down at my hands, wondering how to respond, what I could possibly say that would make anything better.

She added a final comment, "So you see, Jaden, it's completely unfair of you to demand that I love you; I don't even know what the word means."

My eyes snapped up. "Oh, Carly," I said, pushing myself up and reaching for her. She let me pull her out of the chair, and we fell back onto the sofa together. I wrapped both arms around her and held her close, resting my chin on her shoulder. I felt her trembling.

"Listen," I whispered. "None of that is your fault, and you certainly deserve better. I'm in awe of you, now more than ever! Because you *do* know what love is. You're capable of deep, selfless love. You risked your own life to save Len's today. You feel guilt over being annoyed by Lucy's incompetence because, ultimately, you love her, too. You even loved an unknown stranger enough to meet his need for food before you'd even met him. You love like Jesus loves, and that's the purest, most selfless love of all."

She twisted in my arms to bury her face against my chest and asked in a very small voice, "So how come I feel like God hates me?"

I stroked her hair. "I would probably feel the same way in your place, but believe me, it's not true. God never wanted your father to leave the family. God never wanted your mother to feel so hurt by that abandonment that she would hold on to the next man at any cost. God needed your parents' DNA, specifically, to create you, and you are a treasure to Him. He wanted your parents to see you as He sees you, and to stand by you, and to put your needs ahead of their own. But they chose not to, and He wouldn't make them.

"God allows each of us make our choices without interfering. It's a great gift that few people truly appreciate, especially here in the free western world. He wants us to do the right thing every time, but nobody can. So, He sent us His Son, to atone for our mistakes, to make us all perfect in His sight. And to Him, you are perfect, Carly. He loves you more than anything."

She thought for a moment and then whispered, "I didn't think you told lies."

"I don't," I assured her. "There are no truer words than these: God loves you, Carly. And so do I."

She remained silent in my arms for a moment longer, and then something happened that I never expected to experience in my life. She twisted around to face me, pulled my head toward hers and kissed me.

Chapter Eighteen

From the moment our lips touched, I lost myself completely. Nothing existed in my world except for Carly. I couldn't stop myself from kissing her back. I couldn't even make myself wish to stop. I stroked her cheekbone with my thumb and twined my other hand into her hair, letting it slide through my fingers like threads of fine silk.

I moved my lips to her neck and heard her breath catch. At that barely audible sound, my heart rate jumped; heat raced through my body. Nothing I'd ever thought about physical intimacy made sense to me anymore. This couldn't possibly be the wrong thing to do....

My telephone rang.

The world came crashing back.

I opened my eyes and lifted my head, surprised to find myself prone on the sofa, relieved that we were still dressed, but not clear, exactly, how Carly had gotten beneath me.

The phone rang again.

"I'm so sorry," I whispered, sliding off of her and onto the floor. I couldn't look at her. I groped for the phone and checked the I.D. *Chicago P.D.*

"Hello?" I answered, still trying to clear my head.

I recognized the voice that answered, "Doctor Bethany, please."

"Speaking," I said, sitting straighter. Carly got up and moved back to the chair. I could see her out of the corner of my eye, but I was still too ashamed of myself to look at her.

"This is Alex Cindry, Chicago P.D.," said the voice of the man I'd met at the scene today.

"Yes, Officer," I replied. "How may I help you?"

"I wanted to let you know that, thanks to your tip, we've arrested a suspect in the bombing case."

My eyes closed. *Oh, Jen*, I thought, but he continued, "The man is Foster Flautis. We found bomb-making equipment in his shop, and his computer shows recent activity on terrorist websites. He hasn't shut up since we brought him in. In fact, he gave a full confession *with* his lawyer present."

I exhaled loudly and then asked, "Was Carly the target?"

"Just the publisher. Guess they rejected his memoir."

I couldn't help but wonder if Raiser had been affecting Foster Flautis as well as Jen. "That's unbelievable," I said, sensing the officer expected a response.

He snorted. "Jerk'll probably have no trouble getting published now…. Anyway, I thought you'd want to know."

"Yes, I do appreciate the call."

I expected him to hang up, but instead, he continued, "Doctor, that woman today.... She should have died. I've never seen anyone survive after being that badly burned, but they say she's gonna make it.... What's your secret?"

"Prayer, my friend," I answered, "and a sincere belief that God can work miracles."

"Indeed," he replied. "Well... thanks for the miracle." He didn't sound convinced.

"Alex, it really is a simple matter of faith." I wished I had more to offer him, but at the moment, the strength of my own faith was in question.

I ended the call, hung my head and prayed, *How could I have wanted to take advantage of her like that? Will you ever forgive me?*

Have you forgotten why I let them take my life? He asked.

Tears of shame stung my eyes. I would never be rid of the image in my memory of my friend on the cross. No Hollywood actor could fully convey the pain He'd endured that day. And not at the hands of the Romans, either. He'd suffered God's punishment for the sins of humanity, every single one, including my own. He'd even known on that day that I would fail Him nineteen hundred and seventy-seven years later, choosing to pursue my own passions on a black leather sofa in Chicago when I should have been convincing Carly of His love for her. Yet, He'd taken the punishment in my place and gave His forgiveness freely.

"Everything okay?" Carly asked.

I cleared my throat and said roughly, "They've arrested someone, a... disgruntled writer, recipient of a rejection letter."

"You're kidding!" She sounded surprised. I didn't look to see. "We must send out a hundred of those a week."

I shrugged.

"At least there's an explanation this time," she added.

I nodded.

"So... what's wrong with you?"

"I need to pray. Excuse me." I pushed myself up and tried to slip past her, but she put out a hand to stop me. Our eyes met briefly before I had to look away.

"You feel guilty," she guessed. "Jaden, we only kissed. You barely touched me. Even I know that kissing isn't a sin!"

I wrung my hands. "It's not the kissing. It's my selfishness. I wasn't thinking about what's best for you! And that's... that's simply unforgivable. Please, I need to be alone." I motioned for her to let me pass, and she did.

I didn't look back as I made my way to my room and closed the door. I fully prostrated myself on my rug, pressing my forehead into the floor, covering the back of my head with my hands. "Your kingdom come, Lord," I said into the rug and waited until I felt him beside me. "Forgive me," I begged.

There is no sin in loving her, He assured me.

"No, but there is sin in acting on selfish impulses, and my Lord, I can't trust myself not to! Now, I know that I can't. I have to walk away from this."

He replied, *I hear your heart, speaking the opposite of your words. Again you spin in circles, Timon, and there is no time for that. Besides, you are making progress. She heard you today.*

"And then I messed it up by being selfish... How can I do Your work if I can't trust myself to stay focused on what's best for Carly?"

Timon, you act as though, aside from this one moment of weakness, you have never been selfish. But you have.

"I know."

This won't be the last time.

"No," I admitted glumly.

Then rise up, assured of your forgiveness. It is late, and Carly is hungry.

"I can't face her," I whispered, not moving.

She wants pizza, He told me.

"You're laughing at me. Why?"

Because you don't have time to waste in self-abasement. You've asked for forgiveness; it's been granted. You have work to do.

I wanted to agree with Him.

She is hungry, He repeated.

"But how can I trust myself?" I asked.

I trust you, Timon. That is enough.

I returned to the living room where Carly sat, twirling her empty teacup around her finger. She grinned at me.

"Ah… I'm sorry," I said. It was hard to meet her eye, but I made myself do it. I'd expected her to be angry or at least confused by my behavior, but she didn't appear to be either. Quite the opposite, in fact, she seemed amused.

She raised an eyebrow. "For wigging out? Or for kissing me in the first place?"

"Both, I guess."

She clapped her hands together. "Doesn't matter; I've decided to go with it. So what if my new boyfriend's a bit… eccentric. At least he loves me enough to worry that he doesn't love me enough… which is sweet in a sadistic kind of way."

Boyfriend? my brain echoed hopefully. I quickly reprimanded myself, *You're hardly a boy, and it's a bad idea to start thinking about kissing her again!* Of course, I'd already started thinking about it.

I took a deep breath and asked, "So, you're ready to move on?"

"Depends on what you have in mind."

"Pizza."

Her eyes lit up. "Great! I'm starving!"

I reached for my phone. "What would you like on it? And don't say lettuce."

She giggled. "I don't care."

"Really?" I pressed, "Because I'm going to order anchovies and black olives unless you stop me."

"Stop!" she cried in mock-horror. "Hand over the phone."

That night, I had many dreams of Raiser and Trinity, cowering in the damp cold alleyway behind my building, planning, calling others of their kind, attacking me in force. I failed against them, time after time. I'd had enough experience with both to recognize these as dreams and not visions from my Lord, but even so, I could not shake off the nightmares. I tossed on the sofa all night long, tangling myself in the blankets, kicking the coffee table.

I awoke the next morning, tired and sore, surprised to find Carly sitting on the floor facing me. Her eyes were just a few inches from mine. She was resting her chin on her knees with her arms wrapped around her shins, a blanket draped across her shoulders.

"Hey," I said, my voice thick with sleep. "You okay?"

She smiled. "More than."

"What?" I asked suspiciously, wondering if I'd said or done something in my sleep that I shouldn't have. I sat up, realizing that she had one of my Bibles open on the floor beside her.

"It's just... I feel giddy," she answered. "Like, some huge weight has been lifted, you know? They caught that guy already. Len and Lucy will both be okay. I have a really great guy in my life who wants to protect me." She reached over to touch my face. I took her hand and held it there.

"I also have to admit that it feels pretty good not to have any more secrets between us," she added.

"Yeah," I replied. "Same here."

We stared at each other for another minute.

"Are you in here?" she asked, slipping her hand out of mine to pat the Bible.

"I'm mentioned once in most translations. But, Carly, you shouldn't be looking for me in there. That's the place to find Jesus."

She nodded. "I started the Matthew chapter over. Were you one of the fishermen?"

"No," I laughed. "Though, I would like to have been a fisherman. I loved the sea. Still do. Now stop guessing."

"Jesus said and did some really amazing stuff," she commented, "but a lot of it is really confusing."

"Well," I replied, "Matthew was trying to prove that Jesus is the Messiah, or the Christ, as we Greeks like to call Him. So most of that book is better understood from a first-century Jew's perspective, someone who would have known and understood the prophesies about Jesus. You might find Him easier to understand in Luke's gospel."

I reached over her shoulder and flipped forward a few pages. "The words Christ spoke to me are here, too. Luke 9:27." I pointed to the passage and then sat back to let her read it.

"It really is hard to believe," she murmured. "When you were sleeping a few minutes ago, you looked so…."

I raised an eyebrow, worried about how that sentence might end.

"Normal," she finished with a shrug. She folded my Bible closed and gently returned it to the coffee table. "Not to change the subject or anything, but I was wondering…." She paused and lowered her eyes. "Well, since I don't have a job to go to today, and you've already taken the week off… What about that camping trip? I think we both need to get out of the city for a while."

I felt a smile take over my face. "*That* is a fabulous idea!"

I reserved a campsite while Carly took a shower. I had to call three parks to find one with space available. Apparently, we weren't the only ones who wanted to take advantage of the Indian summer weather. Lake Kongatoga, however, had just received a cancellation on one of its private lakeside sites, which they were happy to overcharge me for. I didn't mind paying extra this time. Carly's first camping experience wouldn't have to be in a crowded public lot somewhere, and that was worth it. I thanked God for working this out for us.

Over breakfast, Carly and I discussed logistics. I had a tent and sleeping bags, a camp stove, cooking utensils and food, but she didn't even have a change of clothing. I didn't want her to go to her house and offered to purchase everything she would need on our way out of town. She insisted that I couldn't waste my money while she had perfectly good clothes at home.

"Besides," she added, "Perry's never there on Thursdays."

"Why not?" I asked.

She shrugged. "He just never is. And Mom'll be at work, so I can sneak in and grab my stuff."

Will she be safe, Lord? I prayed.

His answer was evasive and discouraging. *Make your choice, Timon.*

Reluctantly, I agreed to drive her over.

"That's it, just there." Carly pointed to a light-colored, three-story brownstone in the middle of the block, and I pulled my car up to the curb. I cut the engine and started to climb out, but she grabbed my arm. I turned to her, wondering why she'd stopped me.

"I'll go up by myself," she insisted.

No! I couldn't let that happen. Even if Perry wasn't waiting for her, Raiser or Trinity, or both, might be. "I think I should go with you," I told her, trying not to show my alarm.

She shook her head. "It's too embarrassing. No one's there. I'll be right back."

"Why is it embarrassing? I've lived in caves, you know."

She stared at me for a moment. "Right," she said as if she didn't believe me. "But it doesn't matter, okay? I'll just throw some stuff in a bag and be right back."

I closed my eyes and felt around. My soul could sense what was happening spiritually in the surrounding area. I didn't feel the blackness that would indicate demonic activity. "All right," I sighed at last. "But if you're not back in fifteen minutes, I'm coming in."

She patted my arm before climbing out of the car.

I kept one eye on the clock and one eye on the building, all the while keeping myself open to sensing Raiser or Trinity. Nothing felt wrong, but I worried anyway.

Why aren't they here? I asked my Lord.

Because they've chosen not to be, He informed me.

Why would they make that choice? I knew He wouldn't answer that question, and He didn't. I was able to relax, but only a little.

Twelve minutes later, Carly breezed through the front door and skipped down the brownstone's steps, wearing jeans and a tight, white tee under an oversized flannel shirt. Her hair was tied in a thick ponytail. Her lips shined cotton candy pink once more. The only thing about her that wasn't perfect was the small bandage at the base of her neck. I still regretted that I hadn't been allowed to heal her fully.

I jumped out of the car to meet her. "Are you okay?" I asked. "Was anyone home? Did you tell anyone where we're going?"

She pressed her duffle bag into my stomach and announced, "Geez, dude, lighten up! It's a beautiful day, and we are outta here!"

Unable to 'lighten up,' I frowned and asked, "Did you remember a coat? It could get cold later."

"It's in the bag, dude."

"Are you going to call me 'dude' all weekend? Because it's already grating on my nerves." I opened the passenger door and made space on the back seat for her bag, next to the cooler and on top of the tent. Admittedly, it was a tight fit.

"Believe me, you wouldn't prefer the other name I was thinking," she told me. "What's in your trunk?"

"Nothing. Why?"

She shrugged. "Just wondered why you're not using it."

I straightened. "Oh. Well, we'll need that space for firewood when we get there."

She grinned. "A real live campfire? Dude!" She shoved me toward the driver's door. "Let's go!"

Neither of us spoke much as we made our way onto the JFK. I was sensing the air for trouble; Carly was soaking up the sunshine and beaming it back. Before I knew it, we were in Rockford, headed for the state line on I-90.

We made it, I realized. We had not been followed and, even if they could guess that we were together, no one knew our destination. So, no *thing* could track us down. I felt myself relax, finally and fully.

Carly peered at the speedometer, not for the first time. "You've seriously never opened it up?" she asked.

I laughed. There were some good memories along with the dark ones associated with this car and its top speed. "Well... I got it in Europe," I told her, "where speed limits are considerably higher, in places non-existent. So, yeah, I have."

From the corner of my eye, I saw that this excited her. "What was it like?" She petted the dashboard. "How did she respond?"

"It was... sweet. There's no other way to say it."

She giggled. "That word does *not* work for you, my friend."

Probably not, I agreed in my head. "Right. How about I tell you it was like hovering just off the ground with all the world racing by in a blue-green blur."

"Sweet," she breathed.

Carly was right. That use of the word was meant for her, not me.

"How unfortunate for you that we're in Illinois," I teased.

She retorted, "It's unfair to leash her in this way."

"Admittedly.... But I couldn't leave her behind."

"In Paris?" she asked.

I nodded.

"Why on earth did you leave *Paris* to come here?" she exclaimed.

Not such a great memory. It intruded on my happiness. "Had to," I whispered.

"Girl trouble?" she prompted, falsely sympathetic.

I shivered involuntarily at the memories of what Trinity had done in France while God had left me powerless against its evil. But I answered Carly lightly, "Do I seem like the type who'd have trouble with girls?" I glanced at her. I'd never seen her face brighter, her smile wider, her eyes more sparkly.

"Dude, I'm pretty sure girls are nothing but trouble for you."

I returned my attention to the road, patting her knee. "Only this one."

I wouldn't have guessed it possible, but my comment seemed to make her even happier. I found it hard to keep my attention focused on driving. I returned my hand to the steering wheel and said, "I wish time didn't fly so fast when I'm with you."

"*Fast*? We'd be there by now if you'd drive her as she was designed to be driven!"

She pressed down hard on my right knee, to no effect. Or at least, not to the effect of increasing the car's speed, only my heart rate.

Chapter Nineteen

"This is my first time out of state," Carly reminded me, about an hour into Wisconsin. "I guess I've seen pictures and T.V. shows and stuff, but I just didn't expect it to be so empty out here."

I flashed her a grin. "It's not empty; there are hundreds of cows! See? There's one there… and there… Oh, and look, four over there."

"Dude, we are *not* going to count the cows."

"No?"

She shook her head. "But I do love cows. Wanna hear the cow limerick I made up."

"I doubt it," I answered, but she ignored me.

I braced myself as she began, "There once was a cow from Muskegon, whose field was a Garden of Eden. She said as she munched. This is the best lunch! It's a lucky place for me to be in."

Laughter burst from me, uncontrolled.

"It's not that funny," she said.

"But I'd expected it to be dirty, which makes it hilarious, in fact."

"Oh, you *wanted* dirty. Okay. There once was a cow from Nantucket…. Wait. I think I meant a bull…."

"Stop!" I cried through my laughter. "Don't go there. I'll be in so much pain, I'll have to pull over."

Her mood turned serious. "It really causes you physical pain when you hear a bad word?"

My laughter faded to a sigh. "It can happen when I hear profanity, especially in large quantities. It always happens when I hear the Lord's name taken in vain or when I myself contemplate swearing or lying…. It feels like I'm having a heart attack. So, please, don't risk it while I'm driving."

She shook her head. "I want so badly for you to be normal, but you're just not going to be, are you?"

I shrugged. "I am who I am."

She tilted her head. "Okay. Prove it."

"Prove it," I echoed. "How, exactly, do you want me to do that?" I glanced out the window as a blue Chevy passed us. "As I've said, all the real proof is in Greece." I noticed a teenager in the car's passenger seat. He turned to check out my car as they went by. I nodded toward him.

Carly didn't notice. "I don't know…. There must be something you know that no one else does."

"You'd just accuse me of making it up, though," I pointed out.

We were silent for a moment.

"I can speak every human language there is," I offered. "God's Spirit gave me that gift at Pentecost."

"What, exactly, is Pentecost?" she asked. "I know it's like, a holiday, but I don't know what it's about."

"Oh. Well, you know that Jesus was crucified, and we remember that on Good Friday, right?"

She nodded, and I continued, "So on Easter Sunday, we celebrate the day He raised himself from the dead. Fifty days later, after He'd returned to God, He sent the Holy Spirit back to Earth. That's Pentecost."

I decided to add something more personal. "Most of us were huddled up in Jerusalem then, trying to make sense of all that had happened. See, we didn't expect Jesus to die. And then, we didn't expect Him to take back His life. We didn't expect to see Him alive, walking and talking among us, and we didn't expect Him to leave us again after that. But all of those things happened…. And when we received His Spirit at Pentecost, we were able to speak all of these different languages, and we finally understood; our job was to go out into the world and spread the news of God's great love, expressed through His Son, Jesus the Christ, in words and phrases that everyone could understand."

She nodded. "Okay, let's hear some… But use phrases *I* might understand, not whatever you were saying back then."

"Do you know any foreign languages?"

"I took a semester of French my freshman year."

"Okay, then." There really was only one thing to say. "Je t'aime."

She grinned. "You'd like me to believe that, wouldn't you?"

"Oui, c'est vrai…. Ti amo."

Her brow furrowed. "Wait. What?"

"The first phrase was French for, ' I do, indeed' want you to believe that I love you. Ti amo is a different language, but one you like. Can you guess?"

She thought for a moment. "Italian?"

I nodded. "Very good. Wo ai ni."

"Sounds Chinese."

"Mandarin," I confirmed. "And in Cantonese, Ngo oiy ney a."

"Show off."

I grinned. "Ik hou van u."

She hesitated. "German?"

"Close. Dutch. Jeg elsker deg."

"German!" she exclaimed triumphantly.

"Nope. Norwegian. Te amo. Semper eaternaumque te amabo."

"No clue, but that was beautiful."

"Latin. But since it's so close to Italian, I added an extra bit."

"What did you add?"

"I will love you forever and always."

She rolled her eyes at me, but she was still smiling.

"Ta gra agam ort," I said.

Wide-eyed, she shook her head.

"Gaelic," I told her.

"Really?"

I confirmed, noticing that we were almost to the turn off. "Yedadeth-eykh."

"...I give up."

"Here's a hint. It's the language I spoke when I lived in Jerusalem."

"Oh!" she cried. "Jewish!"

I gaped at her for a second before returning my attention to the highway. "Ah, you meant Hebrew."

"Oops," she giggled.

"But you're wrong, anyway. That was Aramaic. In Hebrew, it's Ani ohev otech." I paused a moment and then said, "S'agapo," with as much passion as I could.

She thought for a moment. "You changed it again."

I shook my head. "No; that's still 'I love you.' Do you know the language?"

"I do not. No guess."

I shouldn't have felt hurt by that, but I did. "Really? You can't imagine what language s'agapo might be?"

She must have heard my disappointment because she said, "Sorry," apologetically.

I flipped on my turn signal and took my eyes off the road again. "S'agapo," I repeated, holding her gaze. "It's the truest way I, personally, can say it."

Her eyes lit up. "Greek," she breathed.

I nodded, but had to return my attention to the intersection as we had rolled to the end of the exit ramp.

Carly sighed, "You win."

My eyebrows rose, but I couldn't look at her; there was cross traffic. "You *finally* believe that I've been alive for twenty centuries?"

"Nope, but I believe you love me. So the rest doesn't matter anymore."

I glanced at her, but she'd turned her face away, looking out the window. "Where are we?" she asked.

"Nearly there," I replied as I made the turn. I added, "Help me look for the park entrance. It should be about five miles up the road on the left."

A few minutes later, I pointed to a sign and announced, "Just there."

Carly sat up straighter, taking in the ranger's station, a small, red-brown shack with one window, as we pulled up. "Lake Kongagonga," she mispronounced, reading the yellow-lettered sign. "I thought you'd said Devil's Lake."

I flashed her a crooked smile. "Until you reminded me that he might come for me there."

I got directions from the ranger and paid him for the campsite plus three bundles of firewood.

"Let's set up our camp first," I said, sliding back into the car after loading the wood into the trunk, "and then we can go for a hike."

She smiled, nodding enthusiastically in response.

We had to drive a couple of miles away from the main grounds to get to our private site. The paved, one-lane road twisted and rolled through a tunnel of tree branches as we made our way to the far side of the lake. Carly said nothing, just took it all in, her eyes wide, her glossy lips slightly parted.

Ten minutes later, we pulled into our parking space. Carly sat unmoving, staring out the window in awe. The site was lined with trees and came right to the shore of the shimmering lake. The only ugly distraction was a lime-green port-a-john next to the parking pad. Carly didn't seem to see that, though.

"This is like a picture," she breathed in a tone that was not her usual one.

"What, no 'dude' tacked on this time?" I swung open my door. "Come on."

We walked to the edge of the lake where low waves lapped at gemstone-colored pebbles.

"It's so… vast," she said, her voice still awed.

I laughed. "No one's ever described Lake Kongatoga as vast! Lake Michigan is vast."

"But there's nothing else here," she pressed.

"Sure there is. Rocks, trees, grass… rowboat." The brownish-gray boat was parked at the edge of our campsite with the site number stenciled in white on its side. I hadn't expected that. "Hey, that might be fun after we set up the tent."

Her eyes sparkled. "Where do we start?" She clasped her hands in anticipation, like a child.

She helped me unload the car, and together, we chose the spot for our tent on a soft, grassy area under the trees and away from the water. First, we spread out a tarp. Then, I unrolled the blue and gray nylon body of the tent and laid the framing pieces on top of it. I'd owned this tent for nearly two decades. It had held up well, even though I used it nearly every weekend in summer months and had even lived in it full-time in Iran.

"This is called a spider," I began.

Carly stiffened. "I know what a spider is, Jaden; just kill it!"

I looked at her and then at the piece of plastic hanging limply in my hand. "No, Carly. *This*. This is called a spider."

"Ugh. Why?"

I turned it over. "Well, because it… sort of looks like a spider, especially after you attach all the legs."

"Legs?"

I unfolded one of the tent's poles, three hollow, carbon fiber wands held together by a single length of elastic cord. I showed her how, with little effort, they snapped together into one long piece.

"See?" I held it out to her. "This is one 'leg.' It slips into this point on the spider, and then…" I snapped it into place, "there are just five more."

She looked at me skeptically. "Dude, even *I* know spiders have eight legs."

I shrugged. "How 'bout that? Someone must have pulled two off."

She chortled, fixing me with her beautiful eyes. "You're sick."

She was very apologetic the first time the frame collapsed at her touch. But when she was trying to help attach the fabric to the poles and accidentally pulled two legs out of the spider, we both fell into hysterical laughter. I hadn't felt so young since… well, probably not since I actually was this young.

"Take it easy on my tent, missy. I only have one!" I exclaimed, suddenly realizing that two might have been more appropriate. But I was too relaxed and having too much fun now to worry about it. We were out of the city, breathing fresh air, surrounded by nature. All of the nightmares of the past week had evaporated. I realized that this was the first time, since meeting Carly, that I'd been completely free of anxiety. It felt good.

The tent fell, yet again, when I was staking down the storm shield. I stared at it, mallet still raised, unable to believe that we'd have to, pretty much, start over this close to the end.

Carly looked at me, wide-eyed, very innocent. "I… I just…"

"Ye-e-es?" I prompted, letting the mallet fall to the ground.

She giggled and finished, "touched it."

Bellowing in mock-frustration, I charged her. She shrieked when I scooped her up, but giggled again as I swung her around, carrying her to a boulder near the water. "You. Sit. Stay." I ordered, kissing the top of her head before turning my back.

Whoa, Timon.

I wasn't sure if that was His thought or my own. But I did take a moment's pause to think about what I'd just done. It had felt so natural, but that was probably the problem. I promised myself that I would be a little less relaxed from here on out.

Even so, I couldn't stop myself from glancing at Carly from time to time as I worked to get the tent up for good. She didn't rise from the boulder. She watched me. She watched the water. She batted at insects I couldn't see. Her smile never faded.

I transferred the sleeping bags, pillows and both duffle bags into the four-person tent. It was large enough that I could unroll each bag along an outside wall. I put the rest of our things in the middle.

Satisfied that I was sending the right signals with this set up, I returned to Carly by the lake. "So," I began, approaching her perch. "Want to row now? Or hike?"

She jumped up and chose, "Hike!"

I checked my watch. It wasn't quite three o'clock. "There's a really nice trail back by the ranger's station. I'm not sure we could walk the whole nine miles before dark, but we can start and see how far we get."

Her expression changed. "Nine miles!"

"Or however far you're comfortable with," I assured her.

"Well, if I'm going to be comfortable at all, I'd better put on my boots. Give me a minute to change, okay?"

I looked at her thin-soled sneakers. "Yeah. Good idea."

She dove into the tent, not quite ducking low enough. The frame shook, threatening to fall. I ran my fingers through my hair, holding my breath.

My cell phone rang as I drove us to the trailhead.

"Want me to get that for you?" Carly offered.

I slipped the phone out of my pocket. "That's okay. I think I've got it." We were only driving ten miles an hour on an otherwise deserted road, or I wouldn't have answered at all. I flipped it open without looking at the I.D. and said, "Jaden Bethany."

Brittany's voice replied, "It's me with bad news. You need to come in today after all."

I blinked. "I can't."

"Jaden, they're bumping up the Lambert case. To eight-thirty tomorrow morning! You've got to come in."

I glanced at Carly. "That's Jasper's case," I reminded Brittany. "Madison can help him. That is, *if* he needs help, which he won't."

"Madison doesn't know anything about it!" she snapped.

I tried to calm her down. "It really doesn't matter. Jasper's prepared, even if it's been called early."

She wasn't appeased. "Where are you that you can't come in?"

It never occurred to me to try to lie. "Lake Kongatoga, Wisconsin."

"Why?" She seemed astounded.

"I needed to get out of the city for a while."

"Are you… with Carly?" I heard the jealousy in her voice. She didn't even try to hide it.

"Yes," I answered simply. I would forever count Brittany among my good friends, but, despite her feelings for me, I couldn't go further than that. *I shouldn't be going further than that with Carly*, I added to my thought.

Brittany had been quiet for too long. She suddenly blurted out, "Well, *now* you need to get back to the city."

It wasn't like Brittany to challenge me in this way. "You okay, Britt?" I asked.

"Yeah. Just stressed."

"Well, don't be."

She hesitated. "Tell me you're coming in, and I won't have to be."

I exhaled. "I'm not coming in today. I'll keep my phone on, in case Jasper needs me for anything, but he won't," I repeated, "because he's prepared. Honestly, Brittany, there's nothing to get worked up about."

"Isn't there?" she snapped, and then she hung up on me.

I sighed at my phone and put it away.

"What's up?" Carly asked.

"A change in a court date," I replied. "It happens more often than you'd think."

"So… we need to go?"

I shook my head. "It's not my case. It's a big, bad, ugly case, but Jasper can handle it."

"Are you *sure*? Because I don't want you to get in trouble at work on my account."

I smiled at her. "It's *my* firm," I said as I pulled the car into the parking lot at the trailhead. "I can't get in trouble."

Chapter Twenty

The trail was busy. With warm weather and fall colors to draw them, carloads of outdoorsy types had gotten a head start to the weekend. We waited for another couple to go ahead of us while we studied the oversized map posted, billboard-style, at the trailhead.

"See?" I said, tracing a looping dashed line under the Plexiglas with my finger. "It's nine miles around, or seventeen, if you add this extra section up here.... But the best thing on this trail is the waterfall. Here." I tapped at a set of hash marks on the map. "That's less than two miles in, and we can turn around there if you want to."

She shrugged. "Let's just see how far we get." She reached for my hand, and we followed the well-used path, curving away from the parking lot. Carly walked slowly, swinging our hands and weaving around on the path. The voices of the hikers ahead of us drifted away, and we felt alone once more.

The cars, outhouse buildings, and all other evidence of mankind disappeared from view as the forest enveloped us. The terrain here was very different from my homeland, but being isolated in nature has always brought me a sense of homecoming. I felt at peace.

Even though many of the trees still wore their fall colors, a thick coating of yellow and brown leaves obscured the trail. Carly, in hiking boots that looked like they'd never been worn before, kicked the leaves ahead of her as she walked.

About half a mile in, the trail started to climb. We used tree roots as stair steps to gain elevation. Carly gripped my hand tightly.

I looked down at her, smiling, but she was watching her feet, and I thought perhaps she was only using me to keep her balance.

"What do you think about when you're in the woods?" I asked.

After another silent moment, she said quietly, "I've never been in the woods before."

I motioned, generally, to the space around us. "Well then…. What do you think?"

She looked around and then back at me. "I'm glad you're here," she said, squeezing my hand again, "because I'd be pretty scared otherwise."

I felt my eyebrows rise. "Really? I never feel scared in the woods."

"Not even when you're alone? Because it's like, anything could be hiding in these trees…. Or the rest of the world could have just blown up, and we wouldn't know it."

I couldn't suppress a chuckle at that. "Trust me, Carly, if it were Armageddon, I'd know."

She flashed a conciliatory smile and asked, "So, you've been here before?"

"Often," I replied. "I'm really not much of a city dweller. All of that noise… it really gets to me after awhile. I have to get away."

She hummed. "And what do *you* think about while you're wandering around in the woods?"

I lifted my eyes and looked around. "How amazing it all is. I mean, look at this!" Excited, I stepped off the trail and pulled her over to a large oak tree. I showed her five ants, an aphid and two different types of moss, all climbing over one mere square inch of bark.

"I just get overwhelmed," I told her as my eyes searched higher on the tree trunk, "by the details of creation."

She didn't reply.

"Here's an example." I pointed to a yellowish-green beetle, wedged into the bark. "What do you think of this guy?"

She shrugged. "Just a bug."

"Do you know that, to God, it's not 'just a bug?'" I could hear the excitement in my own voice as I continued, "God knows this beetle personally. He calls it by a name He alone knows. He fed it today, and He's hiding it now, to keep it safe in the sunlight because He knows that, while its colors are very beautiful, they are also eye-catching to its predators. Even though He did that on purpose, because everyone's got to eat, God doesn't want this particular beetle to get eaten today. His plan for life on Earth is detailed, down to the very last creature."

"What if we squished it?" Carly posed. "Would bolts of lightening strike from above?"

I couldn't tell, but I thought she was joking. I answered the question seriously anyway. "Probably not. But God would know He had one less Bark Gnawing Beetle in Wisconsin."

Carly frowned. "Doesn't God have anything better to do than count beetles in Wisconsin? Or, maybe that's the reason everything's going to hell. Because God's too busy counting beetles to bother with people."

Her comment was so absurd that I snorted. "Are you really so blind? God is everywhere all the time! He can care for His beetles and still have as much time for heads-of-state as they are willing to give Him.

"You, personally, have God's attention, Carly, every minute of every day. He watches you, rapt by your beauty, inside and out. He knows you perfectly, and He's waiting for you to notice Him."

She rolled her eyes at me.

"What?" I asked.

"'Rapt' by my beauty?"

"Why not? I know how beautiful you are to me. How much more beautiful you must be to the One who created you!"

She looked away.

"I've heard Him say your name, Carly. I know it's true."

When several more seconds passed without her replying, I prompted, "Is it so hard to believe?"

"Well, yeah." She picked at the tree bark. "If God is right here waiting for me to notice him, then point him out."

"Okay…. If you don't see Him here," I briefly touched the tree with my free hand, "then try looking here." With a finger under her chin, I gently turned her head until our eyes met.

For a good, long moment, I was swimming in the sea of her eyes. Then she cleared her throat and looked away again. Scanning the woods, she said, "We'd better move on, if we're going to see that waterfall."

I silently agreed and led the way back onto the trail.

The sound of water crashing over stones was audible from a good quarter of a mile away. "Hear that?" I asked.

"Sounds like the 'L,'" she replied.

"Nope. That's the waterfall."

A little later, we rounded a corner, approaching the waterfall from the side. The instant Carly spotted its white cascade, her breath caught. She stopped walking, feet planted firmly on the leaf-littered trail. I had to stop as well; I didn't want to let go of her hand.

"You okay?" I asked.

"It's terrifying!" she cried.

That's not at all the word I would have chosen to describe the ribbon of pearly, foaming water as it dropped from a height of a hundred feet through deep green, vibrant orange and fiery red vegetation. But looking at the steep, rocky cliff it fell over and the slick, moss-covered rocks along the creek's banks, I could see her point.

Will she be all right here? I prayed.

That depends on her choices, He answered, *but she seems frightened enough to remain cautious.*

I found myself suddenly desperate to know when He would call her again, how much time we had left. But I didn't ask.

"You're safe on the trail," I promised Carly, squeezing her hand. "Come and look."

There were so many people crowding the steep, narrow trail as it passed near the fall that we couldn't enjoy an unobstructed view. Carly didn't seem too keen on stopping anyway. She looked more often at her boots than she did at the water as we crossed a wet, concrete bridge spanning the stream. The trail continued climbing on the other side. We wove through the polite grouping of gawkers and continued up the trail.

It was much quieter after we'd left the waterfall behind us. There were fewer people, too. Noticing a fallen tree a few yards off the trail and certain that Carly needed a break after such a steep climb in new boots, I led her over to it.

"How are your feet?" I asked, sitting down.

She shrugged, joining me. "Okay…. But if you're offering a foot massage when we get back to camp, I won't turn you down."

I grinned. "Then I'm offering."

"And I'm accepting."

We sat in silence for a few minutes, looking at each other, looking at the forest around us.

"I think I'm also starting to accept some of the stuff you've been saying, last night and today... about yourself and about God," she said.

The statement surprised me, coming out of the blue like that. "Will you share your thoughts?" I asked.

She pouted. "What do you want to know?"

I spread my hands. "Anything.... Everything."

After considering that for a moment, she chose her reply. "Honestly, I've never experienced God the way you have. It's like I'm hearing about him for the first time."

I nodded.

She continued, "I really... *like* God through your eyes, Jaden. But I feel.... You know...."

No, I didn't know. I had no idea what she was trying to say, but I chose to just listen until she'd managed to say it.

"I mean, it's great that God doesn't hate me. Your explanation of all of that made sense. Surprisingly.... But the intensity of his love.... Geez, the intensity of *you*, Jaden! I mean, look at your life! How can anybody live up to that?" She raised her shoulders at me and then looked away, searching the distant trees. "How can I possibly deserve any of this?"

I didn't like making her uncomfortable. I took her hand again. "That's just it, Carly. None of us deserves God's love, me least of all."

She turned back to me. "I thought you were J.C.'s best bud."

"We are close, but I fail Him every day. Take that times three hundred and sixty-five days per year for two thousand and five years, and that makes me the worst offender ever born!"

She raised an eyebrow. "Two thousand and five? Do you know what year it is now, Jaden?"

I sighed heavily. "Yes, but we mark Anno Domini from the time of Jesus' birth, not mine. I am only two thousand and five."

"You're *only* two thousand and five," she repeated.

Had I lost her over that? We were finally getting somewhere! "Just forget I said that, and listen. Love in abundance is God's gift, Carly. Whether or not you think you're worthy of it is irrelevant. He loves you so much that He *died* for you. And all He asks is that you believe it."

I heard nothing but the wind in the trees for several long minutes.

She finally answered, "Suppose I want to believe it... But then I'd be expected to change my life, right? Go through some ritual? Join a church? ...I'm not sure I'm ready for all that."

"You may want to do those things," I explained, "but God doesn't require them. Belief changes your relationship with God. God joins His life with yours. You still make your own choices, but He is there to guide you and to help you manage the difficult and inexplicable times that come along."

I continued, "My experience, personally in my life as well as my observations of other people, is that when you truly believe in God's love and Christ's sacrifice, then you want to tell other people, and you want to be in a community of others who share your faith. You want the rituals, and you want to be more like Jesus. But none of that is required. All you have to do is pray and tell God that you accept His gift."

She frowned again. "If I do that, will Perry... stop?" She didn't have to say what.

I wished I could answer differently, but I told her the truth. "Perry is making his choices, and that won't change until he decides to change. But you can make different choices. For example, you can choose to let me help you move out, which I'm prepared to do, as soon as tomorrow, if you want."

She smiled gratefully but didn't accept my offer. Instead, she tilted her face into the breeze and asked, "Will you teach me how to row, now?

Chapter Twenty-One

It was well past five o'clock by the time we'd returned to our campsite. The hike back down the trail had been more contemplative than conversational for both of us. Carly had held my hand the whole time, though, so I was pretty sure that she was not unhappy about anything I had said.

In the car, she couldn't get a signal with her new phone, so she had borrowed mine to call Jen. I felt guilty, eavesdropping, but it couldn't be helped. From their conversation, I guessed that Jen was pleased that we had gotten away together. Carly also told her friend about the arrest in the arson case, which I could only imagine was a big relief to Jen. They talked until we pulled into our parking space. Carly hung up, tossed the phone to me, and headed straight for the rowboat.

I glanced at the sun's position in the sky and then at the water. I had to make a choice. Either make it a very short trip or light the fire before we rowed out.

Your kingdom come, Lord, I prayed. *What should I do?*

I know you want a definitive answer, Timon. Tonight I will give you one. Light the fire. I will keep you safe, He promised.

Lighting a fire and leaving it was not something I did easily, but my Lord rarely gave such a concrete answer; I had no fear.

I caught up to Carly quickly. "Um," I began. "It'll be getting dark soon. Let's start the fire before we row out. So we can find our way back to our site."

She grinned. "I've been waiting for the campfire all day!"

I held up a cautionary finger. "Can I trust you with fire? Or did the tent incident foreshadow your aptitude toward all things camp related?"

She smacked my finger down, but she was still smiling. "*Dude...*" she began, but then appeared to change her mind about what to say and conceded, "You've probably got a point, there."

She waited by the stone fire ring while I brought over some wood and a tube of long matches. "If you want to help," I told her, "we need some really dry leaves."

"Okay."

I watched her go off in search of them and then turned my attention to making a teepee-type skeleton out of the cut logs. I was nearly finished when Carly returned with an armload of brown leaves.

"Cool," she pronounced. "I suppose you've built a few fires in your two thousand and five years."

"A few," I agreed, stuffing the leaves under and around the wood. "Want to light it?" I offered when I was done.

She blinked. "Sure!"

As I reached for the matches, she joked, "Funny. I thought you'd be wanting two rocks for this part."

"Ha. Ha." I tried to sound annoyed, but I'm sure she heard the laughter behind my words. "Of course, *I* can start a fire with flint," I informed her, "but since you're a novice...." I pulled a match from the tube and closed the lid. "You strike it on the bottom," I told her, handing both over.

"I know how to light a match, Jaden." Fire blazed from the tip of it to prove her point. She touched the flame to the leaves and held it there until they caught.

"Light it on the other side as well," I told her. "So it will burn more evenly."

Once our fire was burning brightly, I went to inspect the boat. It was old and small, but looked sea-worthy... or lake-worthy. There were two life jackets behind the seat nearest the bow. I gathered up the oars and pushed it toward the shore.

"You coming?" I called to Carly who'd been sitting by the fire, staring intently at the leaping, crackling flames, watching sparks drift high in the updraft of smoke.

She pushed herself up, grinning at me as she approached. "I love everything about this, Jaden. Camping is fun!"

I grinned back. Camping is usually cathartic for me, but not always something that I'd describe as 'fun.' I decided that it depended on who was camping with me.

First, I helped her buckle her life jacket. *No sense in taking chances*. I motioned to the boat and told her, "Go ahead and get settled. Then I'll push you out."

She looked from the boat to the lake. "And you'll get in by… walking on water?"

I chortled. "Never tried that, actually, but I think, this time, I'll jump."

"Ah. That'll be a sight."

I held her hand to help steady her as she stepped in. I also took off my shoes and socks and set them on the seat opposite her. Then, I rolled the legs of my jeans up to my knees.

"Ready?" I asked.

"Oh yeah," she answered.

I got down low behind the stern, probably lower than I needed to, and shoved. There was a loud grating sound as the hull scraped against the gravel shore, rushing into the lake, and then the craft became buoyant. I kept pushing until the freezing cold water reached midway up my calf. I gave a final, hard shove and jumped in, spraying Carly with water.

She squealed.

"Sorry," I said. "I didn't mean for that to happen."

She waved me off.

I fitted the oars into their brackets and turned the boat, rowing us away from the shore. Carly, meanwhile, had been studying my bare feet.

"Your feet are girlie," she pronounced. "You get pedicures, don't you?"

"No…." I felt my face turning red. I explained anyway. "You know how I heal very quickly? Well, I don't get calluses, either. It can literally be a pain sometimes. I don't like shoes, especially not shoes with hard, stiff soles." *Like my wingtips*, I added to myself.

She looked confused. "But then... wouldn't you rather have shoes than not have them? Doesn't walking around on hard ground hurt just as much?"

I nodded. "The land, where I come from, is sandy. I love to walk on sand or sandy soil without shoes. That's when my feet are happy."

"That reminds me," she said. "When's my foot massage?"

I looked around. I'd been rowing hard without really meaning to. We were already a good hundred yards out from shore. "Right now, if you want it," I answered, stowing the oars. "We can drift for a while."

Her eyes widened. "You sure?"

Motioning to the still water, I promised, "We're not going anywhere."

Carly removed her shoes and plopped her right foot on my lap, musing, "What could be better than bobbing around on the water at sunset while a beautiful, foreign man rubs my feet? This is heaven!"

Part of me wanted to refute most of that, but I chose not to. Instead, I said, "Here, give me both your feet before you get cold." As soon as she did, I went to work on her arches. Her feet really were very beautiful. I felt her relax almost immediately.

"So, tell me about this sandy-soiled homeland," she said. "What do you miss most?"

I smiled. That was easy. "The Mediterranean Sea. Did you know, on a sunny day, it's the exact color of your eyes?"

She smiled at that.

I continued, "When we were first spreading the Gospel, I sailed as often as I could. Sailing was a dream I'd had since childhood.... Of course, when I was very young, living with my family, we didn't go to the sea. It wasn't far away, but... we were shepherds, not fishermen."

She urged, "Tell me more."

I hummed, remembering. "Okay.... I'm from what is now known as the West Bank."

"Ooh," she said. "Bad stuff's been happening there."

I nodded. "It was pretty safe back then, protected by the Romans."

"Romans?"

"Two thousand and five years ago," I reminded her, "was the height of the Roman Empire."

"I know. It's just...." She changed her thought again. "You know what? I'll just listen. You talk."

What's the point if you're not going to believe me? I wondered, but I kept that question to myself. "The world, under Roman rule, was a pretty mobile place, like it is today. So, while I grew up in Palestine, I'm not Palestinian. My ancestors were Jews who'd been living in Greece for generations. Under Rome, my grandparents, both sets, moved back to their religious homeland. Bethany isn't my last name so much as it is the town nearest to where I grew up."

She interjected, "I'm picturing a dusty hovel where cows wander loose in the streets."

"You're not far off.... There were hills all around with caves, perfect for hiding in when we played."

"Do you have a lot of brothers and sisters?"

I nodded. "I did. I was the third and youngest son in a family of nine children." I hadn't thought about my family in a long time. I had to work very hard now, just to recall their faces. It made me a little sad to be reminded of how much I missed them, of how much time had passed.

Carly, however, seemed quite excited. "Wow! How did your parents manage that?"

I shrugged. "It was fairly normal back then. We raised sheep and spun the wool for a living. Everyone helped out, even the youngest kids."

"But what about cows? Please tell me your family owned cows!"

"Just one…. Named Merriam."

Her smile grew broader. "You did *not* name your cow Merriam!"

"No. My sister Mary did." Mary, two years younger than I, had also named every sheep and every dog that wandered around the hills near our home. She'd been the most gentle and loving of us all, and she was the one I missed the most.

Carly's voice drew me back to the present. "There sure were a lot of Marys in Bible times."

It was an innocuous comment, a simple observation, but I used it to transition. "I'm glad you know that…. One of those Biblical Marys was my neighbor. She had a sister, Martha, and a brother, Lazarus. Sound familiar?"

She frowned slightly and said, "Nope. But I never went to Religious Ed…. Or Sunday School, either."

"Well, Jesus was a friend of theirs. A very good friend. He preached from their house, often. That's where I met him."

"Were you blown away?"

"To say the least! Meeting him changed my life.... Obviously."

"Keep going," she said, and I didn't know if she meant the foot massage or my story. So, I continued both.

"I was twenty-six when I met Him."

She interjected, "So, two years ago." She read the exasperated expression on my face, and quickly added, "I'm sorry. I couldn't resist.... I am listening, though."

I relaxed into a smile. "There are some things, culturally, that you need to understand if you want to know why Jesus means so much to me."

"Okay."

She seemed seriously interested, so I continued, "I mentioned that I'm the third son, born at a time when the first son got almost the entire inheritance. The second son was there for back-up, but the third was pretty much unnecessary."

"Did you feel unnecessary?" she asked.

Hesitantly, I nodded. I had at the time. "My parents loved me, but they didn't have anything to give me, and they didn't lie about it."

"I bet all your sisters were worse off, though, right? Wasn't that a time of arranged marriages?"

"Well, yeah, but my brothers and I could only choose from the daughters of families who found our family worth marrying into. So, nobody really got a choice. My sisters didn't complain, at least not to me. They were all married off by age seventeen. Being a third son, I was not a desirable match, so, at age twenty-six, I was still waiting."

"Hold up," she said. "Really? The girls were married by seventeen, but boys still weren't at twenty-six?"

"My oldest brother got married at eighteen and was given half of my father's wealth... and his own cow." I added that detail, knowing that it would make her smile, and it did. "The second brother didn't have any real reason to marry, so he kept refusing every girl my parents suggested. They had decided on a girl for me, but she was only thirteen, so we were waiting."

Carly looked disgusted. "You were going to *marry* a thirteen-year-old?"

"Well, not until she was fifteen, but yes. I guess I was."

"Fifteen!"

"That's how things went back then."

"Bizarre.... Did you like her?"

"I never met her."

Carly closed her eyes and shook her head. "So, what happened?"

"Like I said, I met Jesus, and He explained the scriptures in terms I'd never before considered. He talked about the change that was coming: the kingdom of God, freedom from Rome, or so we thought, freedom from religious convention, a personal relationship with God, and for me, personally, a purpose for my life: caring for others. He led by example, loving and tolerant, *always* forgiving. I couldn't get enough of His preaching or His miracles. I wanted to be like Him. I pledged myself to following Him and to supporting His cause.

"I was among the seventy-two people whom He chose to go ahead of Him on his mission. You would not believe the things we could do in His name. Healing sick people, restoring hope, driving off demons, it was phenomenal! Here I am, nineteen hundred and seventy-nine years after meeting Him, and I'm still in awe of all He allows me to do in His name."

"Like saving Lucy's life?" she guessed.

I nodded.

"And... mine?"

I nodded again.

"Wow," she said softly. "Did you heal Jen?"

"Yes." *In more ways than you know*, I thought, but didn't say it.

She seemed contemplative after that, gazing out over the open water. So, I let us drift in silence. I tried to concentrate on her feet, but once in a while, she whispered something inaudible. I looked at her then, but her focus was elsewhere. I had to wonder if she finally, truly, believed me.

When the sky had turned purple, and the sun had dropped below the horizon, I interrupted her thoughts. "We should head in, Carly, before it gets any darker."

She looked at me, almost as if she was seeing me for the first time. Then she smiled and agreed, pulling her feet away from me and reaching for her boots in the same motion.

"Want to row us back?" I asked as she finished lacing them up.

She glanced up in surprise. "Really?"

I pressed down on the oars to lift the paddles out of the water and offered them to her.

She took them with a look of trepidation spreading across her beautiful face. "I'm not gonna drown us, am I?" she asked even as the left oar slipped out of her hand and smacked the surface of the water.

I chuckled. "I was about to say no, but... I guess the answer's, 'perhaps.'"

She looked like she wanted to punch me, but both of her hands were gripping the oars now, and I knew she wouldn't let go of them for anything, not even to abuse me, regardless of how much I deserved it.

It took a few tries, but she did eventually get the hang of rowing and moved us in the right direction. I told her to aim for our campfire, burning ever more brightly as the sky darkened. She seemed both proud and relieved when the bottom of the boat scraped the shore pebbles once more.

Carrying my shoes again in preparation for landing, I hopped out of the boat and hauled it onto the shore.

"Great job!" I said as I helped her out. "I mean it. You'll be racing next."

"I wanted to join the crew team in high school," she admitted, "but Mom wouldn't let me try out. She said we didn't have the money, but my guess is she just didn't want to have to drive me to practices."

"You would have been great," I assured her as we walked over to the fire.

The temperature was indeed dropping as night came on. I added more wood to the fire.

"I'm gonna duck into the tent for a flashlight before it gets any darker," I told Carly. "Want your coat?"

She nodded, rubbing her hands near the flames.

I brought back both of our jackets, my camp-pack full of tools and utensils, and two flashlights. Then I made a trip to the car to get our food.

"The turkey dogs should be thawed out by now," I told her as I set the cooler on the ground beside her. I kept them in my freezer at home just so that I'd have them for camping trips. I never ate them otherwise. "Or we could heat up a can of soup." I'd brought a few of those along as well.

She grinned. "If I pick turkey dogs, does that mean we get to roast them on sharpened sticks? Because I've always, sort of, wanted to do that."

"As you wish," I replied, digging out my Swiss Army knife. Finding long sticks was easy in the tree line near our tent, and it only took a few minutes to whittle the ends into points.

By the orange glow of firelight, I showed her how to skewer her hotdog for optimum heating and how to hold it over the flames so that it wouldn't burn. We sat on a dried-out driftwood log with our thighs touching and watched the flames dance and leap, crackle and hiss as we cooked our dinner.

I didn't keep hotdog buns around. I had brought pita bread instead and salsa in place of ketchup. We also ate pears and bananas. I'd brought olives, of course, but Carly politely declined those.

We decided to skip roasting marshmallows for the time being, and snuggled up together by the fire, sipping orange soda. For a long time, we silently watched the waves of flame dancing along the tops of the ashen logs.

Carly broke the trance. "So, I've been thinking.... I'm sort of awe-struck by you, the same way you were by Jesus. I mean, your ability to see things from a different perspective than everyone else, and your conviction in things that, on the surface, don't seem possible, yet, for you, they are very real. Your belief that God protects, loves and fights for you, and the fact that you help people so freely.... I'm sort of jealous of all that. I want what you have."

"All you have to do is ask for it," I told her.

"I think I already have," she answered.

At that, I turned toward her and gazed again into the sea of her eyes. There, I saw His Spirit looking back.

I wanted to jump for joy, to sing my happiness to the heavens. I didn't, though. My hands went to Carly's face and then tangled into her hair. I pressed my forehead against hers. I couldn't believe it. We would have a future together, maybe not in this life, but for all eternity after. I couldn't wait, but I would wait, for as long as I had to. "I love you right now, more than ever," I whispered.

Chapter Twenty-Two

W e stayed by the fire for a few more hours. I added wood when it burned low. Carly occasionally asked a question about her new faith, but mostly, we just sat and watched the stars come out.

I couldn't remember ever being happier. I'd succeeded in what was, to me, the most important challenge I'd ever faced. I had no fear of Raiser or Trinity or others of their kind, now. Nothing about the future worried me. Christ could return in this hour or in another thousand years, and I would be content either way. I spent most of the silent evening offering prayers of thanksgiving to God, who has blessed me beyond measure in this life.

I noticed that Carly was dozing at my side. "Bedtime?" I asked.

She mumbled something that sounded like agreement.

I pressed my lips into her hair and asked, "Want me to carry you?"

At that, she sat up. "No, I'm awake."

"You go ahead," I nodded toward the tent. "I'll put the fire out and be there in a few minutes."

She looked around. "Where do I... brush my teeth?"

"Oh." I dug into my pack for a water bottle and a roll of toilet paper. "You can brush anywhere, just don't spit near the tent," I said, offering her the water first. "And this is in case the port-a-john isn't stocked. It's over there by the car."

She thanked me and started to walk away.

"Hey?" I called, and she turned back. "Take a flashlight, okay? It's dark over there."

I waited by the fire while she finished up outside and made her way into the tent. With the flashlight on inside of it, I could see her silhouette against the fabric. I watched her for a moment, until I realized that she was undressing, and then I turned my back quickly.

Please don't ruin this, I begged myself as I started separating the logs and spreading out the glowing ashes of our spent fire.

I took my time, making sure that the fire had gone out completely. I took care of my own hygiene needs and turned off my flashlight before crawling into the tent so that I wouldn't disturb Carly.

Inside, it was pitch black. As quietly as I could, I made my way to my sleeping bag and slid my legs inside of it. I knew how easily I overheated in this particular bag, so I removed my shirt before lying down, and then I pulled the bag up to my chin, zipping myself in as quietly as I could.

The nylon felt cool against my skin. I shivered, wondering if I should put the shirt back on, wondering if I'd be able to sleep at all.

I heard Carly moving in the darkness and wondered if she was having trouble finding a comfortable position. Before I could ask, I felt a tug on my sleeping bag.

"Do you need something?" I asked.

She didn't answer. I heard my zipper unzip again and felt a draft of cold air. And then, she slid into my sleeping bag on top of me. My hands, involuntarily, went to hold her. All she had on were her socks.

"Carly, what are you doing?" I whispered in alarm.

"Well," she answered, "I know that you love me, and that I love you. And I love me when I'm with you. I even love God when I'm with you.... So, I figure, this is okay now."

She kissed me then, before I could refute. I kept my head this time, realizing that there was something missing here. A promise. I wasn't sure what it would mean tomorrow, but tomorrow was in the far distant future. I could make this right, tonight.

I moved my lips to her ear and whispered, "Carly, I vow to love you forever, to be one with you in body and spirit for all of my life. I promise to be faithful to you and to care for you for as long as we live."

She reared back. "What are you saying? I don't..."

"I'm marrying you," I explained. "I know it's not orthodox, but I am ordained, so I think it counts. Just make your vow to me, and it's done."

She rolled off of me. "We can't get married, Jaden; I've only known you a week!"

"So? I've been waiting for you for two thousand years, and I don't want to wait another second to be with you…. But I can't be, at least not like this, unless we're married."

"Jesus Christ," she muttered, pushing away from me. I cried out in pain, from her words and also from the loss of the moment. Either she didn't notice or she didn't care.

"Are you telling me, now, that you're a two thousand year old virgin?"

"By choice," I whispered, unable get any volume from my voice.

She didn't have that problem. "Nobody makes that choice!" she shouted. "Why do you have to go insane *right now*?"

I didn't know how to answer. I felt so confused. I needed air. I needed my Lord. I crawled away.

"Jaden!" she cried, pleading.

But I'd found the tent's exit, and I wasn't turning back.

I raced for the lake and didn't stop until I collapsed into the frigid water. I knelt there, in water up to my waist with my hands clasped on top of my head, trembling, not only from cold, unable to catch my breath.

I know that you're hurt and confused, Timon, my Lord said before I'd even called on Him. Sympathy flowed from Him. *I am here with you.*

Hoarsely, I replied, "Tell me that I've made the right choice, my Lord."

Few can understand such a choice, He replied compassionately.

"Everything felt so right," I babbled, "and now it's all wrong. Horribly wrong! All Carly needed was someone to show her Your love. Why couldn't I do that? Just that? Why did I let myself believe that I couldn't live without her? Why did I let things get physical? Why did I even bring her out here?"

Timon, do you believe that all things work together for good, for those who love me?

"I do, Lord."

Then this, too, I shall work for good. There is a time now of pain, for you and Carly, both, and I truly wish that it were not so. However, you will also both be there on the day I take all pain away. Then we will rejoice together.

He made it sound so easy, just a simple matter of time. But how long would I have to wait? "When will you come, Lord?"

He didn't answer that question. *Draw strength from me, Timon. If certain choices are made, I will need you soon.*

A few minutes later, I made my way out of the water and over to the fire ring. I didn't think I could enter the tent for a change of clothes; I couldn't face Carly. So, instead, I placed a couple of new logs over the old ashes and relit the fire.

My jeans dried out faster than ordinary physics would have predicted. For that, I said a grateful prayer. Overhead, the stars turned slowly. I figured I'd been out there for a couple of hours when I heard a rustling sound. I looked over at the tent. Carly was coming out, fully dressed, carrying my jacket slung over her arm. She offered it to me without speaking.

I took it with one softly spoken word, "Thanks."

She sat down on the log a few feet away from me, resting her elbows on her bent knees, her hands clasped together, her head bowed.

I pulled my coat on, not sure if she wanted me to apologize or if she wanted me to keep quiet. She broke the silence before I could decide. "I guess I just don't know how to do the right thing," she said into the ground.

"Me neither."

She looked up. "I thought you had all the answers, dude."

I smiled in relief; my nickname was back. "Well, I have one: I wouldn't still be here if I didn't still have a lot to learn."

She smiled weakly.

"Will you come closer?" I asked.

"Do you trust me?"

I held out my arms. She scooted into them and asked, "Is this the line?"

I nodded. "I think it has to be."

"Okay," she agreed. "But can I ask you a really personal question?"

"You can ask me anything," I answered truthfully.

Still, she paused before asking, "If you've really been twenty-eight for two-thousand years, how can you *possibly* still be a virgin?"

The entire truth was that no one had ever offered herself to me the way Carly had, and considering how my body reacted to her, it didn't seem likely that I would have been able to maintain my chastity if they had. But I thought she might feel guilty if I was that honest. "Well, the sexual revolution is, actually, a very recent event. I grew up in a time and place where no 'good' person even considered it before marriage. Jesus reiterated the importance of keeping the sexual relationship sacred for marriage, which is why I made that lame attempt to...." I let my sentence die.

Carly frowned. "Well, why haven't you gotten married then? And why would you even consider it now?"

"I've, uh, never considered it in the past because I worried about how my... halted status would affect the relationship. Can you imagine growing old while I don't? I mean, it might not matter for twenty or thirty years, but eventually, I'd appear to be a twenty-eight-year-old man married to a seventy- or eighty-year-old woman. Even if you could ignore the gossip or find a way to lie, it would be awkward at best."

"You could dye your hair gray," she suggested. "Or take up smoking. That would age you."

"It wouldn't age me," I assured her.

"So what's different about me? Did you think I'd get off on being a cougar?"

I couldn't help but chuckle at that, even though I chose not to comment on it. I did answer her first question. "There are two things: I love you like I've never loved anyone." She snuggled happily against my side at those words. But I had to continue, dropping my voice to just above a whisper, "And... you don't have even twenty years to be with me."

She swore, softly, so it didn't hurt too much. Her physically pushing me away hurt worse. "You just have to keep on ruining everything, don't you?" she asked. "Every time I think I can move on, you *say* or *do* something so enormously…." Her sentence died out.

"Stupid?" I finished for her.

"Insane," she corrected and looked at me, sadly. "I'm gonna try to get some sleep. I want you to take me home tomorrow."

I let her get halfway to the tent before I called, "Wait!" but she didn't stop, and she didn't answer. I didn't have time to even think about following her before my Lord spoke to me.

Timon, Raiser comes!

It took a moment for his words to sink in. "What?" I whispered, "Here?"

Yes. It will arrive in thirty-three minutes. There is time to flee, if you choose not to face it, but if you choose to fight, you may use the power of my Spirit, as I've promised.

Clearing my head to consider my options was not easy, but I made myself focus. Allowing Raiser access to Carly, here, felt like I was personally signing her death warrant. But I couldn't easily pass up the chance to send Raiser, right now, to judgment.

"How did it find us?" I asked to stall the decision.

He sent me a vision: Trinity, in possession of a court official, had turned up at my office with a change of date notice on the Lambert case. Trinity couldn't possess Brittany, but the demon had preyed on her innate need for things at the office to run smoothly and also on her jealousy of Carly. It had influenced her to call me, but I was the one who'd freely told her where I'd gone. I couldn't fault her for passing that information on; Brittany wouldn't have recognized the danger.

The vision changed.

Raiser, having been in possession of a dog ever since I drove it out of Jen, had introduced himself as a stray to a man packing for a weekend trip to Lake Kongatoga. The man, himself, didn't understand why he'd gotten up in the middle of night to make the three hour drive, but he would be here, with his new dog, very soon.

The vision faded.

I gave that man several opportunities to make a different choice, my Lord told me, *but the demon's influence is too strong.* There was no sense of surprise in His statement.

"How is Carly?" I asked.

Sad. Angry. Confused. But she is talking to me. We'll work through this.

I hung my head in shame.

He continued, *Yet again, Timon, you have no time for self-pity. Have you made your choice?*

"Yes," I answered. "I will fight Raiser, here."

Chapter Twenty-Three

I took a few minutes to build up the fire and to plan my strategy. If Carly was sleeping, there was a chance that I could dispatch the demon without it ever seeing her, without it even knowing that she was here, and without her sensing it, either. Of course, there were risks in that approach. The demon might attack the tent, or Carly might hear me fighting and come out. There was no chance of Raiser possessing her now, but that wouldn't keep her out of physical danger. If she had to go before Christ's throne, I didn't want it to be at the hand of such an ungodly creature as Raiser.

Fifteen minutes, my Lord warned me.

"Carly?" I called urgently at the tent's entrance. "Wake up, Carly!"

She replied sleepily, "I am awake."

"Can you come out?" I asked.

There was a pause. "Why? I'm all tucked in."

Why indeed. How can I explain this? I decided that the whole and complete truth was really my only option at this point. I squatted down, nearer to eye level with her, even knowing she couldn't see me. "Do you remember me telling you that... that there are things hunting me?"

"Yes," she said slowly, as if fearing where this conversation might lead.

I had to convince her that this was real and that I was going to protect her. "You have to believe me; one of them has found us."

After a brief pause, she asked, "How do you know?"

"Our Lord told me."

"Jesus?"

"Yes.... Carly, I want you to hide... just in case."

A rustling sound came from the tent again, and then Carly's head poked out. She looked around. "Where is it?"

My head jerked, involuntarily, toward the sound of a baying dog, suddenly echoing through the cold night. "That," I replied, "was it."

She stepped out of the tent, still dressed, wrapped in her coat. "But that was... It was just a... a dog," she stuttered.

"A dog possessed by a demon," I explained.

"A demon?" she repeated. "Wait a minute; are you telling me that a *demon* attacked us at the Art Institute?"

"Yes," I said, "but not this one."

"How many demons are there?" She sounded alarmed.

"More than you want to know about. This one is called Raiser. It's not quite as nasty as the one that attacked us before, but I don't want it to get near you all the same."

She shook her head. "No... That's just... You're a lunatic, Jaden. You've got to be."

I wished that were true. She'd be a whole lot safer if it was. "Listen to me," I pleaded. "We don't have much time. It's very important that this demon doesn't see you. I think you should row out onto the lake."

She looked at me. I could smell her fear. That meant the dog certainly would. I wished I could say something to assure her, but time was not on my side. I dug into my pocket for my car remote.

"Here," I handed it to Carly. "If anything happens to me...." I decided not to finish that sentence.

"Why don't we just get in the car and go now? Together," she offered.

The dog howled again. *Ten minutes*, my Lord informed me.

"There's no way to get past Raiser now," I answered, "and I have a better chance of destroying it if I let it come to me."

She continued to stare at me like I was crazy.

"You'll see me for who I am soon enough," I promised her, reaching for her hand.

She allowed me to lead her to the rowboat. We quickly buckled her back into the life jacket.

"Row out at least as far as we went today," I told her as I pushed her and the boat into the water. "Don't let Raiser see you," I repeated.

"When can I come back?" she asked.

"When it's gone," I answered. "You'll know."

She headed out, not in a straight line, but moving in the right direction. I couldn't be certain that she'd ever stop. I could imagine her rowing across the lake and seeking a ride back to the city with a stranger rather than taking her chances with me.

I couldn't dwell on that. Her choices would be what they would be. What mattered was that God was with her, and she was as safe…. So long as I did not fail.

I watched until I couldn't see her anymore, praying that she would stay out of sight. Then, I turned my attention to our campsite, kicking the dirt around, hoping to dispel not just her footprints, but also her scent. I zipped the tent closed to hold it inside, and then I added more wood to the fire. Before long, it lit up the entire site from my car to the shoreline.

Danger heightened my senses, so I heard Raiser coming: an erratic clicking of toenails, sniffling, snuffling, more baying. I prayed. And I waited.

The dog came alongside my car, nose down, ears up, white-tipped tail wagging happily in the air. Raiser had taken a beagle-mix, a young dog, larger than a purebred, but with the same coloration. It smelled me, but hadn't seen me, yet.

As it sniffed its way down the length of the tent, I held up my hands. Filled with the Spirit's power, I spoke, "In the name of Christ Jesus, I command you; come out of the dog, Raiser!"

The puppy yelped, shying away. Then, against its will, it stumbled forward again into firelight.

"Come out!" I repeated, using the Spirit's power to try to pull the demon away from its host.

The demon, not the dog, barred its teeth, growling. I actually preferred this possession to that of a person. *At least the dog can't talk to me.* But in that one thought, I completely underestimated the strength of Raiser. It didn't need words to communicate. Again, it sent images at me, straight into my brain. I saw a series of terrible crimes it had influenced: murders, suicides. It wasn't going to Christ's throne for judgment willingly.

I tried to force the Spirit's power into a shield against Raiser's images, but one more got through. The demon may have created this vision from my own worst fears, or it was possible that it had actually been party to the crime. It didn't really matter. However it had created the image, the effect on me was total. My control of the Holy Spirit became unstable as I was forced to watch Carly being raped by a much older, drunken man.

She was thrashing beneath him on a ripped, plaid sofa. He was bellowing profanity, calling her disgusting names. I heard her cries for help, her shrieks as he struck her, her voice pleading with him to stop.

The pain I felt from helplessly watching this vision was nothing like I'd experienced from mere cursing. Not even memories of the fiery furnace compared. This felt as though my soul was being ripped from every cell of my body. For a moment, I even thought I'd gladly die here, if it meant an end to the violence I was being forced to watch, perpetrated against a person I deeply loved.

But then, God's voice broke though, reminding me that He was with me and that right now, Carly was sitting out on open water, vulnerable to this monster demon if I let it destroy me. With His help, I found the will to wield His power once more.

I gave the ugly vision to God, wrapping the Spirit's power around it until it disappeared into Him. I'd never done anything like this with His power before, but it worked. My vision cleared.

Filled with wrath, Raiser made the dog attack. It charged me, snarling, and clamped onto my ankle. I felt searing-hot pain as its sharp teeth sank into my lower leg. I fell to the ground and kicked it hard with my other foot.

It let go with a yelp and scooted away, taking refuge behind the fire. I struggled to my feet, ready to defend myself as Raiser tried to force the dog to attack again.

Somehow, it, too, found the will to reject Raiser. It braced itself, barking, bleeding from its nose, but it refused to approach me.

I wanted to help this dog that was obviously fighting with me. I tried wrapping it in the Spirit's power, wondering if I could separate its body from the demon that way.

Nothing I did seemed to be enough; Raiser held firm, working the dog's mouth, making it snap and snarl rapidly and ferociously. In the process, the animal's jaw broke. My compassion for the dog weakened my concentration and, thus, my hold on the Spirit's power. Simultaneously, it fueled Raiser's anger.

As my attention turned to the puppy's bleeding mouth, wondering if the little dog could be saved, once again, Raiser slipped from my grasp. Violently, it exploded from the animal, tearing the poor thing in half.

Raiser rose into the clear night like a thick, black fog. Wafting and churning upward, the demon expanded to the size of my tent, fixing its dozens of flaming eyes on me. But in its fury, it had destroyed its only available host. Its only possibly defense now was to distract me, but there was no longer anything to distract me with.

Shrieking in victory, I wrapped Raiser in a shimmering ball of the Holy Spirit's power, sealing the demon inside. The ball rose into the air like an iridescent soap bubble, high enough that I was sure Carly could see it from the lake.

Raiser thrashed, pushing against the sides, but this was no bubble of soap. The sides deformed, but held tight. I could hear its shrieks and see its glowing eyes, but the demon could not escape.

"Glory to God in the highest!" I cried "Thank you, Lord, for the use of your Spirit's power, which I now return to you!" I let the power go, sending it back to the Lord, complete with its captive. Instead of popping, the bubble brightened as it collapsed in on itself, like a dying star. There was a final, bright white flash that split the night sky. Then, there was nothing but blackness, a hole in the heavens, which the stars slowly filled in.

Exhausted, I knelt on the ground near the fire and continued to pray. *Thank you for helping me, my Lord.* I knew it wasn't over, though. *How long until Trinity gets here?* I asked.

Trinity has been sufficiently delayed, He answered. *Rest, Timon. Your work is done for now.* I felt Him repairing the gash in my ankle.

I took a few deep breaths, but I couldn't relax. *Was it real, Lord? The vision Raiser showed me?*

It was history, my Lord replied, *history that you already knew about, history that you cannot change.*

Yes, but it nearly killed me to see it! And I don't know if I'll ever get past this anger I feel.

It is not for you to be angry over, Timon. You must continue to love.

I do love her! I love her more than ever.

Which is exactly what she needs. Now. She comes.

I heard the boat pull up to the shore. I heard Carly splash out of it and into the shallow water. Relief flooded over me. She was alive, and she hadn't left me.

I whispered an end to my prayer and then stood, watching Carly approach. Her face was white. She was quaking, but whether from cold or fear, I could only guess.

"Geez-O-Petes," she said softly.

Ordinarily, I would have laughed at that, but I was so drained, I couldn't even smile. I lifted my hand toward her, and, to my relief, she rushed into my arms.

"Jaden, are you okay?" she asked my breastbone.

I rested my head on hers. "Now, I am."

"You were glowing," she said.

"His spirit," I told her.

"You were amazing!"

"His spirit," I repeated.

"You're really…!" Her exclamation died out. "Who are you really?"

I didn't answer.

"I'm never camping again." She pushed back slightly, to flash me a relieved smile.

I kissed her forehead and pulled her back to my chest.

She didn't seem able to keep silent. "So… is it gone for good?"

"That one is."

"Where'd it go?"

"To kneel before the throne of Christ and receive its punishment."

She shivered.

"You need dry clothes," I told her.

"I need a smoke!"

"Carly?"

"Yeah?"

"My knees are about to buckle."

She laughed. It sounded like heaven. "Does that mean I can drive us home now?" she asked.

"Not on your life," I answered, intending to make a light comment, but instead, it crushed my soul. "Carly," I whispered.

"You need to lie down," she replied.

Holding my hand, she led me to the tent. I crawled inside first and fumbled for my flashlight. I switched it on. "Are you coming?" I called.

"Damn bet'cha," she answered, quickly amending, "I mean, *yeah*."

I moved away from the entrance. She looked sheepish as she crawled through. "Sorry. Old habits."

"It's okay." I curled into a ball on my sleeping bag, facing away from her. "Change into something dry," I told her. "I won't look."

A split-second later, she said, "You can look."

I smiled at the fabric wall. "Better not."

"Your loss."

I know.

I lay still, listening to the zipper of her duffle, the softer zipper of her jeans, clothes coming off. I couldn't suppress my memories of our earlier time together or how my body reacted to those memories.

I tried to think of something else, and my brain picked the image Raiser had shown me of what Perry had done to her.

Every muscle of my body tightened. I exhaled and tried to remember the sea on a bright, summer morning.

Dressed in my sweats, which I hadn't realized that she'd kept, Carly curled up beside me. She slipped her arm around my waist. Here, at last, was the experience I'd been waiting for my whole life, a woman I loved fitted against my body, not sexually, but supportively.

"You're sad," she said, resting her chin on my shoulder.

"How do you know?"

"I heard you sigh."

I considered my reply carefully. Real or simply imagined, Carly wouldn't want to know that I'd seen a vision of her nightmare. "That demon... it was able to show me things, pictures in my head. Disturbing stuff."

"Anything you want to talk about?"

I shook my head. "I'm too exhausted."

Taking the hint, she switched off the flashlight. "Can I tell you one thing before you fall asleep?"

"Yes, but you'll have to hurry," I muttered.

"I've decided to take you up on your offer."

"You want to marry me?" I asked hopefully.

"No! …Sorry. I mean… I meant your offer to let you get me out of my mother's house. Tomorrow."

Relief mixed with exhaustion and overwhelmed my ability to reply, but I fell asleep happy.

Chapter Twenty-Four

Carly woke me from a deep, dreamless sleep, whispering urgently, "Jaden!" She jabbed me with her sharp elbow and repeated, "Jaden!"

"Huh?" I mumbled, rolling onto my back. My shoulder ached from sleeping on it all night. I'd never turned away from the outside wall. Carly had slept at my side, using her sleeping bag as a blanket over us both.

Enough light filtered through the fabric to tell me that it was morning. "What's the matter?" I asked sleepily.

She answered in a low voice, "Something growled a minute ago.... I think your demon's back. Listen! It sounds like it's taking a piss on the tent!"

"The demon can't come back," I assured her, waking up enough to realize that it was raining. I pinched the bridge of my nose. "And they don't urinate, Carly. It's raining."

Thunder rumbled in the distance to prove me right. Carly gasped and clung to my arm, burying her face against my shoulder.

I shifted to wrap my arm around her properly. "Honestly, it's just a storm."

"I'm afraid of storms."

"You're kidding?"

"Go ahead and laugh, demon-slayer."

I kissed her temple, the only place I could reach. "I'm not going to laugh at you. What would make you feel better?"

I felt her shrug. "The one thing that you're *not* going to do."

"It's not that I don't want to," I assured her. "Can we change the subject, please?"

"It's just not fair," she continued, a lilt in her sultry voice. "What's the point of being so darn attractive, then? You should gain eighty pounds and grow a scraggy beard. Then I wouldn't want you."

"Wouldn't you?" I replied. "Because if you gained eighty pounds and grew a scraggy beard, I'd still think you were the most beautiful woman in history."

She chortled. "Yeah, right you would."

"I would."

She was quiet for a moment and then asked, "Are you really going to move me out of Mom's house today?"

"I'm really going to move you out of your mom's house today."

She smiled and snuggled closer. "But where will I go?"

"In with me, until we can find you a place... or you can marry me and stay."

She thought about it. "You haven't exactly proposed."

She was right. I pushed myself up onto my elbow so I could see into her eyes. "Carly Bell Benson, will you marry me?"

She grinned and answered, "Yes. When I'm twenty-five. If you still want me."

I sighed, looking away, and she added, "Jaden, if you say one word about me being dead before my twenty-fifth birthday, I will *kill* you!"

Of course I'd been thinking about that, but I was also thinking what I said out loud, "I'm just wishing we didn't have to wait that long."

The rain let up about an hour later. We emerged from our tent to a fresh, wet, piney morning. The sky remained overcast, the lake gray and rippling with low waves.

Carly grinned at me. "It smells like a fresh start, doesn't it?"

I had to agree.

Because it was so late, I made instant oatmeal with water heated on the camp stove, and then we packed everything back into the car. Fortunately, my Lord had taken care of the dog's remains, and the rain had washed the gore away. No sign of the battle I'd fought here last night remained. I could almost forget. Still, I was happy to be going before Trinity came looking for us.

The demon would have a hard time attacking us so long as we stayed within the walls of my penthouse, but I would have to track it down before Carly went back to work.

She interrupted my thoughts. "I know you were planning to stay out here all weekend," she said, pulling her hair up into a ponytail again as I backed out of the parking space. "But I'm really excited about moving today, getting on with my life."

I nodded. "Me, too. Shall I call Jasper to help us? He's got a big truck."

"I thought he was in court today," she reminded me. "The Lambert case?"

I checked my watch: eleven forty-five. "They're probably done by now. If not, they certainly will be by the time we get back to town. I could have him meet us at the house."

Carly shook her head. "I don't have enough stuff to warrant a truck. All I'm bringing are my clothes and maybe my iPod. I don't want anything that reminds me of where I came from."

I thought about that. "If you want, you can leave it all behind. We can hit the outlet mall on the way home and buy you all new stuff, whatever you want."

She considered it, but finally decided, "No. I can't leave the sweater you gave me. Or the earrings.... Let's just get my stuff from home."

"Not 'home,'" I corrected. "Your mother's house."

She grinned. "Right. *Mother's.*"

The sun had come out by the time I pulled up to the brownstone, dry patches already appearing on the pavement.

"Give me a minute," Carly began. "Can you believe it? I need to pray before I go up there."

My heart leaped with joy at the reminder that His spirit really was with her, but I left her in the car without comment.

I stood for a moment on the sidewalk looking up. Movement in an upper window caught my eye. When I looked fully, though, the person ducked out of sight.

Carly finished her prayer and stepped onto the sidewalk with me.

"Which apartment is your mother's?" I asked.

"Top left. Why?"

I stared at the window. "I just saw a man up there… in the window."

"Scary Perry."

My spine tingled. "We'll come back later," I said, turning her toward the car.

She stood her ground and shook her head. "No. I want him to know that I'm leaving, and that he'll never hurt me again."

It felt too dangerous. "You sure about that?"

She looked at the now-empty window. "Yeah…. Yes, I am." She seemed nervous, but not afraid.

Are we in danger, Lord? I prayed.

He sent me courage and answered, *You must let Carly make this choice.*

I held Carly's hand as we climbed the two flights of stairs. She tested the doorknob. It wasn't locked. She glanced at me, apologetically, then popped open the door.

The apartment was dim; no lights had been turned on. Perry, a man of indeterminable age, leaned causally against the doorframe that divided the living room from the kitchen, holding his hands behind his back. He wore torn jeans and a ribbed tank top. His hair was disheveled, and he hadn't shaved in at least a week. His eyes were rimmed in red.

It was the same man from Raiser's vision. I turned my head and saw the plaid couch. A piece of old, curled duct tape mended the tear. I thought I might vomit and swallowed hard. Anger burned behind my eyes.

"Hey, Carly baby," Perry crooned. "Got yerself a new boyfriend there?"

She glanced at me, but only briefly. "Where's my mom?" she asked.

"Passed out in the kitchen. Yep, left me hangin' again." He rubbed the front of his pants with the palm of his left hand.

I tensed, drawing his attention. "Is your rich boyfriend here to party?" he asked.

"He's not the partying type," Carly replied, her voice surprisingly calm.

In response, Perry whipped his right arm around and leveled a gun at us. I hadn't seen, or even suspected it. My blood turned to ice. Carly's breath caught. We both stood frozen, unable to react.

"Let's see if we can't change that," Perry said smoothly. "This here's my new toy. Ya like it?" he asked, as if he were not using it to threaten our lives. I'd seen a comparable one before, a Glock 9 mm. This one had a silencer, about 8 inches long.

"Where'd you get that?" Carly whispered.

"Friend loaned it to me," he replied. "Yeah, I had a job last night…. Didn't pay very well, though.

I still owe some people some cash." He turned his attention to me. "Maybe Richie Rich can float me a loan."

I held up my hands, praying. The Lord gave me strength and peace, but no power. Perry was not possessed, just unloved. *And drunk or high or both*, I added.

I searched my mind for a way out of this, or barring that, a way to get Carly out safely. Perry could shoot me all he wanted, I wasn't going to die here.

"My wallet's in my pocket," I told Perry, "with about eight-hundred dollars inside. I'll leave it on the floor, and you can let us go."

He grinned. "If you've got eight-hundred bucks, man, we'll be having us one hell of a party."

He pointed the gun at Carly. "Come over here."

It was not her usual voice that replied, but one belonging to a frightened girl, "No, Perry, please. Take the wallet."

"Oh, I'm gonna take the wallet," he answered. "And we'll see how much Richie really has before anybody goes anywhere." His voice changed to something far more sinister. "Come here, Carly, unless you wanna see if this really is the quietest gun money can buy."

Locking her gaze on mine, she obeyed. I tried to assure her with my eyes, even while realizing that we had run out of time. But I knew one other thing just as surely. I was still in control of my choices, and I would do my very best to keep her alive, with or without my Lord's permission.

As soon as she'd crossed the room, Perry seized her ponytail, yanking her head back. She cried out in pain, but he didn't flinch. He stroked her neck with the barrel of his gun. "Your boyfriend know we've been together, Carly?" he asked. "Does he know how much you like it? Whataya think; wanna feel *this* barrel between your legs?"

She whimpered.

"Tell you what," he continued. "Maybe we should let him watch." He began walking backward, dragging Carly with him. "Come in the kitchen, Richie," he said in a friendly, disturbing, voice.

I had no choice.

The kitchen smelled like garbage. There were dirty dishes piled in and around the sink. Boxes and bags of convenience foods covered the counter.

Carly's mother lay sprawled on floor, the likely victim of a concussion… or of an overdose. Prescription pill bottles and empty beer cans littered the table. But I could do nothing for her, either. The Spirit's power still would not come to me.

Perry shoved Carly to the floor. He pointed the gun at her head but spoke to me, "Put the money on the table, Richie."

I moved slowly, slipping the wallet from my back pocket and laying it down gently. I knew the difference between a bluff and a threat.

If only he'd point the gun somewhere else. I could distract him, and Carly might have a chance, I planned. But for now, it seemed like if I did anything, Carly was going to pay for it.

"Good," he said. "Have a seat." He indicated the nearest of the mismatched, taped-up vinyl chairs.

As I obeyed, Perry snatched my wallet and backed to the door. There was no other way out of the room, not even a window. He didn't count the money, but grinned at how much he saw. "So, Richie don't lie.... I got a call to make," he added and ordered, "Get up, Carly."

Quivering, she obeyed.

He sneered at her. "Take that duct tape, there on the counter," he motioned with the gun, "and tie Richie to that chair real good.... If you don't do it, or if either of you distracts me, I'm gonna blow your frickin head off. Understand?"

I sat perfectly still and whispered, "Do what he says, Carly."

Her eyes were terrified, but full of trust in me. I saw the Holy Spirit there as well, and knew He would be comforting her through this.

I mouthed the words, 'I love you,' as she began to wind the tape around my body.

While I was being immobilized, I listened to Perry's phone conversation.

"Hey. It's me. Just came into some cash. Wanna settle my score." He listened, then went on. "Yeah, and bring some good stuff.... I *said,* I can pay."

In one motion, he hung up the phone and lunged for Carly, yanking the roll of tape from her hand. He shoved her away from me, hard. She cried out in pain as she fell against the countertop behind me.

Perry didn't acknowledge her. He tugged on the tape, which wrapped my torso three times, pinning my arms to my sides, holding my back stiffly to the chair. He grunted in satisfaction and ripped it off the roll. Then, he tore a smaller piece, and slapped that over my mouth.

For a few seconds, Carly was not in immediate danger, but I couldn't speak or move, and she chose not to run. All I could do was pray.

"Come here, Carly!" Perry roared, returning his attention to her. He patted the tabletop. "Hop up so Richie can get a good look."

She shrieked and dove beneath the table, emerging on the opposite side, near her mother.

Aiming the gun, he shouted, "I don't have time for this sh…!" Someone banged on the front door before he could finish.

Perry froze. "If that's some neighbor who heard you scream, somebody dies," he threatened.

He resumed his previous pose, leaning against the doorframe, facing the living room and the front door, the gun hidden behind his back. I sat behind him, unable to see past him. Carly was on the other side of the table, trying to revive her mother.

Perry pointed the gun at me and called, "It's open."

I heard the door creak, but couldn't see who came in.

Perry's response was, "How'd you get here so damn fast?"

The reply had an accent, one I'd heard before. "We were in the neighborhood. You have our money?"

"Right in here," Perry replied, stepping aside.

I did not recognize the face of the African man who entered the kitchen. But the entity within him was no stranger to me: Trinity.

It knew who I was as well. "We have been looking for you," it hissed, gliding into place across the table from me, "for a very long time."

"You know Richie?" Perry asked. Stupidly. He was on my right. To my left, Carly rose to her feet. The demon was a few steps away, directly ahead of me.

"It is not called Richie," Trinity replied, looming over the table, "We are forbidden to speak its name."

Perry started to say something else, but at that moment, I felt the Holy Spirit's power surge into me. I stood up, the bindings and the gag falling, like paper, to the floor. My hands flew up, power exploding from them. "Come out of him, Trinity! In the name of Jesus Christ, come out!"

The possessed man stumbled backward, but Trinity seized control and resisted me. "No. We need not obey you while you are sinning, and he is ours," it hissed, stroking the African man's face with his own hand. "Beautiful, no?" The man's head turned toward Perry. "That one is ours as well. It is waiting for us."

I glared at Perry.

"Ahh," sighed Trinity, shivering with pleasure. "That feels good....You *hate* him."

"Obey your King!" I shouted, wishing I'd had more time to recover from Raiser. I already felt weakened. I wasn't about to admit that my abhorrence of Perry had anything to do with that. "Come out!"

"Do you think *we* are Usher?" the demon screamed. "Do you think *we* are Raiser? WE ARE TRINITY!" Trinity shook the African man violently. "And we need no human shell to fight you, sinner!"

The possessed man convulsed. His head lolled back, and he began bleeding from his nose and ears, then his eyes, then his fingernails.

Horrified by what I feared the demon was attempting do, I concentrated hard on binding up the possessed man, holding his flesh together with the Spirit's power.

But Trinity was too strong for me. The African man's skin cracked with a sound like that of breaking glass.

I felt the string of expletives from Perry more than I heard them.

"Quiet!" I commanded him, but the pain of his words had already distracted me, which increased my anger. The power slipped through my fingers. My bindings around the African man loosened. His body exploded into trillions of droplets of flesh and blood, water and bone. Vaporized.

Trinity rose up and took form: three dragon's heads, nearly reaching the ceiling, a serpentine body below, a thick tail barbed in blade-like spikes, twitching. A thousand furnace-like eyes blazed at me.

It was an illusion, I knew. Trinity had no body of its own.

"You've been called to your judgment!" I shouted, trying to wrap the beast in the Spirit's power as I had done with Raiser. It didn't work this time. Trinity slithered around my attempts to capture it.

"You are weak, sinner," it laughed, thrashing me with its tail. It left a long, burning gash across my cheek. My hand flew to my face and drew away smeared with blood. I felt the Spirit's power, already knitting the wound back together. Even so, I was shocked. Trinity shouldn't have been able to touch me, not without a host. I glanced at Carly who had pressed herself against the far wall, a look of horror on her beautiful face.

I refocused my concentration, drawing the Spirit's power around myself, creating a shield. I was about to extend it out toward Carly when I heard the gun go off.

Chapter Twenty-Five

My shield evaporated. Trinity laughed. I heard it hiss, "Poor, pathetic sinner. How sad that your hate far exceeds your love." It licked me with a forked, fiery tongue. My skin bubbled where it burned me. I still couldn't figure out how that was possible.

I didn't care. My eyes were on Carly, who clutched her stomach and crumpled to the floor. I wanted to go to her, to save her if I could, to die with her if I could not.

Trinity moved toward Perry, ready to claim his body for its own. Desperately, I re-formed the shield of power and threw it between them. Perry was the last man I wanted to save, but I knew from experience how dangerous Trinity could be with a gun in its hands.

Perry stood confused, immobilized, apparently wondering how the bullet had passed through the monster before him without harming it. I couldn't tell if he'd even realized, yet, that he'd shot Carly instead.

I cried out to God, begging Him to reveal the sin in me so that I could wield His power effectively.

Trinity struggled toward its desired victim, spinning and swirling, pulling open cupboard doors, crashing dishware to the floor. Blinding me by exploding sacks of flour, boxes of cereal, whatever it could find as it tried to tear its way through my shield.

I held on, somehow, and kept it from reaching Perry, who continued to stare at his gun as if it held some answer for him.

The solution I needed came to me as I recalled Trinity's words about my hate exceeding my love. If Dimitrius had been right about the exponential effects of love, it stood to reason that the effects of my hate were exponential as well. I realized, to my horror, that I would have to let go of my hate for the man behind my shield if I was ever going to defeat the beast before it.

"God, give me the strength to do what I must!" I prayed before turning to Perry. I spoke sincerely, believing my own words, knowing that they were true because it did not hurt to speak them. "I forgive you, Perry, for raping Carly repeatedly since she was a child and for shooting her here today, for abusing your own body and Carly's mother, for stealing from me and for holding us at gunpoint. God loves you, Perry, and I will not hate you any longer."

Perry gaped at me, confused, but Trinity shrieked. "No! You loath him, sinner. He has debased your woman and taken her life from you! You cannot forgive what he has done!"

My eyes shot to Carly, slumped on the floor, a pool of blood spreading out behind her. In that moment, my heart was too full of love for her to hate anything. But if I was going to have a chance to say goodbye to her, I had to get rid of Trinity now.

A roar escaped from my throat, fueled by my passion for Carly. I wielded the Spirit's power like a sword, slashing at the swirling three-headed monster, and at last, I felt the Lord's power make contact with the beast.

Trinity seemed shocked, temporarily unable to fight back as it examined the tear I'd made through one of its necks. That head hung limply from the shoulder, it's mouth jawing.

I slashed at it again, severing that head. Immediately, I wrapped that piece of Trinity within the Spirit's power, even I as struck again, splitting the other two heads apart in a single stroke. Trinity was once again three separate demons, greatly diminished in power.

I compressed the bubble of Spirit that already contained a third of Trinity while the remaining two demons made a break for Carly's still-unconscious mother.

"To judgment!" I shrieked, scooping them up in the Lord's power, barely able to feel their resistance, they were so weakened.

Screaming and weeping, they compressed into an implosion of red light.

The sudden silence was shocking.

As the air began to settle, I rushed to Carly, kneeling on the floor at her side. "Oh, my love," I said, lifting her into my arms to examine the wound. The bullet had entered just below her sternum in the front and blasted a three-inch wide crater through the right side of her back as it exited. I inhaled sharply at the sight.

Behind me, I heard Perry dialing the phone. I listened as he calmly gave the operator his name, Peregrine Johnson, admitted to shooting his girl-friend's daughter, gave the address and promised to remain at the scene. But that was all background noise for me.

To my surprise, Carly was still conscious, her eyes searching for mine. "It hurts," she whispered.

"I know." I held her eyes, wondering if I'd ever again be lost in their depths, wondering how I'd sur-vive the loss of the sea this time.

I sat against the wall and cradled her on my lap. I held her head against my heart and prayed, *Please, Lord, may I heal her?*

I felt His sorrow, as real as my own. *You may ease her pain, but she must come to me now. I need her.*

His power came through my hands again, a gentle, water-like flow that entered her body where I held her. I felt her relax, but no matter how hard I tried to direct the power, I could not heal her.

"Better?" I asked, wiping the tears from her face.

She nodded and whispered, "But I can't stay with you…. He's calling me, Jaden." Her next words actu-ally sounded excited, "Jesus! I can hear His voice."

I nodded, my own voice breaking as I made a final promise to her, "When He comes back, with you, to bring his kingdom to the Earth, I'll be here, waiting to hold you again."

For several long and painful moments, she was quiet. Then, weakly, urgently, she whispered, "Jaden, tell me your real name."

"It's Timon."

She spoke again, the last words I'd hear from her for what would feel to me like eternity, "Timon, I love you."

I pressed my forehead against hers and answered, "I love you, too, Carly. I always, always will."

And then, ten days after the first time I'd saved it, Carly's life slipped through my fingers. She was the sea, and I could not hold her.

I cried. And then I wailed, pressing Carly's body against mine.

I prayed for relief, and my Lord responded, *She is with me. I have wiped away all of her tears. There is great joy in Heaven today! Be at peace, Timon. I still have gifts to give you, and you* will *be with her again.*

I knew His words were true, but that did not lessen the pain of losing her.

Look around you, Timon, my Lord suggested. *There is more you could do, if you choose.*

I lifted my head. Perry knelt at Carly's feet, quiet tears trailing down his cheeks.

He sensed my eyes on him and croaked out, "I didn't mean to shoot her. I swear I didn't! I loved her."

Again, I had to fight the urge to vomit. *Don't talk to me,* I thought at him, but apparently, he couldn't read my mind.

He sputtered, "If only... that talk of forgiveness... had been real."

It was very hard to say, but I managed to whisper, "It was real; I do forgive you."

His swimming eyes found mine. He asked softly, "How is that possible?"

I didn't want to answer him, but I forced myself. "Only by following the example of my Lord, Jesus Christ, and taking my strength from Him." It sounded like a rehearsed line. It *was* a rehearsed line. I had nothing original to say.

He considered my words for a moment. "I've done things that can't be forgiven," he confessed.

What can I say to that? I wondered, since I agreed with his statement. But then I remembered Saul. If I hadn't forgiven him for murdering Stephen, God's word would not have spread as it did. I did not know God's plan, but I did know His mind. "Anything can be forgiven," I promised Perry. "Simply pray." Slowly, I stretched my hand out to him. "If you want, I will pray with you."

Perry did not take me up on that offer. Instead, he sat down contemplatively next to Carly's mother, where he remained until police and emergency crews arrived. He looked at me with resolution in his eyes and then rose to meet them.

A group of three medical technicians rushed to my side. They checked Carly's vital signs and examined her wound. Then they told me what I already knew, that there was nothing they could do; she was already gone.

I asked if I could hold her a while longer. No one objected. They moved on to her mother, determining that the best course of action was to try to pump her stomach here and now.

I bowed my head over Carly, listening as Perry chose to tell the truth. He admitted to the officers that he'd purchased the gun illegally, that he'd supplied Carly's mother with the drugs and alcohol that fueled her overdose. He told them that he'd robbed me at gunpoint and intended to rape Carly.

He stopped short of telling them about the possessed supplier or of my battle with the demons. He simply said that the gun went off while he was hallucinating, and he was too high to know if he'd intended for it to or not.

I witnessed all of this as if I was floating near the ceiling. It was a complete out-of-body experience for me. I couldn't feel the wall behind me or the floor beneath. There was only the weight of Carly's body leaning heavily against my chest.

I let her hair down and stroked it smooth while I talked myself into believing that, eventually, I would be okay. I imagined that soon, Carly's body would be taken away. I'd be examined at the hospital, but not even a scar from the dog bite would be found on me. I'd be sent home to my empty penthouse to plan and prepare for Carly's funeral. There would be a ceremony and many more tears. I predicted months of numbness before I could feel again.

After that, I didn't know. I didn't think I could stay in Chicago. I knew I couldn't return to the Mediterranean Sea, maybe not ever. But I certainly didn't have to make any decisions about my future today.

What I could not have anticipated, what I'd heard of, but had never witnessed myself, was that, standing before the Most High King of Creation, Carly Bell Benson of Chicago, Illinois was asked a question. She was allowed to make choice very few people get to make. And she chose me.

An hour and twenty-four minutes after her lungs had exhaled their last breath, her tiny body gave a shudder against my chest. As I watched in stunned incredulity, her wounds were healed. I heard her inhale sharply, then deeply. She opened those beautiful sea-colored eyes and smiled at me.

Author's Note

Saint Timon is mentioned only once in the Bible, in Acts 6:5. He was a Hellenistic Jew, a Jew of Greek culture, though perhaps not really of Greek descent. He served with Saint Stephen as a Deacon in the early church, caring for widows and orphans in Jerusalem. It is believed, but not Biblically documented, that Timon also served Jesus as one of the seventy-two disciples Christ sent ahead, early in His ministry, to heal the sick and to preach that the kingdom of God was near.

After Stephen was stoned for preaching that Jesus is the Messiah, Timon's history becomes muddled. He fled Jerusalem and either landed in Syria or in Greece. Regardless, he continued his ministry, preaching the gospel and caring for the needy. It is widely accepted that, having received the Holy Spirit, Timon healed the sick and cast out demons in the name of Christ. Various histories site his martyrdom by furnace at the hands of a Syrian governor, or by crucifixion in Greece, or both, saying he survived the first by a miracle of God. In a few records, he is assumed to have died of old age. Others claim that nothing at all is known of his life after Jerusalem.

As far as I know, the possibility that he has not yet died is a history of my own creation.

Acknowledgments

This book would not have been possible without the love and support of my husband, Chip, and my children, Kayleigh and William. From the bottom of my heart, I thank you.

I also wish to thank my extended family, Denise for her excellent editing, Mom, Dad, Amy, Scott and Joe for reading early copies and offering their encouragement!

Thanks to my small-but-mighty writer's group, Mike and Anne, for helping me through the hard parts and for fixing many, many errors!

My dear book club members: Kristi, Holly, Alicia, Laura, Susan, Tina, Lisa, Sue, Amy, Becky, Kim, Andrea, Chris, Monica and Nancy, I thank you for treating the manuscript as though you did not know the author, for showing me where the story was strong, where it was weak, and where you saw yourselves. To our founder, Ginger, I offer special thanks for reading the first drafty outline of Lenity, and for pressing me to make a novel of it.

Thanks to other friends who read early copies: Kinga, Bill, Anne, John, Todd, Merry, Jen, Lee, Rebecca, Elaine, Jennifer and Cathy. I know there are others, and I beg you'll forgive me for not mentioning you by name, but my love and appreciation are genuine.

Special thanks to my stylist, "Fancy Nancy" Klein for the cover photo!

My pastor and my small groups at church have taught me much about lenity. I love you and am grateful to all of you.

Thank you to William Creed for that unexpected phone call and for setting me on this path. Your words meant so much to me!

I thank Jack Walton for reminding me of Isaiah 40:31 and for answering my questions about P.O.D. publishing with kindness and understanding.

I sincerely appreciate the efforts of everyone at Xulon Press.

I prayed that God would give me a significant story to tell, and I praise Him for answering that prayer! May He use this work to His glory.

aVergne, TN USA
) June 2010
87953LV00001B/2/P